Granny Probyn
& the Great
Theatre Royal Drury Lane
Mystery

DCG
Publications

First Published in Greece 2011

© Douglas Foote

The author's moral rights have been asserted.

Douglas Foote
DCG Publications
www.dcgmediagroup.com

ISBN 978-960-99470-7-7

Typeset by
DCG Publications

For
Rousselle,
Puccini & Sweeney

Prologue

Once upon a time is as good a start to a story as any, whether it's a good story I'll leave that for you to judge. Whether it's a true story, well they say that truth is stranger than fiction, and in the build up towards the Second World War many bizarre things were happening so who knows...?

But where to actually start that is the question. There have been so many deaths I suppose I should start with the first. But no, let's go back just a little bit further, to a village just outside London not too far away named Dulton, and the last small cottage before farmer Nichols' fields begin. Set back from the road by a small rose garden and surrounded by a picket fence. Rose Cottage named after its garden is the perfect picture postcard of any country village. Its thatched roof hangs low over the bay windows situated either side of the front porch with its stable door, the top half always open in the summer to allow the breezes in to cool the interior. Baskets of hanging flowers adorn the porch, while a cracked glazed path leads from the slightly rickety wooden gate to the front step.

This then is the home of Granny Probyn. A widow not too old who thanks to a healthy lifestyle and a cheery outlook on life is remarkably sprightly for her age. A mop of silver grey hair tops her small features. Her eyes still sparkle and at times, an impish smile appears on her lips.

Ever since she was a little girl, in fact as far back as she could remember, Granny Probyn had always wanted to be an actress, she dreamed of standing on stage flooded by light, taking bow after bow from her adoring audience, signing autographs at the stage door, mixing with the *in* crowd, but this was before she met her husband, Abercrombie. A tall handsome man Granny Probyn fell instantly in love. Abercrombie was a quiet man, working in the city for a firm of stockbrokers spending most of his time on the floor of the stock exchange, dealing in whatever stocks & share came his company's way. Although not rich himself he had, through careful trading, provided well for himself and family. Their three children; Berty, Billy, & Beryl, grew up in the comfort of Edwardian England. But as the years rolled by the world had changed and so had Granny Probyn though she still occasionally dreamed of "treading the boards" as they say.

Then one day over muffins with Mrs. Dorfellwaffer, she was ruminating about how when quite young she had been in the school play and according to her teacher had been, 'remarkably good.' Well Ethel Dorfellwaffer was not one to be outdone… no siree… and, in the process of adding another dollop of rich yellow butter to her muffin, exclaimed that her son Napoleon Packard had booked a ticket for her to see the pantomime at the Theatre Royal, Drury Lane and what did Granny Probyn think about that!

Well at that precise moment Granny Probyn didn't think anything about it, she was more concerned about that dollop of butter being waved precariously around on a knife edge and landing on her Axminster carpet. She had only just managed to get the jam stain off the arm of her chesterfield from Mrs. Dorfellwaffer's last visit and didn't relish the thought of days of scrubbing carpets.

'Hmm!' Was all she could say as her eyes followed the yellow blob of butter in its airborne course before it landed with a flourish on top the hot crumpet. With a sigh of relief Granny Probyn stroked the head of Fluffy, who lay curled up beside her on the divan.

Fluffy, or Fluffy Yeomans to give him his rather grand name for such a small cat, opened an eye, to observe progress. He knew from previous occasions that these little tea parties could become a war of attrition at any moment and he felt it was up to him to keep Granny Probyn on an even keel… so proceeded to purr quite loudly in order to calm her.

Ethel Dorfellwaffer continued unawares… and naturally of course she wouldn't be going on her own. No her thoughtful son,

Napoleon Packard had insisted that they all go, meaning Granny Probyn thought, "her son, his bore of a wife Veronica, and that brat of a child Beauregard Henry Packard. Thank God that my three grew up normal," she mused as Mrs. Dorfellwaffer waffled away about how they were going and what they would see when they arrived in London.

Granny Probyn thought on the tragedy of her own two sons, lost in the Great War. What a waste it all seemed at the time. Of course the boys themselves were eager to go, as everyone was at that age. How could you stop them? Bright eyed and bushy tailed they marched off to the recruiting office in the town hall along with half the town. Children ran about and danced in the street, mothers with tears in their eyes waved and cheered as their boys passed by. Oh what a happy time it was. But that was soon to change. Abercrombie didn't go. At the start they weren't expecting the war to last as long as it did, and by the time Abercrombie was needed at the front he was already head of the home guard here in Dulton, and so thankfully he managed to stay out of the trenches. Granny Probyn remembered so well the day that one of her neighbours received their first telegram. What an awful experience she never thought that it would ever happen to her, and then it did, twice. At least Beryl was still here, well not exactly here, she had been a land girl working at the local farm where she met her future husband whilst ploughing a field of mangelwurzels. Now married and having moved north, they lived in some dreary town in the midlands.

Granny Probyn was in her own little world when finally, having exhausted the topic of conversation, Ethel Dorfellwaffer came to the crux of the matter and Granny Probyn was aware that she was being asked a question.

'I'm sorry dear what did you say?' she asked slightly embarrassed, as she knew that Ethel was aware she had no interest in the antics of Napoleon, Veronica or Beauregard Henry Packard.

'I said,' Ethel Dorfellwaffer continued slightly indignantly, 'that the old school friend of my son, Mucus Drillby who is stage manager for the Theatre Royal, Drury Lane was in a predicament, and that I would ask you, but seeing that you have better things to think on maybe I was mistaken.'

'Well now, don't take on like that Ethel, and tell me what the problem is?'

Fluffy Yeomans closed his eye again knowing whatever storm that had been brewing had just blown over and the butter knives weren't in danger of becoming evidence for the prosecution.

'I already have, that the Theatre Royal Drury Lane have been holding auditions and have not been able to find the star of the show and that was when I said that you would be able to help.'

'Me? Star of the Theatre Royal Drury Lane Pantomime? Well of course I would love to help, but do you think that I could play such a role, such a demanding part? I know I was pretty good in my school play but I mean, I haven't had that much experience, of course I always knew I was destined for greatness somewhere but this is such an honour I hardly know what to say...'

'What on earth are you talking about?' Ethel said, most exasperatingly, 'Who said anything about you?'

'Why you did...' just then Granny Probyn realised she had made a terrible mistake. 'What is the name of the pantomime that you are going to see?'

'Why *Puss in Boots* of course.'

Act i

Scene 1

Fluffy Yeomans did not want to be a theatre cat. Born in the local rectory his mother had warned him, well not just him but his seven siblings as well, that no kitten of hers was ever going to be in the theatre. They were God fearing felines and the road to wrack and ruin lay on the great broad way. No, stick to the straight and narrow and keep the church and graveyard clear of pesky vermin. His mother was most fervent. A little moggy Fluffy Yeomans had four white stockings on his legs and a white patch that covered his right eye, the rest of his coat was jet black. As a kitten his white feet always proved to be his downfall when playing in the coal cellar, as his mother, ever of clean mind and spirit cuffed him round the ears, whilst expounding the virtues of a clean body & soul. But it was those selfsame white feet that had also caught the attention of Granny Probyn. She had adopted him straight from the litter and took him to her little cottage five miles from the village of Dulton. Alone Fluffy Yeomans had grown up with his mother's mantra ringing in his ears, 'find a nice home and keep it clear of vermin, whatever size and shape,' and apart from the odd visit of Mrs. Dorfellwaffer and her brat of a grandson Beauregard Henry, so far he had done a pretty good job.

Granny Probyn lived by herself now that her children were no longer with her so he only had to keep her in trim, and as soon as these theatre plans had been mooted he had tried all ways to tell Granny Probyn that he was not interested in a life on the stage. He clawed the chintz covers of her best armchair by the fire, he climbed the chintz curtains in the front room, only used on special occasions, knocked over one of her porcelain figurines, the one of a shepherd girl with her hat blowing in the breeze, a particular favourite of Granny Probyn's, and as if that wasn't enough he refused to drink the cream that she had saved especially for him. No he wasn't going to be in the theatre.

But Granny Probyn had other ideas and set about making preparations for the trip to London and their first steps towards stardom. It had all been settled. Mrs. Dorfellwaffer had communicated to her son that Granny Probyn was interested and through him a time had been arranged to take Fluffy Yeomans for an audition at the theatre. Of course all expenses would be reimbursed, in fact if Fluffy Yeomans was successful in securing the part a full wage would be paid depending upon the number of performances a week. This was just extra icing on the cake as far as Granny Probyn was concerned, she had at last got her foot, if not on stage, well into the stage door and she was determined she wasn't going to have it removed too easily.

Granny Probyn sat back and smiled an exhausted smile. It had been a hard day since Mr. Hogben the postmaster had hand delivered her a letter. Always one for probing into other peoples business Mr. Hogben was well placed at the local post office which was a constant source of gossip. Of course nothing on earth would have induced Mr. Hogben to open somebody else's mail, but there were other subtle ways of getting information that most times he knew what was going on before the person who had received their letter. But today was the exception to the rule. Apart from the occasional postcard and letter from her daughter in Middleton, Granny Probyn rarely received mail and so, out of special service of the Royal Mail and a natural curiosity, he had left the boy in charge of the shop and went to knock on the door of Granny Probyn's cottage. The letter from the Theatre Royal Drury Lane had an embossed crown on the front which further piqued the imagination of Mr. Hogben, and having loitered on the doorstep for what seemed an inordinate amount of time, his patience was finally rewarded by the invitation to have a cup of tea to steady the nerves of Granny Probyn as she read the contents of the letter that gave the time and place of the auditions.

Granny Probyn could hardly believe her eyes as she scanned the simple card which held the instructions. She had to read it twice before all the information would sink in. Mr. Hogben, who now sat with his cup of tea delicately placed on his knee, waited to hear the full story and what if any would be the repercussions for the village. As a member of the town counsel and general busybody he was always one to have the village and its reputation at heart and with this juicy bit of news and being convinced that it couldn't harm his village Mr. Hogben couldn't wait to return to his counter to inform the local gossipmongers of the strange doings up at Rose Cottage.

Sitting with her feet on the pouffé in front of the fire and her Ovaltine steaming in a mug on the little occasional table by her chair, Granny Probyn could finally relax as the fish paste sandwiches lay wrapped in their grease proof paper on the kitchen table. The thermos flask, cleaned and drained in anticipation of the boiling water for Granny Probyn's tea, sat on the old slightly spongy wooden drainer of the kitchen sink. Her husband Abercrombie's old suitcase, cram packed full, blocked the foot of the stairs awaiting the taxi to take them to the station and Fluffy Yeomans's wicker-work basket with its metal grill door sat on the settle in the hall stuffed with a bright tartan travel blanket and his favourite toy Nippy, a stuffed mouse filled with catnip. Fluffy Yeomans was still showing his reluctance and was refusing to sit on her lap, but Granny Probyn thought it was because of all the upheaval of packing and that he would come around to her way of thinking eventually. How she would sleep tonight she had no idea as her head was filled with images of backstage dramas and on stage glory... which as it turned out lead easily into peaceful slumbers.

The taxi arrived promptly at 8am to take them as far as Dulton station where they would get the express train to Paddington.

Excitement ensued as Fluffy Yeomans was somewhat unceremoniously bundled into his basket and whisked off by the taxi driver onto the back seat of the car as Granny Probyn eased herself in to join him there. She hoped that she wouldn't want to go to the loo again until well on the train, but the excitement of the moment meant that she had to have at least one more try just in case and fled the cab. Fluffy Yeomans gave Stan, the taxi driver, a knowing look as Granny Probyn disappeared down the garden path, but Stan had seen it all before and waited patiently until she returned rushing back flushed with success and her skirts tucked into her knickers.

The train journey wasn't nearly as exciting as Granny Probyn had imagined it would be, in fact it was rather boring. After the initial rush of seeing the houses whiz by it all became a blur and the green English countryside flashed by without her giving it a second glance. Scanning the compartment her travelling companions weren't that exciting either as they sat and read, something Granny Probyn regretted she couldn't do as in her rush to leave that morning she had left her intended choice of book, neatly on the settle. Any chance of conversations were interrupted by either the ticket inspector or the lady with the tea trolley so she had to content herself by humming tunelessly, something which greatly annoyed her travelling companions, and smiled to herself as she daydreamed of stardom.

London on the other hand was exciting; from the moment Granny Probyn stepped from the train she knew she was going to have a good time. The station bustled with people. Granny Probyn was slightly overwhelmed by the noise and smoke from the engines which echoed about the great iron & glass canopy of Paddington before being funnelled out through the huge opening at the end of the platform into the bright winter sky. Porters were running up and down the platform grabbing cases and trunks and loading them onto dolly's and trolleys to be transported to taxis waiting at the main entrance of the building. The large clock on the platform informed her that it was nearing midday and she would have a little time still to see

London before the audition at 1 o'clock.

Outside on the pavement while waiting for the porter to find a taxi Granny Probyn surveyed a vast kiosk selling newspapers and books, but with so much to choose from and all the advertisements to read, she only managed to grab the latest paperback called *Murder is Easy,* before the porter had her bags and Fluffy Yeomans ensconced in the back seat of yet another taxi ready to take them to the theatre.

Granny Probyn asked to be taken there via Buckingham Palace, as she wanted to show Fluffy Yeomans where the queen lived. Of course Granny Probyn had been in London before when she married Abercrombie and had seen all the sights then. They had honeymooned in a hotel in Bloomsbury spending a glorious week walking the capital from Regents Park to Pimlico. But now, alone except for Fluffy Yeomans, she wanted him to be a part of her life. As they travelled in the taxi down the Edgware Road and then on to Park Lane, memories of that happy time came flooding back and she recounted them all for Fluffy Yeomans who sat wide eyed listening to all that Granny Probyn said. Travelling down Constitution Hill with Green Park on their left and the palace gardens to the right past Victoria's monument and the gates of Buckingham Palace down the Mall on to Trafalgar Square, The Strand, Aldwych and finally to the stage door of the theatre all became one large blur and Fluffy Yeomans was glad to be back in his basket before passing under the colonnade and entering the hallowed stage door of the Theatre Royal Drury Lane.

Walter sat behind his desk in a small vestibule of the lobby just behind the stage door. Everybody knew Walter, he was the first person anybody ever saw when entering and the last person they saw when leaving. He had been at the theatre all his life. His father had been a stagehand before him and at the age of seven he had secured a job as runner and call boy on the second level and had finally worked his way up the backstage social ladder to becoming the stage doorman, a post he had held now for nearly 30 years. In fact most people said

11

that Walter and the theatre ghost were permanent fixtures and nobody could imagine them not being there. His friendly smile put Granny Probyn immediately at her ease, especially as Abercrombie's case was now taking up most of the entrance space and people had to perform the most ridiculous contortions just to gain entry into the building.

'Just leave it there, my lovely,' Walter said. 'We'll soon have a place for yer.' At which point he removed a key from the pegboard behind him and passed it to a rather large gentleman in a charcoal gray coat with an Astrakhan collar, who had just entered and now filled what little space was left in the lobby.

'Afternoon Mr. Stutlz,' he said.

'Gut hafternoon, Valter,' came the reply as the gentleman squeezed past Granny Probyn squashing Fluffy Yeomans's wickerwork basket against the door jamb.

'Oh, excuse me, gut lady,' he said and tipped his hat as he made his way through the inner door and down a corridor.

'Oh dear,' said Granny Probyn, 'it's a very small theatre. I thought it would be a lot larger.'

Walter smiled a knowing smile just as a young girl of twenty five stuck her head round the door.

'Ah you're here, good,' she mumbled removing a pencil from her mouth. 'My name is Miss Plimple; I'm Mr. Reed's secretary.' Thrusting her clipboard beneath her arm and her pencil in her pocket she extended her hand and gave Granny Probyn a rather hearty handshake. 'And this must be Fluffy Yeomans,' she said immediately looming in on the wire door of Fluffy Yeomans' basket. 'If you would like to follow me, I'll take you directly to Mr. Reed.' With which she turned and was off down the corridor at a virtual trot. Granny Probyn unsure what to do looked for encouragement from Walter who nodded his head as if to say "You'd better follow," and added, 'Don't worry about yer bag; I'll get young Jimmy to keep it safe.'

Granny Probyn had a job following Miss Plimple, ever efficient; it seemed Miss Plimple rushed everywhere, even when standing still

Miss Plimple exuded energy like a greyhound waiting for the starting signal. As Miss Plimple turned a corner she opened one of a pair of heavy double doors and beckoned to Granny Probyn who had finally managed to catch up. 'Straight through there,' said Miss Plimple as she turned and walked briskly back the way she had come.

With trepidation Granny Probyn entered the dark area of the stage. She could make out in front of her a table in the middle of the stage beautifully illuminated, while she herself was standing in the shadow of the wings. She took a deep breath and whispered to Fluffy Yeomans in his cage, 'This is it,' and walked to the table in front of her. The lights bathed her in warmth as she placed Fluffy Yeomans and his basket on the table. She then looked around. To her left was darkness and to her right at her feet were a row of lights casting pink hues over the stage. But beyond that all was darkness again. Granny Probyn was a little lost and didn't quite know what to do next.

'Hello?' she said rather quietly at first. Her voice seemed to have disappeared for some reason. 'Hello,' again, this time a little louder.

'I divin't want that bloddy thing on my bloddy stage,' boomed a disembodied voice from the auditorium.

'Excuse me,' replied Granny Probyn to no one in particular.

'I said I divin't want that bloddy thing on my bloddy stage,' said the voice again, even louder.

'Sorry Mr. Reed,' came a reply, which sounded suspiciously like Miss Plimple. At which point she appeared in the far corner of the stage from somewhere beyond the footlights. She walked briskly towards Granny Probyn and whispered, 'In the middle of a lighting rehearsal, do you mind waiting over there,' pointing back the way she had come.

'Not at all,' said Granny Probyn, relieved to see a friendly face. She picked up Fluffy Yeomans as the voice boomed out, 'Next cue, Joe!' And the lights snapped out, leaving Granny Probyn stranded halfway between here and nowhere in total darkness. 'This is Mr. Pleach's entrance,' boomed the voice again, as the lights snapped on once more blinding Granny Probyn.

'Oh dear,' she said, turning around and coming face to face with a painted backcloth she was sure hadn't been there a few moments before. She quickly turned again this time running to the side of the stage as a tall handsome young man dressed in a bright blue satin costume with little pink bows in his shoes and a hat with large blue ostrich feathers made his entrance with a rather flouncy flourish, nearly knocking into Granny Probyn.

'Stop,' boomed the voice again. 'What *is* that woman doing on my stage?'

'Sorry Mr. Reed, this is Mrs. Probyn, she's brought the cat.' Said Miss Plimple from somewhere in the dark.

'Well why didn't you say before? Lights!' Boomed the voice again. Just then the lights blacked out leaving Granny Probyn once again in the dark, then what seemed like a single bulb backstage was turned on and the auditorium materialised out of the gloom as the house lights were raised.

Granny Probyn, stood amazed as she looked at the beautiful auditorium, with its rich red velvet seats and gold and cream painted balconies.

Fluffy Yeomans if possible was even more amazed and star struck than Granny Probyn. Having spent the time on the train sleeping, London was bigger and busier than anything he had every seen before. In fact St Swithains Church where he was born in Dulton was the biggest building he had seen up to that point in his life, but the taxi ride through the streets of London on Granny Probyn's lap, had proved quite an eye-opener. So much so that by the time they had reached the theatre, he was glad to be able to go back to the relative safety of his basket. That was of course until Miss Plimple scared him witless by taking him unawares like that and thrusting her face at him. 'Oh my,' he meowed, 'who would want to be a theatre cat?'

'Well where is he?' Boomed Mr. Reed from the auditorium.

'In here,' Granny Probyn said, holding Fluffy Yeomans basket close to her bosom as if it were in danger of being snatched from her hand.

'Then let's all see the next star of my theatre.' Mr. Reed boomed once more.

At which point Granny Probyn unceremoniously bundled him onto the table top in the centre of the stage. Bringing the rehearsal to a standstill Fluffy Yeomans was soon surrounded by members of the cast and chorus all cooing and clucking. 'Humph,' he meowed, to even more "ohs" and "ahs" from the expectant crowd.

'Alright everyone,' the disembodied voice boomed again, 'this isn't Piccadilly Circus, this is the theatre! So let's get on with it, Mrs. Probyn could you please do your act.'

'Oh, but I don't have an act,' she replied timidly as the crowd disappeared into the shadows leaving her and Fluffy Yeomans exposed on stage.

'Surely the cat can do something,' boomed an exasperated voice, 'can he sit to command? Jump through a hoop? Surely he can stand on his hind legs and make a bow? That Mrs. Probyn is what I would expect of a real theatre cat!'

'Oh, no he can't do any of those things; at least I don't think he can.' Replied a nervous Granny Probyn close to the brink of tears, 'I'm afraid he's just my Fluffy Yeomans, I didn't think he would have to do all those things.'

'Then why are you wasting my time?' Boomed the voice even louder, 'Miss Plimple, kindly remove this menagerie from my stage at once, Joe let's continue with act two. Lights!'

At which point the stage was again plunged instantly into darkness.

'Mr. Pleach…'

'Yes Mr. Reed.' Answered the young man in the blue satin costume who had been standing nervously on stage trying desperately not to be noticed but not knowing whether to leave or not.

'We will continue with your entrance,' came the voice from the darkness.

'Yes Mr. Reed,' and as the lights resumed, the young man dressed in blue silk with pink bows but hatless flounced once more onto the stage and stopped dead in his tracks as Fluffy Yeomans, holding Mr. Pleach's blue hat with ostrich feathers on it gave a rather elegant bow and meowed, 'How do you do?'

'STOP!' Bellowed the voice even louder than before.

'I'm sorry Mr. Reed,' said Miss Plimple hurriedly running onto the stage and ushering a rather confused Granny Probyn off into the wings, 'it won't happen again,' she said rather lamely.

'Why that cats a natural, a genius, an Irving of the feline variety. Let me see it again,' bellowed the voice. And so Fluffy Yeomans, this time but slightly more nervous, made his bow out over the footlights to the disembodied voice, and meowed the first line of the only poem that he knew.

Unaware that he had just heard, 'I wandered lonely as a cloud, over hill and dale,' a favourite of Fluffy Yeomans mother, the disembodied voice suddenly appeared on stage attached to an enormous man with a huge beard.

'My word,' he continued, as he knocked Mr. Pleach out of his way to stand in front of Fluffy Yeomans who was now cowering in the shadow of this giant. 'I'm going to make you a star,' at which he bent down and lifted Fluffy Yeomans high into the air before clasping him under his arm. He then turned and pointed out over the footlights into the darkness. 'See that?' he boomed. It seemed Mr. Reed boomed all the time. Having only two scales of volume to his voice. Loud, (stage whisper) and very loud (King Lear!). 'See that?' he said again. 'One day all this will belong to you. You'll have the public eating from your tiny paw.'

'Miss Plimple!' he boomed again.

'Yes, Mr. Reed.'

'Take Fluffy Yeomans here to the star dressing room; give him a script and a contract,' then to Fluffy Yeomans, 'sign one learn the other and I want to rehearse act one in full tonight!'

'Yes, Mr. Reed,' replied Miss Plimple. With which Fluffy Yeomans was handed to Granny Probyn who quickly followed Miss Plimple as she ran off into the wings followed by a disembodied voice bellowing, 'Okay Joe, from the beginning of act two, Mr. Pleach your entrance if you please and this time try doing it with a certain flair. You'll be working along side a real actor so hopefully you should learn something.'

'Yes Mr. Reed,' was all poor Mr. Pleach could reply as voices in the dark shouted orders from all directions.

Scene 2

Granny Probyn sat in a daze. The day's events still hadn't sunk in. Here she was sitting in the star dressing room of the Theatre Royal Drury Lane, her star dressing room (well to be exact her and Fluffy Yeomans's star dressing room) and it all seemed like a dream. Everybody in the cast had knocked on the door to congratulate her and welcome her to the theatre while a young man had nailed a large gold star on the door and painted Fluffy Yeomans's name on it in big letters. Now as she sat facing the mirror surrounded by lights she sighed a happy sigh as Fluffy Yeomans, exhausted from rehearsing all evening, lay asleep on her lap. Abercrombie's case, or so she had been told by Jimmy the call boy, had been sent to her hotel, but she didn't want to leave just yet. Not just yet. It had all been much too exciting.

Suddenly another knock at the door brought her out of her reverie as Jimmy the call boy shouted out, 'Yer taxi's waiting, Mrs. Probyn.' Such a nice young lad she thought and made a mental note to buy him some sweets once she had settled in. 'Thank you,' she called back, 'I'll be right along,' as she bundled a rather disgruntled Fluffy Yeomans back into his basket.

As she was leaving their dressing room all wrapped up in her coat and scarf she heard snatches of a heated conversation coming from the room next door. Of course all the cast had come and introduced themselves but there had been so many new faces that Granny Probyn couldn't quite remember who had said what and who was in which dressing room and who if any said that they were neighbours. Out of curiosity she slowly made her way to the open door further along the corridor as quietly as she could. She held a finger to her lips as Fluffy

Yeomans in a pique of stardom and tiredness with a meow objected loudly to being left in a draughty corridor. As Granny Probyn neared the door she could distinctly hear a man and a woman arguing.

'It's no use,' said the man, 'she'll have to go.'

'But how? I mean, what with the chorus milling about there isn't time. And as you know I shouldn't be there anyway. It would make things very difficult. And we don't know if she has it anyway.'

'That's your problem. Orders are orders.'

'Yes, but I don't see how I can,' the woman replied.

Granny Probyn took one more step and tried to see through the gap of the open door but was met only with her own reflection in the dressing room mirror and the back of a young lady sitting in a chair. Just then the door slammed shut as the voices carried on muffled now by the closed door.

Granny Probyn wondered if she should knock at the door and find out if there was a problem, but she also had the distinct feeling that she had been seen and the door closing was no coincidence.

'Yer taxi's here Mrs. Probyn,' said Jimmy, having reappeared wondering where she was.

At which point Granny Probyn clutched her heart. So engrossed was she that she hadn't heard him walk up behind her.

'Oh, thank you, thank you,' she replied as she turned to follow Jimmy who had picked up Fluffy Yeomans's basket and was half way back down the corridor. Granny Probyn had to hurry to catch up with him and as she reached the far end of the corridor before turning into the stairwell she turned once more to look at the door of the dressing room only to see that it was being closed very quietly. Somebody had been watching her leave. Unsure as to what she should do Granny Probyn hesitated on the stair until the voice of Jimmy calling out once more prompted her to finally go down to the stage door and the waiting taxi. Thanking Jimmy and Walter as she left the theatre she climbed into the waiting taxi unaware that she was being watched from a first floor window. As the taxi drove away, she tried to remember who it was who had said they were in the next dressing room but try as she might she just couldn't recall.

The next morning at breakfast, Granny Probyn was sitting by the window of the dining room overlooking the gardens of the hotel where she and Abercrombie had honeymooned all those years ago. Of course it had been redecorated since then but it was still more or less as she remembered it. Fluffy Yeomans after a pleasant nights slumber was now enjoying a fresh kipper. Granny Probyn had her usual soft boiled egg, cooked to perfection so that she could dip her toast soldiers into the soft runny yolk. She poured herself another cup of tea before delving into her handbag to produce the script for the pantomime.

'Come along, dear,' she said, 'we must be word perfect for Mr. Reed. He wants to rehearse act two this afternoon.' Then as an afterthought, 'Oh, and I must find out whose dressing room is next to ours don't you think? I do believe something not quite nice is brewing.'

Fluffy Yeomans was beginning to regret performing that bow. He had so wanted to make Granny Probyn happy it just sort of happened but now there was all this work and hanging about he wished he was back at Rose Cottage. But he had to admit to himself that once you were on stage it was also fun. He had learned his lines very carefully with the help of Granny Probyn going over and over again until he knew not only his but those of Mr. Pleach as well. But it was the interminable waiting in the wings with nothing to do which was such a bore. Some of the chorus and dancers sat and giggled in little groups around the dark recesses of the stage, while others practiced their dance routines. But as Fluffy Yeomans only had a few scenes each with Mr. Pleach and Mr. von Stutlz, he just had to sit and wait until it was his turn again on stage.

Of course at first everybody made a fuss of him and Granny Probyn, being new to the cast and all, but the pressure of putting on one of the biggest pantomimes in the country was getting to everybody and soon he and Granny Probyn were left to their own devices.

Granny Probyn was in her element. She soon had the dressing room just as she wanted it with the help of Walter and Jimmy. It was amazing what they could come up with and, by the next day, she had an armchair just like the one at home, only without the chintz covers and Fluffy Yeomans had a large basket stationed by the old fashioned radiator which gurgled as the hot water ran through the pipes. In fact the room looked more like Rose Cottage than the star dressing room at the Theatre Royal Drury Lane, but as Walter had said, 'that was all part of the magic of show business.'

Two days later, opening night loomed and everybody was nervous and excited. Sitting in their dressing room, Granny Probyn and Fluffy Yeomans were reading all the telegrams and cards they had received from friends and well wishers and one particularly from Ethel Dorfellwaffer saying that she hoped all would be well on opening night as she, her son Napoleon, his wife Veronica, and her grandson, Beauregard Henry would be right there with them sitting in one of the boxes.

'Good grief,' said Granny Probyn, 'I didn't think I would be this nervous. I'm sure I wasn't this nervous in the school play.'

Fluffy Yeomans meowed, a nervous meow.

'Of course then I was only playing a sheep,' she continued, 'along with half of my class. We were doing a version of the nativity, and Fanny Clampkness was playing the Virgin Mary and got her robe caught on a nail and showed her knickers to the entire school before anyone realised.' And she burst out laughing at the memory of it.

Just then Jimmy the call boy knocked on the door of the dressing room calling for act one beginners and somewhere in the depths of the theatre a hush descended as the overture started to play.

Picking up Fluffy Yeomans, Granny Probyn whispered, 'This is it,' more to reassure herself then anyone else and joined the others in the corridor who were on their way to the stage ready for beginners.

Down on stage the overture came to an end and the great red velvet curtains swept open to reveal a beautiful village scene full of people milling around in various guises as typical villagers, well theatrical versions thereof. Then very soon it would be Fluffy Yeomans turn to make his entrance. He and Granny Probyn waited nervously in the wings for his cue. All of a sudden it was nearly time.

The scene set in the store room of the miller's house was surrounded by bags of flour. In the centre of the stage raised slightly on one of the hydraulic lifts stood a counter and to the side a large safe. Upstage stood a large windmill, its sails revolving slowly around and around. The designers of the pantomime, Messrs Beech and Co. had been very clever in their designs as the room below and the windmill above blended perfectly together giving the illusion of seeing inside the windmill.

Mr. Maltravers, who was playing the oldest son Hovis made his entrance followed by Herbert Beleno playing the dame and Mr. Younger who was playing the second Brother Be-ro.

'Oh, dear, what's to become of us,' cried the dame. 'I've worked my fingers to the bone and what have I got to show for it?'

'Boney fingers?' answered Mr. Maltravers.

'What's to become of us?' cried the dame again, 'Your poor dear father, has worked himself into an early grave.'

'Don't fret mother, we still have the mill,' said Mr. Maltravers.

'And the house,' said Mr. Younger.

'What more do we need?' asked Mr. Maltravers.

'Dough,' answered the dame. 'Dough and lots of it. Otherwise the Black Baron with throw us out.'

'Why that's easy,' said Mr. Younger, 'anybody can make dough.'

'Leave it to us,' said Mr. Maltravers as they both left the stage.

Granny Probyn was becoming very nervous. Soon Fluffy Yeomans would be making his entrance. Mr. Pleach who was playing the third and youngest of the miller's sons then made his entrance.

'This is it,' whispered Granny Probyn to Fluffy Yeomans shivering in her hands with nerves.

'There you are, Jack,' said the dame as Mr. Pleach entered the stage.

'Hello, Mother,' he replied.

'Jack, Jack, Jack, what are we to do? Your father's gone and left the Mill to Hovis, and the House to Be-ro, and to you…' The dame waved a large scroll in her hand. Made by the props department it had on it written in large letters 'Will' across the top.

'What has father left me mother?' asked Mr. Pleach.

'The cat.' Answered the dame.

'The cat!' exclaimed Mr. Pleach.

'Yes the cat.'

'Only a cat! But how am I to live?' asked Mr. Pleach walking towards the safe. Mr. Pleach then sat on the safe and said the lines, 'My brothers may make their living easily enough yet I may soon die of hunger and want.'

That was the cue for Fluffy Yeomans. He burst through the cupboard door as he had rehearsed, stood centre stage and said his opening line, 'Meow!' to thunderous applause. After that it was all plain sailing, everybody played their parts superbly, Mr. Maltravers and Mr. Younger did their tumbling routine, the dame led the audience with the song sheet, Mr. von Stutlz as the Black Baron was suitably booed as the villain, and Miss de la Mouche and Mr. Pleach sang their love duet together beautifully and, as the curtain descended at the end of the walk down with everyone dressed in rich blues and silvers, a great cheer arose from the cast to say, 'We did it.'

Back in the dressing room, Granny Probyn sat with Ethel Dorfellwaffer as she twittered on about the show and how much Beauregard Henry had enjoyed it. Fluffy Yeomans was signing pawographs for the young dancers in the cast, while Ethel's son Napoleon and young Beauregard himself were getting a tour of the understage hydraulic mechanism by their friend and stage manager Mucus Drillby. The whole backstage area was a buzz with people coming to congratulate friends and family, all apart from the dressing room next to Granny Probyn.

Augustus Reed knocked and stuck his rather large head around the door just as Ethel was recounting that Beauregard had eaten three ice creams on the way to the theatre, when a scream was heard from the corridor outside.

'Who's screaming in my theatre?' boomed Mr. Reed half in and out of Granny Probyn's dressing room, as Miss Plimple hurriedly ran past him and down the corridor to the stage door. 'What on earth is going on?' he boomed again to no one in particular, as some of the young chorus members looked at each other in confused amazement. Everybody was now in the corridor, looking to see what all the commotion was about. All except for Miss de la Mouche, who had the dressing room next door to Granny Probyn's. Of all the doors on that corridor, hers was the only one to remain very firmly closed.

Mr. Maltravers, came to the front of the crowd and suggested that they should knock to see if she was all right.

'A good idea,' boomed Mr. Reed and cleared his throat, 'Ahem,' then knocked quite quietly on the door. 'Miss de la Mouche?' he enquired. Silence. The whole corridor held their breath. 'Miss de la Mouche?' he knocked again. Silence, then slowly the door opened and a very ashen faced Miss de la Mouche stuck her head around the door.

'Is everything all right Miss de la Mouche?' boomed Mr. Reed.

'Yes Mr. Reed, thank you.'

'Then what was that scream we all heard?' he tried not to shout.

'Ah... well... you see,' she stammered trying to think of an excuse, when Miss Plimple reappeared through the crowded corridor.

'That was me, Mr. Reed,' she said somewhat more composed. But no reason was forthcoming.

'Well,' boomed Mr. Reed slightly at a loss what to do, 'if everything is all right, then why are we all standing about like lemons? Come along and clear the corridor.' His voice resumed its natural loud level as the chorus members dispersed back to their dressing rooms to gossip over what had just happened while getting ready to leave. Granny Probyn, was still standing in the doorway of the dressing room with Fluffy Yeomans between her feet as Mr. Maltravers, who was last to leave gave Miss de la Mouche a look which Granny Probyn couldn't quite make out. Just then Beauregard Henry bounded around the corner of the corridor and espied Fluffy Yeomans and made a beeline for him. Fluffy Yeomans having been mauled by Beauregard Henry before and not wanting a repeat performance dashed down the corridor and into the dressing room of Miss de la Mouche just as she closed the door.

Mr. Maltravers nodded politely to Granny Probyn and walked off to his own dressing room on the next floor as Napoleon and his friend Mucus rounded the corner and nearly bumped into him. Their conversation was very animated as Napoleon being a hydraulic enthusiast, albeit in an amateur fashion, discussed the finer points of Mucus' improvements to the theatre hydraulic system.

Ashley de la Mouche sat at her dressing room table. The lights around the mirror enhanced the paleness of her skin. She hadn't seen Fluffy Yeomans enter as she closed the door and was surprised when he brushed himself up against her leg.

'Oh,' she gasped as she Fluffy Yeomans brushed between her legs, 'you frightened me.'

'Meow,' said Fluffy Yeomans.

'What am I to do?' she asked as she bent down and picked Fluffy Yeomans up, placing him on her lap and tickling him underneath his chin.

If there was anything better than a tickle under the chin, Fluffy Yeomans couldn't think of it. He purred quite contentedly and started to knead Miss de la Mouche's lap careful not to expose his claws, before sitting down with a smile on his face and his chin held high in anticipation of another tickle.

'You are a lovely thing, but don't you think you should be in your own dressing room?' she asked knowing that she wasn't going to get an answer from Fluffy Yeomans except a meow. But Fluffy Yeomans didn't meow, and wasn't going to give up the opportunity of another chin tickle especially with the young Beauregard tearing up his dressing room at this very moment. So he curled up on her lap and purred some more.

'Oh what am I to do,' she asked to no one in particular looking at herself in the mirror. She had a confession to make but couldn't tell, and Fluffy Yeomans was as good as anyone to confide in. 'If I don't do as I'm told there's going to be a lot of trouble, but I just can't.' She continued then burst into tears. 'Oh what am I to do?'

Granny Probyn knocked quietly at the dressing room door, 'Hello dear, I don't suppose you have seen Fluffy Yeomans anywhere,' she said as she opened the door. 'Ah, there you are you naughty boy, running away like that. I was getting quite frantic with worry. You ought to be ashamed especially when Mrs. Dorfellwaffer and Beauregard Henry came backstage especially to see you.'

'It's not his fault,' said Miss de la Mouche, 'he was just keeping me company for a while.'

'Is everything all right, my dear?' enquired Granny Probyn solicitously, as she could see that Miss de la Mouche had been crying. She was determined to find out if this young woman was the same person who she had overheard on her first night in the theatre.

'Yes, thanks. Just first night nerves I expect,' she replied.

Granny Probyn smiled, and called Fluffy Yeomans who reluctantly jumped from Miss de la Mouche's lap and slinked his way to Granny Probyn at the door. 'We'll I won't keep you any longer then. It's been a long day and we need to get back to the hotel. Good night.' With which Granny Probyn shooed Fluffy Yeomans out into the corridor with the inside of her foot and closed the door behind her. 'Now you listen to me Fluffy Yeomans,' said Granny Probyn in a stage whisper so as not to be overheard, 'you keep away from that young lady. There's something fishy going on and it's not one you can eat. You heard that argument as well as I did. Somebody is going to get hurt. Oh dear! We really should tell someone, but who?'

Fluffy Yeomans went straight to bed as soon as they had arrived at the hotel, but Granny Probyn in too much of an excitement over the day's events tried to calm her nerves a little by doing a spot of reading. 'I have just the thing,' she thought as she fished into her bag to retrieve the paperback she had bought on her arrival at Paddington. Soon she was engrossed in the novel about an old woman who shares a carriage on a train with a young man and happens to tell him of a series of murders disguised as accidents which have taken place in her little village. Although the local police are out of their depth she knows who the murderer is and is on her way to Scotland Yard to impart her news. But, she never makes it. The young man reads of the accidental death of an old lady who has been hit by a car... just then the clock chimed and broke her concentration.

'Oh, dear, just look at the time, and we have to be at the theatre early tomorrow.' Granny Probyn placed her marker in the book and crawled into bed as Fluffy Yeomans grudgingly made room for her.

The next morning Granny Probyn along with the entire cast were standing on stage waiting for Mr. Reed to make his speech and tell them of any changes that he thought would be necessary for that evening's performance.

'Well this is intolerable, where is the man?' boomed Mr. Reed's voice from the back of the auditorium. By now Granny Probyn was used to Mr. Reed and his blunt way of addressing people and wasn't in the least scared of him now.

'I'm sorry, Mr. Reed.' Said Miss Plimple, 'but he's nowhere to be seen. In fact according to Walter he never left the theatre last night.'

'Probably drunk in a corner somewhere. How am I supposed to give notes if the stage manager isn't here? Well don't just stand there, go and find him. Meanwhile we'll go through the changed positions for the walk down.'

'Yes, Mr. Reed.' With which Miss Plimple made her way through the pass door back stage as Mr. Reed boomed out. 'Right, ladies and gentleman, everyone places for the finale if you please.' Back at the stage door, Miss Plimple enlisted the help of Walter and some of the backstage crew to help look for the missing Stage Manager. According to Walter she learned that Granny Probyn had a lady friend and her son with his family visiting backstage and it turned out that Mucus and the son of Granny Probyn's friend were pals from school and had been on a tour of the theatre. The family had left with Granny Probyn and Fluffy Yeomans as they had said their goodbyes to each other right here at the stage door, before Granny Probyn climbed into one taxi and her friend and family climbed into another. He remembered he said as Granny Probyn's friend had left twice, 'She had left something in the dressing room,' he said. Mucus had stayed behind; obviously he had a lot of work still to do.

'Well I suppose we had just better search every room until we find him. You do back stage and I'll do front of house.' Said Miss Plimple and strode off leaving Walter to arrange someone to look after the door while he and Jimmy the call boy went in search of the stage manager.

Mr. Reed was not in a good mood, although the show had gone very well the previous evening he was not happy with the ending and wanted to rehearse the walk down. The scene, set in the palace ballroom had a large staircase upstage upon which members of the cast made their entrances. This meant that one of the upstage stage lifts had to be used as the back area with steps added, and without Mucus Drillby the stage manager nobody knew how to work the controls for the newly improved hydraulics that worked the lifts.

'Surely there must be someone else in this theatre who can work the lifts,' he bellowed out to anybody who wasn't cowering on stage. The crew backstage knew when to keep quiet and out of range and with all the actors on stage in full view it was a good chance that one of them would cop the storm that was brewing. Meanwhile, Mr. Perry the assistant stage manager was desperately twiddling knobs and buttons in the vain hope that something he did would release the mechanism and raise the backstage lift so members of the cast standing on it could eventually make their walk down.

Suddenly Granny Probyn, along with Julian Pleach, started to come into view above the heads of the rest of the cast, as the stage lift started slowly to rise.

'At last,' bellowed Mr. Reed. 'At least Mrs. Probyn can get the damn thing working, now place the treads.'

Looking slightly embarrassed at this remark both she and Mr. Pleach were waist height above the people in front of them and rising, when the rest of the cast turned to see just how she had managed to make the lift work, then one and then another of the young girls of the chorus started to scream.

'Who's screaming in my theatre?' boomed Mr. Reed from the back of the auditorium.

'Shut that woman up, I divin't want all that bloddy noise on stage,' he bellowed as he made his way to the front of the orchestra pit as the cast on stage parted to reveal the now elevated Granny Probyn and Mr. Pleach clinging together on top of the bridge as the drop was becoming quite substantial while beneath, hung by the neck, was the limp body of Mucus Drillby.

Scene 3

The police kept everybody waiting about for ages as all had to be questioned and statements taken but of course nobody had seen anything or knew anything. There was a discussion as to whether the show should go on that night but Mr. Reed had insisted in the good old theatrical tradition that the show *must* go on, though nobody felt in the mood and the entire production felt like lead. Of course the audience knew nothing of the death of Mr. Drillby and so were disappointed by the flat performances when they left the theatre that night.

Granny Probyn and Fluffy Yeomans were questioned along with everybody else, but alas she had no news about the unfortunate man, only that he was a friend of the son of a friend of hers and that they had met the previous night and he had an animated discussion about hydraulics with Napoleon Packard. Why he should want to take his own life…? Well anybody could guess. The police went to the law offices of Napoleon Packard to enquire of the nature of their conversation, but soon got bored as Napoleon described in intimate details the current workings of the hydraulic lifts at the theatre and how Mucus had improved upon the system. Of course one piston and ram is very much like any other piston and ram, and Napoleon was no orator so the police in question left as soon as they were reasonably able. And soon everybody put the unpleasant event behind them and got on with the daily routine of doing the pantomime.

Dormanston School was a huge Victorian building in the centre of London. The two entrances still bore the original inscriptions: *Boys* over one; *Girls* the other. As space was at a premium when the town planning development committee met to decide where they would want to build the school, a plot of land had been donated by a wealthy patron but, there wasn't enough room for a school yard, and so someone came up with the bright idea of putting it on the roof. Shoppers new to the area would sometimes hear the sounds of children playing but never a trace could be found of the little tykes running and chasing each other no matter how hard one looked. This was the old school of Mucus Drillby and his friend Napoleon Packard and now, aged 9½, Napoleons son Beauregard Henry was ensconced on his favourite stair just by the newel post of the first bend. Surrounded by his gang, this was an advantageous spot from where any teachers could be espied coming up to the play yard and as always he would be first to the dining room at lunch and break times.

Granny Probyn had been right in her description of Beauregard Henry in that he was a brat. But as long as his bore of a mother Veronica ruled the roost Beauregard Henry could do no wrong, and he knew it. He still got the occasional clip about the ear if his pranks got too much out of hand but most times it was just put down to high spirits and he was encouraged all the more.

Edward Cebris Jones dawdled. From the time that the doctors pronounced him to be a sickly child he never in his entire life was ever seen to break into a run. He ambled as usual along the street towards Dormanston School. He had no friends and no particular reason to rush to school as all his classmates picked on him. Maybe it was the way that his pigeon chest ribs stuck through his tee shirt during P.E. or how his teeth braces glinted in the cold classroom lighting or maybe it was because of the thick pebble jam jar bottom glasses that he wore, but his classmates always played some prank or had another new name to call him. He had just turned the corner of the school when he heard the school bell ring. He could hear the voices of his classmates shouting as they played in the school yard above before the start of lessons. If he hurried he might just be in time for assembly and so uncharacteristically for him he picked up speed. Having started to climb the three steps that lead to the boys' entrance a voice called to him.

'Hey there, you boy!' Came the call.

Edward Cebris Jones stopped for a second. Surely it couldn't be for him. Nobody ever wanted to speak to him. And so he started again up the steps.

'I say, you boy,' came the voice again. This time seeing that there was no other boy in the vicinity Edward Cebris Jones stopped and turned to look to see who had shouted. He looked myopically through his one good eye. The jam jar bottoms seemed to enlarge it to unnatural proportions. His other eye was encased in a rather shabby looking peachy coloured sticking plaster. The doctor had said that he also had a lazy eye and this would counter balance it. And so he looked out at the world with a sort of one-eyed squint. Standing in front of him was a man in a trench coat and trilby.

'I say, boy, you don't happen to know of a young man called Beauregard Henry Packard do you?' the man enquired.

This seemed a rather silly question to Edward Cebris Jones who spent his entire days at school trying to find ways to avoid meeting Beauregard Henry Packard, he being one of the many who teased and bullied him, but he nodded his head in reply.

'Well,' said the man, 'I have a package for him. Special delivery. I don't suppose you can tell me who he is?' At that point a light seemed to turn on in Edward Cebris Jones's mind. "Here's my chance for revenge," he thought. "At last after three years of torment I can repay all the taunts and beatings." 'I'm he,' he said quietly.

'You?' the man queried looking at this small bag of skin and bones with match sticks for legs and large knobbly knees showing beneath his school uniform shorts.

'Yes sir,' he said again a little more emphatically. 'If you please, sir I'm late. If you could just give me the package.'

The stranger dug his hands into the side pocket of his coat and produced a small gold cardboard box wrapped in a red ribbon. 'It's a sort of belated Christmas present,' he said, 'from my boss,' he added as an afterthought, handing over the box.

'Thank you, sir,' Edward replied turning as quickly as he could and trying to mount the last two stairs in his haste to get away. 'Thank you, sir,' he repeated as he pushed open the large wooden door that led into the main entrance hall of the school. For once Edward Cebris Jones managed to break into a trot as he made his way to his form classroom. As everybody was at school assembly he managed to get to his desk and hide the package before anybody could stop him and enquire as to his business.

For the rest of the morning the thought of that box sitting in his desk gnawed away at his mind to such an extent that he couldn't concentrate on any of his lessons. Finally the bell rang for lunch and, as the rest of the school made its way to the dining hall, Edward Cebris Jones headed for the only place of safety he could think of. Many a time when he was being chased he would make his way to the basement office of Mr. Duttheridge the caretaker and behind that the boiler room with the great furnace which roared during the winter months eating up the great stack of coal which was delivered once a week through a coal chute directly from the road above. Next to the boiler was the store cupboard where Mr. Duttheridge kept all his cleaning materials, mops, buckets, brooms, rat traps and poisons, this was the best place to hide. Nobody ever went in there during the day. Mr. Duttheridge locked himself into his office during school hours and only came out in times of emergencies like when someone in too much excitement was sick in the corridors.

Edward sat on one of the upturned buckets with his prize glinting on his large bare knobbly knees. He had been thinking all morning about what could be inside. Oh how he would gloat knowing that he had eventually got one over on Beauregard Henry. He slowly undid the red ribbon savouring every moment as he slid the lid off the box to reveal a layer of chocolates. By the depth of the box he estimated there must be three layers, each with four lovely tempting chocolates in each tray. This was just too much for Edward as he picked one of the forbidden fruits and placed it to his lips. His mother never allowed him to have chocolate. Another of her doctors decreed that chocolate caused catarrh and in one so young with a weak chest could prove fatal so not for him the pleasures of that rich creamy taste.

The temptation was just too much for young Edward. He just had to have another then another, and before he knew it he had already finished two layers of the box. But instead of feeling triumphant he had only succeeded in making himself feel sick with over indulgence. He began to feel guilty about stealing the box which was meant for Beauregard Henry. How was he going to get rid of the evidence? What would happen when Beauregard was questioned by the man who had given him the box only to find that he hadn't received a gift? An enquiry would be made and surely the man in the trench coat would point a guilty finger at him in front of the whole school. He would be taken away to prison and there left to rot. He had read the *Count of Montecristo* and knew all about the hardships of being abandoned in prison.

He had to get rid of the evidence but he couldn't face the task of eating any more chocolate. He was feeling decidedly queasy, his pulse had started to quicken and his breathing was becoming more laboured. Maybe the doctors had been correct after all he thought, as he started to gasp for air. He had to get rid of the evidence then surely it would be his word against that of a stranger's. If only he could be sure that no trace could be found of the box. Then it struck him, the cavernous boiler's fire next door was roaring away keeping the winter chill at bay. Although warm in the basement, the cold seemed to keep its grip on the rest of the building except for small pockets around the few radiators dotted about the building. His breathing was becoming even more laboured; gasping like a fish out of water Edward made his way to the furnace.

He lifted the heavy handle of the door burning his fingers on the hot metal and was obliged to use the hem of his jumper to pull the door open before throwing the box with the remaining chocolates inside. The box instantly burst into flames for a second as the hot air inside the furnace burst through the open door. The pain in his stomach had intensified and brought Edward out into a sweat which, mixed with the heat of the furnace, increased his inability to breath. His tongue felt as if it was swelling within his mouth and constricting the flow of air down to his lungs. With a final effort he managed to close the door of the furnace before collapsing on the floor. Bent double from the pain in his stomach, his eyes bulging from the lack of oxygen which he was desperately trying to get into his lungs he lay grasping at his throat which was slowly closing.

The bell finally rang to inform teachers and pupils alike that school was finished for another day. Mr. Duttheridge the caretaker opened his office door making his way to his cleaning cupboard to pick up his mop and bucket before starting to clean the mess from the hordes of kids that infested his lovely school. It was only then that Edward Cebris Jones was discovered. Dead.

Scene 4

The next day Ethel Dorfellwaffer couldn't wait to tell Granny Probyn. Sitting in the dressing room Ethel Dorfellwaffer recounted all the grisly details. 'Oh how lucky they were that the unfortunate accident didn't happen to poor Beauregard Henry.' As if poor Beauregard would eat rat poison. But one death in a school and all the parents were up in arms. Why keep poison in a school? It was an accident waiting to happen. Nobody seemed to ask the question as to what the boy was doing in the basement in the first place, but Ethel Dorfellwaffer was convinced that Beauregard Henry had escaped death by a hair from Fluffy Yeomans head and she wasn't going to relinquish the telling of a good story even if it was a little gruesome.

Granny Probyn sat patiently with Fluffy Yeomans while Ethel Dorfellwaffer described the scene of the accident as recounted to her.

'Oh that poor boy,' lamented Granny Probyn. 'Such a shame.'

'But just think, Granny Probyn, it could have been any one of the little darlings?' said Ethel clutching her breast. 'And such a horrible death too. His tongue so I'm reliably informed was black and the size of a cucumber!' Her reliable informant of course was no other than darling little Beauregard Henry who had embellished the story slightly for dramatic effect.

In the law firm of *Pritchett, Snickertt and Fox*, Napoleon Packard paced his office. The day before he had received a letter by the early post which was worrying him. He had tried to talk to his wife Veronica about it but what with that unfortunate accident at Beauregard Henry's school he couldn't quite seem to get her attention and so it was up to him to make a decision as to what to do.

But what should he do? The letter had only said that he would be contacted shortly by person or persons unknown and if he didn't do as was ordered another tragedy would befall the house of Packard. As far as he was aware there had been no tragedy to date other than the death of his one time school friend Mucus more than a week before and now the unfortunate accident with the child at his old school but should he go to the police? Even though the note expressly forbade it. He could just see himself trying to explain to some sergeant that he believed he was the subject of blackmail and that something very bad was going to happen to him if he didn't co-operate. And upon what evidence? None. No he would just have to wait and see who, if anyone, would contact him.

Granny Probyn just knew they were going to be late. Trying to cross London was going to be a nightmare and today there just had to be a matinee and the entire cast was called for extra rehearsals. It seems that Mr. Reed still wasn't happy with the walk down. Finally the taxi drew up outside the stage door, so that Granny Probyn with Fluffy Yeomans in his wicker work basket could rush inside and prepare for the rehearsal.

'Good morning, Walter,' she called as she dashed through the small vestibule of the stage door before bumping into Miss de la Mouche who was making her way out of the theatre.

'Oh excuse me, dear,' she said, 'not looking where I'm running, we're terribly late you know.'

Miss de la Mouche mumbled something into her handkerchief before rushing out.

'Ere, where's yer going Miss Mouche?' Walter called after her, 'rehearsals starts in five minutes. Mr. Reed'll do his nut!'

'I wonder what could be the matter with Miss de la Mouche, I didn't bump into her that hard,' said Granny Probyn. 'Maybe I hit her with Fluffy Yeomans's basket? Oh dear!'

'I don't think it had anything to do with that, Mrs. Probyn,' replied Walter, 'more'n likely to do with that letter that was left for her.'

'Oh, from who?' asked Granny Probyn whose curiosity was piqued?

'No idea,' answered Walter, 'I was away from me post less than two minutes. Went to get some hot water for me flask and when I returned there it was stuck in her pigeon hole.'

'Oh dear, I do hope it isn't too serious,' said Granny Probyn before turning into the corridor, 'well there's nothing we can do about it, is there Fluffy Yeomans? So we'd better just get ourselves ready and see what happens.'

Miss de la Mouche didn't turn up for rehearsals at all that morning and Walter's prediction of Mr. Reed's reaction was correct. He exploded. What sort of actress was she that she couldn't turn up for rehearsals when needed? Why, if he didn't have a beard, he would play her part himself and probably do a better job of it. After all, what does she have to do except smile, look pretty, and say her few lines in the proper order. It wasn't that difficult.

Miss de la Mouche was playing the part of the princess who marries the Marquis de Carabas the alias name of the third son Jack played by Mr. Pleach. In the end they had to improvise and use one of the stage hands to take her place so that they could rehearse the duet together and hoped that she would eventually turn up for the matinee performance.

Jimmy, the call boy knocked on Granny Probyn's door to call the half hour when Miss de la Mouche finally got to the crux of her story.

'It's so silly, Mrs. Probyn, but if I don't do as they ask, I'm afraid that they will do something terrible.'

'But what is it that they want?' asked Granny Probyn slightly confused. 'And who are they?'

'I received a letter saying that if I didn't do as I was told they would tell the authorities about my mother.'

'Why don't you go to the police about it? Surely they would be able to help.'

'No I can't do that, the note said that I mustn't and anyway, they would find out about mother and she'd be deported I'm sure. And I couldn't bear that. Where would she go? Since my Uncle died we have no family left. Only ourselves. No I couldn't go to the police.'

'Then we'll have to do something ourselves. I tell you what, my dear,' said Granny Probyn, 'don't say another word. Leave it to me and do as the note says and wait to be contacted.'

Scene 5

The Oppenheimer laboratories were one of the largest in Berlin. Professor von Meis, head of sciences, had his own set of rooms and a staff of twenty doing research for the National Security. Hydrodynamics had become its own science and Professor von Meis was its undisputed leader and champion. As yet nobody could see the potential for applying the new science but for the past few years von Meis had been working on combining aeronautics and hydrodynamics to design a whole new breed of aircraft. The NSDP had funded the project, and were now looking at different aspects of jet engines and aeronautics. This was soon to be the age of Jet rockets. Herr Hitler himself had made a rare visit to the Oppenheimer factory especially to be kept up to date on the latest developments.

Karl Leibknecht had been working closely with the professor on using the principal of hydraulics in aircraft when one night von Meis approached the young man.

'Karl, my boy,' he said, 'I know how fond you are of working here, but have you ever thought of what is going on in the outside world?'

Karl was a shy man, 25 years old he had studied hard to get himself educated. After the First World War he had been left orphaned, and life had been hard for the young Karl. Securing a job at the Oppenheimer factory had saved his life. Karl thought about the question, it didn't really affect him, he was safe in his job, what did he care what the NSDP did to others? He shrugged his shoulders in response to von Meis.

'Karl, my boy, you have to get out of here,' von Meis was now not asking but telling the young Leibknecht. 'Germany is not safe anymore; the factory is not safe anymore.' Karl looked at the professor. 'I'm leaving shortly Karl, and I want you to be with me. You're as close to me as a son. I want to carry on working this project through but not here. It will be used for evil and I don't know if my conscience will ever forgive me.'

'But professor, where will you go?'

'I have friends; they will help us out of Germany. But I'm not a young man anymore. If I don't make it I would like to know that the research will be finished.'

Karl looked at his mentor, unable to take in the enormity of what he was asking. His whole life would change. But what else did he have? Nothing.

'Where would we go?' he asked again, this time adding himself into the equation.

'We would have to leave separately, you first to London, via Amsterdam, then a few weeks later I would follow possibly going through Italy and down to Greece. The final details haven't been worked out as yet. I just wanted to know if you would come with me.'

Karl again looked at the man who for the last five years had taught him everything he knew.

'When do we leave?' he asked.

'The plan has already been put into motion. You will need to be ready to travel at a moments notice. Once everything is in place Levi will contact you.'

'Levi?'

'Oppenheimer, he has been a good friend, as you know it is dangerous for Jews in Germany, he will be leaving along with his family.'

Karl nodded. He had seen himself the daily struggle which the Jews were facing, and along with a great many of the German people he turned a blind eye.

Miss Plimple wrapped her coat around her to keep the winter chill from biting into her bones. What did she think she was doing, waiting here on the train station? Someone was bound to see her? But then of course a train station is also the best place in which to be concealed, that was why she chose this location in the first place. A station is always crowded with people waiting so why should anyone query a young woman waiting by herself? Finally, after fifteen minutes a man crossed the concourse from where he had been observing her, and introduced himself then, taking her by the elbow, led her into a waiting taxi. But of course this didn't go unnoticed.

Herr Delfger whistled quietly to himself practicing a new harmony which he would introduce into the act. His wife of course would complain. It seemed nowadays she was always complaining. He sometimes wondered why he had married her but at the time it was a marriage made in heaven. How many women siffleurists where there, and one so beautiful? Well, she was beautiful once but a life of gin and touring had taken its toll and now what had they left but touring second rate variety theatres? This could be his big break, give him the money he needed to get away. This was what he had been waiting for. He followed the unsuspecting Miss Plimple and the mysterious gentleman across the concourse. He'd made his exit just in time to note the number plate of the taxi, not that he needed it, Delfger knew who the gentleman was and where he was staying. It was just a matter of conjecture as to where they were headed. He guessed it would be the hotel of our new friend so he hailed a cab himself and asked for the Waldorf Hotel.

When he arrived there was no sign of the gentleman or Miss Plimple so he decided to wait in the lounge and see if she left with the package. He ordered tea and made himself comfortable feeling quite pleased with himself. As time wore on the feeling of smugness evaporated. Where could she be? She should be at the theatre shortly or she would miss the performance. Had he been outwitted? Then he saw the gentleman enter through the large turnstile door. Taking

42

his chance he rushed up to the man and very quietly said 'Mr. Oppenheimer, would you care to follow me please? I may say if you don't something very nasty could befall your lovely niece.'

Levi Oppenheimer looked about. Here he was standing in the middle of a very crowded reception hall of a very busy hotel and he felt like the loneliest man in the world. How had they found him? He thought he had been extra careful in his planning. They had checked into the hotel under false names and he had used some of the considerable Oppenheimer fortune on keeping them safe and yet somehow had they got hold of Hetty? And what about Odel was he safe? What he didn't know was that Herr Delfger was bluffing. In his panic Herr Delfger had said the first thing that had come into his head hoping to be able to get Mr. Oppenheimer out of the building and to quieter surroundings.

'Where are they?' Oppenheimer asked. 'If you have hurt her, I swear I shall kill you all myself.'

'If you please, sir, I would keep your voice down.' Herr Delfger looked about to see if they had been over heard. 'They are perfectly safe,' he continued. 'If you would just like to come with me we shall see them presently,' said Herr Delfger in his most sinister voice. He couldn't believe how simple this seemed to be. 'If you would just hand over the package, I can assure you that they will come to no harm.'

'It's too late for that now, I don't have it,' replied Oppenheimer, 'it's already far out of your reach. How much are they paying you for this? I will double it for the safe return of my niece.'

How just like a Jew to want to barter Herr Delfger thought to himself, but this wasn't what was supposed to happen. They should be outside in a taxi on their way to somewhere quiet rather than attracting attention in the middle of one of London's biggest hotels. Thinking quickly he said, 'That can be arranged. If you would like to follow me I can show you where your niece and nephew are being held, and maybe we can come to some arrangement, but I warn you it won't be cheap.'

'It never is with you people,' said Oppenheimer. To the last he was going to be in control. All his life he had been forced to take difficult decisions even though he was the youngest of three brothers. 'For the past six years your people have been bleeding us dry, I didn't expect anything less, come on lets get this over with,' at which he spun around and marched for the door.

It took Herr Delfger a moment to realise that his prey was already halfway across the foyer and willing to get into a taxi and he had to break into a trot to catch up with him.

Outside the doorman hailed a taxi, and when both were inside Herr Delfger gave the address of the boarding house in which he and his wife were staying. He hoped that fool of a landlady was out and his wife wasn't too much in her cups to realise what was going on. He also hoped that this might just be worth his while, getting money from Oppenheimer and at the same time retrieving the package. After all he knew of the whereabouts of Miss Plimple.

'May we say that some pecuniary reward be given before we arrive, as a matter of good faith you understand?' Herr Delfger was trying to sound obsequious and sinister at the same time.

Mr. Oppenheimer looked at him in disgust. Just like all of the others and they said that the Jews were the money grabbers. He was right to get out of that damned country. Too late now, he should have done it years ago, but his elder brother thought he knew best. He knew how to control these thugs he said "so leave it to him." Well where had that got him? Carted off to some camp. Well now it was up to him to save what was left of the family and its fortune. He opened his coat and pulled out his wallet. All he had was one hundred pounds. He was sure that that wouldn't cover it. Then he saw the look of greed on the other man's face.

'Here take it. It's all I have,' he said.

'This will do very nicely,' said Herr Delfger pocketing the money, 'on account so to speak.'

'Humph,' was the reply.

The taxi pulled up outside a small Victorian house in one of the less salubrious areas of Hackney. Herr Delfger made a big show of handing over a one pound note and telling the driver to keep the change, then after having checked that the street was quiet, he indicated the steps that took them up to the front door. So far the landlady hadn't put in an appearance. She lived in the basement with her own door from the light well. So far so good he thought as he opened the door and with a flourish bade Mr. Oppenheimer enter.

The hall was small and cramped with a staircase immediately to the right. And a large art deco coat stand with a central mirror to the left. He was bustled down the corridor by Herr Delfger as a voice from upstairs called out, 'Heinz is that you? Where've you been? That old bag downstairs says she wants some money.'

'This way if you please,' said Herr Delfger, 'in here a moment. Can I get you a drink perhaps?'

'This isn't a damned social call; just show me to my niece and nephew,' Oppenheimer replied.

Herr Delfger was just about to answer when loud steps were heard descending the stairs and again the voice shouting, 'Did you hear what I said? That bag downstairs has been threatening to chuck us out if we don't come up with some money soo...' the shouting stopped the moment that Madam Delfger turn the last step to be confronted by Mr. Oppenheimer and her husband behind, cowering and waving his arms about.

'Oh, begging your pardon, I didn't know we had company,' she said, leering at her husband who was frantically trying to tell her something. Madam Delfger was suddenly aware that she was still in her nightdress and hurriedly pulled each half across her ample bosom. If ever there was an archetypal German frau then Madam Delfger was it. She was a big blonde buxom woman, who would not be out of place carrying steins of refreshing German beer to thirsty clientele in one of the many beer cellars of the Fatherland. With her hair in plaits either side of her ears she could be easily play the part of Brunhilde which indeed she did with her husband doing various selections from Wagner.

But all that whistling and blowing had reddened her cheeks and strengthened her lungs so that she had become the harridan that she was today. 'And just to whom may I have the pleasure?' When she wanted she could still turn on the charm. Or so she thought.

'Madam, it is no pleasure that I am here. Kindly show me to my nephew and niece and we shall leave this place forthwith.' If Oppenheimer was disgusted before, he was even more repulsed now and his face showed it. 'Now get out of my way,' he said pushing Madam Delfger aside and starting to climb the stairs.

''Ere, just who do you think you are coming in here and pushing people around?' retorted Madam Delfger. She wasn't one to be pushed around so easily.

'Now, now, dear,' said Herr Delfger, trying to placate her.

'Call yourself a man?' she said to her whimpering husband, 'letting a stranger into my house, and look at the way I've been treated. Oh stop your whimpering.'

In truth Herr Delfger couldn't get a whimper in anywhere when his wife was in full flow. 'Just who does he think he is?' Madam Delfger repeated, then the thought struck her, 'and what is he doing upstairs?'

She looked at her husband who could only lift his shoulders in a sort of a shrug. "Don't ask me," was the expression on his face.

'We'll see about this.' Madame Delfger started to climb the stairs.

Meanwhile Mr. Oppenheimer, calling out, searched through the two bedrooms and the small box room. 'Where are they?' he screamed. 'Where are they? If you have harmed them I swear I will kill you both here and now.' His face was livid. Arriving back at the top of the stairs, as the approaching bulk of Madam Delfger reached the turn at the top step, he grabbed her by the shoulders.

'Where are they?' he screamed.

'What are you on about? There is nobody here,' she said, pulling herself away from the madman.

'I know that they are here, but where are they?' he repeated as once again he made to grab Madam Delfger. But she was having none of that thank you very much and using her not too inconsiderable strength brushed him away. Unfortunately, being left handed as she was, her sweeping arm knocked Mr. Oppenheimer out of the way, his foot lost its hold on the top step and he crashed head first then backwards down the stairs ending in a crumpled heap at the bottom.

Herr Delfger looked at the mangled figure in the hallway and then up to his wife who, in a state of shock, was silent. 'What have you done?' he said to his wife, and whistled his new harmony.

Fluffy Yeomans was bored, it was all very well being a theatre cat but, when he wasn't on stage, there did seem to be a lot of waiting around. Back at Rose Cottage he could come and go as he pleased as he had a flap made especially for him in the kitchen door. Granny Probyn had young Luke the apprentice carpenter come and fix it to the stable door so that she didn't have to keep getting up every time Fluffy Yeomans wanted to come and go but now, at the theatre, he was feeling a little hemmed in. He had already searched the entire theatre from top to bottom and had put paid to a few rats which were scurrying around under the stage, but, apart from that, there didn't seem to be much to do. He liked to sit in the green room occasionally with the rest of the actors and crew before the performance. He usually got his chin tickled by a chorus member or one of the young dancers which was always something to look forward to, but it seemed his mother was mistaken in her view that the theatre was a house of ill repute and full of sin. In fact there seemed very little that was disreputable going on. Here he was between matinee and evening shows and the theatre was deserted. Granny Probyn was taking a nap in the dressing room. She said there was little point in returning to the hotel only to turn around and travel back for the evening performance so, for the days when matinees happened, she took her nap in the dressing room. He just had to do something. At that moment he noticed Miss Plimple walking by the open door of the green room holding a rather large packet. "Hello, hello," he thought, "let's see what's in the bag." So he followed her down the corridor to the stairwell that led to beneath the stage.

Miss Plimple was being very careful to avoid being seen, or so it seemed to Fluffy Yeomans, and so he intended to be as discrete as possible and once under the stage managed to find a small corner beneath the hydraulic machinery from where he could observe what was going on. Except that nothing was going on, Miss Plimple took the package she was carrying and hid it amongst some crates in a far corner away from prying eyes and left the way she had come. What was in it? Unfortunately it wasn't going to give up its secret easily and so Fluffy Yeomans gave up trying to open it, and decided to wait and see what would happen, meanwhile keeping an eye out for Miss Plimple.

That very day both Napoleon Packard and Miss de la Mouche received the second letters that each had been waiting for. Both were thrown into confusion as to what they should do. Miss de la Mouche knocked at Granny Probyn's door. 'Are you there?' she enquired, sticking her head around the door to see if she was in, knowing that she always took a nap between shows.

'Come in, dear,' Granny Probyn said, smiling sweetly. 'What is it?'

Miss de la Mouche passed the letter to Granny Probyn to read.

'Oh, dear,' Granny Probyn said, as she had finished reading, 'this is serious isn't?'

Miss de la Mouche buried her face in her handkerchief. What was she to do? Her mother was sure to be deported if the authorities ever found out, but what was she to do? She just couldn't do what the letter asked of her.

'Well it's obvious that we can't go to the police,' Granny Probyn said, 'so we'll just have to do as they say.'

'But how?' Miss de la Mouche whimpered through the lace of her hanky, 'Miss Plimple is always backstage, that's her job, she's Mr. Reed secretary, she's his eye's and ears throughout the show. You've seen her sticking her nose into everything. How are we supposed to keep her away from the theatre?'

'That, my dear, is something that we will just have to work out, the other question is why they want Miss Plimple out of the way?'

'I hadn't even thought about that, there must be something back stage what they want, and can't get at with Miss Plimple always being there.'

'Precisely!' Exclaimed Granny Probyn, 'so we have to find out what it is they want and who these people are.'

'Oh, dear Mrs. Probyn, I didn't mean for you to become involved, it's just that I've no one else to turn too.' Cried Miss de la Mouche into her hanky again.

'There, there, we'll find a solution. You just wait and see, it'll all turn out for the best,' said Granny Probyn, although she didn't really believe what she was saying. And she still hadn't forgotten that conversation she had heard that first night in the theatre.

Scene 6

The Thule society gathered once a month in the house of the current president. Tonight was going to be a special occasion as a talk was to be given by Wilhelm Tost, London correspondent for the *Volkischer Beobachter*. The sliding doors to the dining room had been opened and the dining table removed so that extra chairs could be placed. Expectation amongst society members was high. Of course everyone knew what was on the agenda. Wilhelm Tost was a close friend to Alfred Rosenberg who it was said had the ear of Hitler himself. Such was the closeness to power. Many in the society supported the NSDP, quietly of course. It wasn't wise in these difficult times for Germans in England to be too outspoken as far as their belief in support for Hitler was concerned. It seemed the British Press was having a field day of anti German propaganda making fun of the little man with the moustache and the cowlick. But there were still some true believers in the cause. Many of whom were gathered in a large Victorian house in Hackney.

The street was in darkness as Maltravers knocked at the front door. The three story Victorian house seemed ideal as there was a tall hedge surrounding the small garden at the front of the property which shielded anyone who was waiting from prying eyes and in this house the guests didn't want to be seen. The door opened quickly to allow Maltravers to enter and was silently closed behind him. He made his way directly into the front room through a doorway on the left. He was the last to arrive and, as he entered into the room conversations between the other guests stopped.

'Ah, Maltravers,' said a man extending his hand in welcome, 'we've been expecting you.'

'Yes, sorry for the delay,' he replied, shaking his head at the offer of a glass of sherry. 'I'd rather have something stronger.'

'Not losing your nerve?' asked the man with a slight menace to his voice; all ears in the room seemed to be listening to the conversation.

'No, no n-not in the slightest,' stammered Maltravers, although he could feel a trickle of sweat run down the centre of his back. After the death of that boy the police were asking a lot of questions, nothing that could be linked to the organisation, but it didn't help the cause. He would just have to bluff his way out of the mistake and hopefully lay the blame elsewhere.

'Then come and tell us what news you have, and Forsythe here will fix you a whisky.'

Just then a little man, dressed in evening suit, stood before the assembled company and with an 'ahem' cleared his throat to attract their attention. He wasn't too pleased with von Marenbach and had made a mental note to himself that he must have words with the upstart. After all wasn't he, Albert Hessen, President of the society? Hadn't he been working for the cause all these long years and now it was nearly coming to fruition?

'Ladies and Gentlemen,' he said turning his attention back to the crowd. 'May I thank you all for coming, and beg your forgiveness for the cramped accommodation. Our guest speaker tonight needs no introduction. I'm sure many of you have read many of his intelligent and interesting articles, so without any further hesitation on my behalf I present Herr Wilhelm Tost.'

With that there was a small smattering of polite applause as Wilhelm Tost stood and walked to the front of the room. Albert Hessen made his way to the rear and took the elbow of Maltravers. 'Perhaps you would like to join us upstairs,' he whispered in his ear. It was more of a command than an invitation, and for the second time that night Maltravers, felt a trickle of sweat. They made their exit from the room accompanied by von Marenbach and climbed the stairs to Hessen's study. The rest of the German committee were already waiting for the president and Maltravers to arrive. 'Gentleman,' Hessen said as he entered the smoke filled room, 'I must apologise for our friend's tardiness, but I believe that Mr. Maltravers may have some news concerning Project Pantomime. Mr. Maltravers, if you would be so kind as to brief the committee on what progress we have in finding our friend Professor von Meis?'

'Well, as you know gentlemen, I got myself hired so that I could keep trace on the goings on at the theatre. After the unexpected death of Mucus Drillby, our only link now to the professor is his niece Miss Plimple. We know von Meis and his assistant left his laboratory two weeks ago and nothing has been seen or heard of him since...'

'Yes, yes,' interrupted von Marenbach, 'but have you managed to locate him?'

'Well, err...' Maltravers was now on very shaky ground. 'We've tried contacting his niece, but she has been reluctant in joining our cause, so we have had to use other methods.'

'Yes, yes,' interrupted von Marenbach again, 'but have you managed to locate him?'

'If you would stop interrupting the fellow we may learn what has actually transpired.' Hessen said, slightly annoyed. He would definitely have to have words with von Marenbach but now would not be the appropriate time for a scene, especially with a houseful of Thule members below. Best to keep any bickering amongst the committee in house so to speak.

'Pray continue with your briefing, Maltravers,' he said with an air of authority.

'Well that's about it really,' said Maltravers rather weakly. 'Until we can get Miss Plimple to tell us of his whereabouts it's like trying to find a needle in a haystack.'

'And you are sure that she has been in contact with her uncle?' asked Hessen.

'Most definitely,' replied Maltravers as he looked around at the stoney faces in the room, 'it's just a matter of time before we get the information. I myself have been putting pressure on certain people.'

'We all know what a cock up you've made of that,' remarked von Marenbach, 'had the bloody police sniffing around for a week.'

'Yes well, there's no use crying over spilt milk, I have used some of my considerable influence to put a check on any activities regarding the police, but I warn you any more stupid mistakes will have to be dealt with severely.' Hessen was staring at Maltravers who for a third time felt that trickle run down his spine. But the threat wasn't for Maltravers alone, Hessen had a chain of command beneath him but still had to answer to his own superiors in the Fatherland and this information was not going to be warmly received.

'I'm sure everything will be fine, believe me, we are almost there. Once we have his whereabouts it will be impossible for von Meis to defect to the Americans,' said Maltravers trying to instil in his voice a note of confidence which he didn't quite feel he had.

Just then a knock at the door interrupted the conversation.

'Yes!' Barked Hessen. 'Come in!' The door opened and Forsythe entered. 'Forgive me sir, but Herr Tost has concluded his talk and wishes to have a private word.'

'Thank you, Forsythe, if you would care to show him in? Gentlemen if you will excuse us?'

At which point the five members of the German committee as well as Maltravers made their farewells.

'Be careful you don't make another mistake, Maltravers,' said von Marenbach as they were descending the stairs to join the rest of the Thule Society in leaving, 'failure can be a very nasty business.'

Fluffy Yeomans spent the next week assiduously keeping an eye on the package that Miss Plimple had secreted under the stage. At every given opportunity he checked to make sure it hadn't been moved or tampered with, meanwhile trying to open it himself to investigate its contents.

Something fishy was going on and, like Granny Probyn was fond of saying, it wasn't one that you would want to eat. He had tried to get Granny Probyn to open the package, but the only time that she was under the stage with him he was about to make his entrance and Miss Plimple as well as some other members of the cast were milling about waiting for their cues so it was impossible for him to make himself understood and Granny Probyn would never start rummaging around in other people's belongings, it just wasn't done. No, he would have to find a way of getting inside that package for himself. As for Miss Plimple, she ignored the package entirely. It was if she was unaware of its existence.

For a whole week Granny Probyn wracked her brains as to why Miss Plimple should be of interest to these people who seemed to be blackmailing Miss de la Mouche. She had followed her as much as she could around the theatre, but as she had no reason to be front of house etcetera, it was rather awkward trying to keep a track on all her movements. Miss de la Mouche seemed to be forever in her dressing room, wringing her hands around the lace hanky that she always carried, and was definitely beginning to look the worse for wear. The pantomime continued as if nothing was the matter; audiences came and loved the spectacle, the sparkle and the glitter. It seemed there were dark clouds gathering on the horizon and a lot of people just wanted to escape everyday life and where better than the pantomime at the Theatre Royal Drury Lane?

At the end of that week, Ethel Dorfellwaffer called on Granny

Probyn after one of the matinees. Having made herself comfortably ensconced in Granny Probyn's chair, she dived into the hot crumpets which Granny Probyn had prepared for her arrival.

'And how is life on the boards treating you, my dear?' she said using the latest phrase she had picked up from the stage door. 'I must say it seems all very exciting and colourful and...' waving her hand around in a vague gesture that encompassed the room, 'you have made this lovely little room just like Rose Cottage.'

Granny Probyn followed the hand that also held a knife and a blob of raspberry jam.

'Yes, well one has to have one's little comforts, don't you think?' she replied, still keeping an eye on the knife that had come to rest on the crumpet. 'But it's terribly hard work though. I didn't think there would be so much to do. Poor Fluffy Yeomans is exhausted after every performance; although I must say he is rather good at it.' Such was the praise that Fluffy Yeomans had been getting in the daily press that Granny Probyn had started to keep a scrap book in which were pasted all his cuttings and photographs.

'So what has brought you into town today?' she asked. 'I must say I was quite surprised by your telegram, it sounded so serious.'

'It is, my dear, it is,' Ethel Dorfellwaffer looked from side to side to make sure that she wasn't going to be overheard then leaned forward conspiratorially and whispered, 'something fishy is going on.'

'Oh,' said Granny Probyn as nonchalantly as possible, 'in what way?'

'Well, you know that poor Mr. Drillby,' she said, 'Napoleon Packard thinks that he was murdered!'

Once more, 'Oh,' was all that Granny Probyn could say. In all her thoughts about Miss Plimple and Miss de la Mouche she had totally forgotten about the death of poor Mr. Drillby. Supposing they were connected!

'Why would he think that?' she enquired, not really wanting to know the answer.

'Well, Napoleon says,' Ethel continued, 'that prior to Mucus taking a job in the theatre, he had been working on some theory of hydronauticals or hydrodynamicals or something like that, and he has just read that some professor has disappeared from his laboratory in Germany without a trace. What do you think about that?'

'But what could any of that have to do with the theatre and poor Mr. Drillby?' asked Granny Probyn.

'Well isn't it obvious? It has got to be something to do with those hydraulics under the stage.'

Granny Probyn couldn't quite see the connection. What possible reason could link a set of hydraulic theatre lifts with the suspected murder and disappearance of some professor? It all seemed so bizarre. But then again there was Miss de la Mouche and her letter.

'But my dear that's not all,' Ethel was twittering, 'there has also been another murder which nobody seems to have linked to poor Mucus.'

Granny Probyn stopped her musing to try and concentrate on what Ethel was saying as she continued, 'The poor man was found drowned in one of the canals. Of course the police haven't made the connection but they don't know about his history.'

'And how do you?' asked Granny Probyn.

'You know, while I was a small girl growing up in Berlin, we didn't have the privileges that you have had. Indeed, I went into service as a lady's maid and nanny so as not to be a burden on my family, well it seems this young man who the police have found is no other than little Levi. Of course he's not so little anymore, poor thing...' Ethel cut short her diatribe to blow her nose into her hanky. Granny Probyn wasn't sure if this was from grief, or learning of the death of her young charge, or the onset of a cold.

'Why was he here in England?' enquired Granny Probyn, 'You yourself know it's not all that pleasant for Germans at this time to be around and about.'

'That, my dear, we shall never know.'

'I still don't see the connection. What has the death of this poor man got to do with Mr. Drillby?'

'Why Levi and his family are exceedingly rich, one of the richest in Berlin, they own the factory from where this professor disappeared. Now do you see?'

'Yes.' Granny Probyn said quietly. It seemed that something decidedly fishy was going on.

Scene 7

K arl was lost. Having found a small room in which he and the professor were going to sleep he went out to find someone who could help them travel to Gibraltar. The back streets of Athens teamed with vendors selling all sorts of merchandise. And in the maze of Monasteraki he had totally lost his bearings. Above him he could see the ramparts of the Parthenon and knew the direction he should be walking but couldn't seem to find the street to lead him back to Omonia square and the room they had rented.

Professor von Meis slept fitfully. The escape from Germany had been brought forward and so what had been planned had to be quickly altered. It was decided that both he and Karl would work their way through the Balkans down through Greece and find a way to Gibraltar and then on to the UK, while Levi would leave first with his family and go via Amsterdam, taking with him all of von Meis's notebooks and research which he would leave with von Meis's niece, none other than Miss Plimple! Now that they were in Athens, it seemed what was a good plan in Germany had failed, as travelling to Gibraltar was not going to be as easy as they thought. Von Meis awoke in darkness; the slatted shutters were closed against the winter chill. He looked across the room to the other metal framed bed which was the only other piece of furniture in the room only to see the grubby mattress. Karl still hadn't returned. The professor made his way to the door and looked out. He stepped out onto the corridor which was open to the courtyard below; downstairs the family who owned the house were sitting eating. Von Meis walked down the exterior stairs into the centre of the yard to be greeted by Manolis Kastanas, a large man dressed even in the winter chill only his vest. 'Please come and join us,' Manolis said.

His wife Eleftheria, silently stood and removed their three children to the kitchen, as the professor took his seat. Eleftheria returned with another plate and a glass and placed them before the professor, as Manolis set about filling the plate from an array of dishes.

'Your friend he no has returned?' Manolis asked.

'It seems not,' replied the professor as he took out his pocket watch to check on the time. 'I do hope he will be alright.'

'Of course, I shall send my cousin to find him if he no come back.' Manolis said. 'Eat. You look tired.'

'Thank you, yes; travelling is not what it used to be. Our next problem is to get to Gibraltar,' said the professor as he started eating.

Odel and his sister Hetty waited quietly for their uncle. They had not left the hotel in nearly a week and both were now beyond distraction. Levi had left for a meeting and instructed them on what to do if he should not return but neither of them wanted to acknowledge the fact that Uncle Levi wasn't or couldn't return home. Odel being the eldest felt that it was his responsibility to do something. Should he follow his uncle's wishes? He wanted to go to the police but knew he couldn't. No, they would just have to work something out between them and try to make contact themselves. Odel picked up the phone, 'Hello operator? Could you put me through to the Theatre Royal Drury Lane please? Yes I'll hold.'

"Was this wise," he thought to himself? Anybody could be listening to the conversation but he had to find out about Uncle Levi.

'Yes, hello, Theatre Royal?' he asked of a tired sounding response.

'Who else is it gonna be?' replied Walter. Really some people rang the theatre and did asked the most stupid questions.

'I wonder if you could help me I'm looking for a Mr. Plimple?' Odel asked.

'Sorry, Guv, can't help you there, we ain't got no Mister only a Miss,' said Walter. 'You *Miss*-ed out on that one,' he continued, chuckling to himself at his own joke.

Odel was taken by surprise; he hadn't expected his uncle's contact to be a woman. The note left by his Uncle stated only the name Plimple and the phone number of the theatre. 'Would it be possible to speak to her?' he enquired, hoping that there weren't two theatres with a Plimple in them.

'Sorry, Guv, can't help you there neither, ain't nobody here yet, show don't start for an'uvva three hours. I can takes a message for yer if yer want.'

Odel was having difficulty in following Walter's accent, although from an old German family, Odel had been educated in England and spoke perfect English. 'No thank you,' he replied and hung up.

'What did they say?' Hetty asked.

'This Plimple turns out to be a Miss and she wasn't there,' he replied. 'Get out your glad rags, Hetty; we're going to the theatre.'

Mr. Marchmount cut a dashing figure in his great grey overcoat and top hat smiling at patrons and holding open the large doors which led into the foyer of the Theatre Royal Drury Lane. Inside there was a buzz of excited chatter. Children had an expectant gleam in their eyes as they waited impatiently for the grown ups to finish saying their hellos to friends and take their seats in the auditorium.

Odel joined a queue of people waiting to collect tickets from the box office counter. All around people were chatting. Hetty was feeling rather nervous. This was her first outing since the disappearance of her uncle, of whom she was very fond. She couldn't help thinking that everybody was looking at her. In fact nobody was looking at her except Herr Delfger. His patience had finally paid off. Waiting outside the hotel he had followed Odel and Hetty. 'At last,' he thought. 'This is where I am able to get the package.' Things were looking up for Herr Delfger since the untimely demise of Levi Oppenheimer. His wife once such a harridan had been subdued. They had easily got rid of the body in the canal. They had placed it in one of the travelling baskets they had for their costumes. Borrowing a cart wasn't so easy, but with a pocket full of money, it seemed anything was possible. Even paying off the landlady what they owed had sweetened her temperament so it was she who had arranged the cart. Now all he had to do was retrieve the package and then it was easy street here we come.

Odel finally managed to get a pair of tickets and rejoined Hetty who was standing against the wall behind a pillar. 'Come on', he said, 'don't look like that or people will suspect something.'

'I'm sorry, Odel,' she replied, 'I can't help it, I feel as if everybody is watching us.'

'Well let's give them something to look at,' was his reply as he took her gently by the elbow and led her through the double doors into the auditorium.

Herr Delfger waited until Odel & Hetty had entered the auditorium then slipped out the front and made his way to the stage door. Walter as usual was at his desk fending off the autograph hunters and well wishers. The little vestibule of the stage door was crammed. Herr Delfger was not going to be able to slip by unnoticed. He was just going to have to wait until the performance started and somehow bluff his way in.

Odel felt exposed sitting in the middle of the stalls at Drury Lane, but what could he do. He had left a note with the stage door during the interval and was glad when finally the house lights came up at the end of the performance. He rushed out with Hetty by his side to wait in a quiet part of the foyer. He hoped that the man with whom he had spoken to at the stage door had delivered his message, and that he would be met by Miss Plimple. As the crowds filed past on their way to the exits the noise of chatter and buzz filled the foyer. Odel didn't hear his name being called at first. Hetty drew him to one side and introduced him to a slightly tense young woman.

'Please come with me,' she said after the initial exchange of pleasantries. Miss Plimple ushered them quickly into her little office and before she had shut the door questioned Odel. 'Why are you here? I have already spoken with your uncle, and the package is safe?'

'The package maybe safe but my uncle isn't,' replied Odel. This wasn't what she was expecting. 'He hasn't been seen since he left the hotel to visit you.'

'Oh,' said Miss Plimple. Just then a group of dancers walked noisily passed the office. 'We can't talk here, there are too many people. Can we meet later?'

'Just tell us where our uncle is,' Hetty said, almost ringing her hands in her distress around her handkerchief.

'I'm afraid I don't know where he is,' she replied. 'The last I saw of him he had dropped me off here at the theatre and returned to his hotel. I'm sorry I don't even know where that is.'

'Thank you for all your help, Miss Plimple,' Odel said, 'I think it's about time we left, Hetty.' Odel took hold of Hetty by the elbow at which point she burst into tears and hugged her brother.

'He's dead, I know it, I just know something awful has happened to him, poor Uncle Levi, what shall we do?'

'There now, don't take on so. We'll just have to follow his instructions. He knew what danger he was getting into; he always said that there would be no getting away from these people.'

'Maybe we should go to the police,' said Miss Plimple. 'See if they have any information.'

'Police don't give out information Miss Plimple, they only gather it, and if by any chance Uncle Levi is safe and hiding somewhere, going to the police might alert whoever is after the package. No it's best that we stick to his original plan. Somehow we have to leave for America as soon as possible.'

Karl finally found the house in which he and the professor were staying. He knocked at the street door which Eleftheria opened and ushered him into the courtyard. Von Meis had retired back to their room while Manoli had gone in search of Karl. Eleftheria tried to explain to Karl that her husband was out looking for him, when von Meis appeared at the top of the stairs.

'It appears you have given us all a bit of a stir, I was worried about you. It is not safe roaming strange city streets,' said von Meis as he descended the steps. 'But I'm glad that you are safe. Where have you been?'

'I went looking for someone to help us. But I have made a great discovery, someone who can get us to Gibraltar.'

'That is indeed good news, it seems we have both been lucky as Manoli our host, also knows of a way for us to reach England. Have you eaten?' he asked. Then to Eleftheria, 'please could my friend have some food.'

Eleftheria nodded and left for the kitchen to return with a plate of beans and a loaf of bread. Karl had just finished eating when Manoli returned with a couple of men who he introduced as his cousins. These were the men who could help in their escape. Later that night Karl and the professor crawled to bed knowing that in the morning they would be nursing a hangover, but that arrangements had been made for getting the pair of them to London.

Julian Pleach was descended from a long line of the noble house of Leach. His mother a one time music hall artiste by the name of Rita Marzoni had managed to catch the eye of young Septimus Macalister Leach who, in line with family tradition and inbreeding, had left him somewhat lacking in the brains department. His only interests were horse racing, and his club, which, after his marriage to Miss Marzoni, who it turned out was actually by name Gertrude Basher, he resumed. After Septimus's early and untimely demise the family paid a small annuity to the widow on the stipulation the she renounce any claim to the title. Even though her son was tenth in line to inherit the baronetcy.

At the age of seven it seemed young Julius had a very pleasant voice and his mother who always had delusions of grandeur as evident by her sons name Julius Ignatius Alfred Norman Percival Leach, decided to give him singing lessons, and although his voice wasn't strong enough for opera it certainly gave him a chance of a career on the stage.

Determined to make his own way in life rather than constantly begging for handouts from the family he incorporated all his names into the shorter version Julian Pleach and had the start of a very good career in the theatre.

Odel and Hetty left Miss Plimple's office after giving assurances that if Levi Oppenheimer turned up then they would inform each other. Miss Plimple desperately wanted to go and check on the package to make sure that it was still safe but she decided, in case she was being watched, she had best let sleeping packages lie. Odel and Hetty made their way to the end of the corridor and the stone stairwell which would take them down to the stage door level.

Hetty was now crying. What were they going to do about Uncle Levi? She was sure that he had been murdered and that they would never see each other again. Odel tried to be brave but sensed exactly what Hetty was thinking and knew it to be true. Halfway down the stairs Hetty could no longer suppress her tears as she collapsed on the cold stone staircase. Just at that point Mr. Pleach was going up to his dressing room. Being between shows he had quickly gone down to the stage to check his props for that evening's performance and was just returning for his lunch and afternoon nap.

Dressed only in his dressing gown and with his face still in makeup, he looked rather out of place when he enquired of Odel if the young lady required any assistance? 'Thank you,' said Odel, 'but no we shall be fine, thank you, my sister has just had some bad news, that's all.'

'Oh, I am sorry to hear it,' he replied, as Hetty looked at him for the first time.

Her eyes wet with tears she looked at the half dressed, made up face of Mr. Pleach and smiled.

'There, that's better,' he said. 'Allow me to introduce myself, Julian Pleach, descended from a long line of Leaches, but that's a long story. Would you care for a cup of tea? I'm just about to have my luncheon, and you are most certainly welcome to join me if you wish.'

Hetty looked at Odel, who replied, 'Thank you, for your kind offer but we really must be getting home.'

Hetty somewhat disappointed nodded her head, and stood up to leave.

'Then maybe we could do it at another time?' said Julian, 'I'm at the theatre every day and we only have matinees, Wednesday, Friday & Saturdays. Perhaps we could meet then?'

'Yes, I would like that very much.' Hetty said as she started down the stairs. Odel astonished by his sister's forthright manner could only shrug his shoulders at Julian, before having to run off after Hetty. Finally catching up with her at the stage door, he took her by the arm which he gave a friendly squeeze as they left the theatre.

It hadn't been difficult for Herr Delfger to get backstage. Walter it seemed was a permanent fixture at his desk and Herr Delfger couldn't risk being identified, so he gave up trying to enter through the stage door. The large scene dock doors were closed during performances. There to get large flats and set pieces of scenery into the theatre, they were not usually opened, but the small pass door was and it was only a matter of time before a couple of stage hands appeared for a quick smoke. Herr Delfger waited until they had returned before trying the door. Luckily they had left it unlocked and he soon found himself in the pitch black of the scene dock area. He could hear the performance on stage and see shadows as they moved around in the darkness getting ready for the next cue or scene change. Used to being backstage he knew that it would be impossible for him to get through the pass door from the stage to the dressing rooms without being seen by some member of the cast or crew so he searched around for an alternative. Finding himself in a large darkened room he saw a huge paint frame against the sidewall, used to paint the elaborate backcloths for the pantomimes, Herr Delfger knew the paint frame was an essential part of the theatre workshop and that there must be a pass door somewhere, and sure enough, after having made his way carefully around the room he found himself through the pass door and backstage at the Theatre Royal Drury Lane.

Granny Probyn needed an excuse. 'Now you listen to me Fluffy Yeomans,' she whispered. 'I need to follow Miss Plimple, and I shouldn't be front of house so you are going to be my excuse.'

Fluffy Yeomans looked at Granny Probyn.

'Now there's a good boy and get yourself lost so that I have to find you.' Granny Probyn said opening the door to their dressing room and assisting Fluffy Yeomans to exit with a carefully placed foot up his derrière.

Fluffy Yeomans took this as his chance. At last he could get Granny Probyn interested in that package and he made a beeline for the under stage area.

Granny Probyn waited for a few minutes then opened the door and checked that the corridor was empty. She could hear Jimmy the callboy singing and clanking down the stairwell at the far end of the corridor, but elsewhere all was clear.

At the same time Miss de la Mouche sat in her dressing room ruminating on how she was going to get Granny Probyn to sort out the sniping Miss Plimple. She had received another letter that morning from von Marenbach. He was becoming impatient. He said that the movement couldn't wait, that action was demanded of every loyal member of the party etcetera, etcetera. She had heard it all before, but she had never been on the receiving end. And now she was afraid that she wouldn't be able to do as she had promised and she knew first-hand the price of failure. All her attempts at encouraging Granny Probyn into action seemed to come to nothing, it seemed she would have to do the deed herself and on top of everything else her mother was becoming difficult. Most time Ashley could handle her, but of late she was losing her hold over the old lady and she feared that something unexpected was gong to happen. Just then Granny Probyn knocked on the door and opening it slightly poked her head around. She smiled at Ashley and said, 'Chocks away, at last we might see what Miss Plimple is up to,' and as quickly as she had come the door was shut and she vanished down the corridor.

Granny Probyn slowly made her way to the manager's office and looked through the grubby window which also served as a hatchway for the payments of money every week. She was in luck. Miss Plimple was alone and on her way out to do her rounds before the evening performance. This was Granny Probyn's only chance of finding out why she wasn't wanted in the theatre. Miss de la Mouche insistence that she should do something struck a raw nerve with Granny Probyn, but she disliked seeing people upset and if she could help, well all well and good.

Miss Plimple could contain her curiosity no longer. As she sat in her office her thoughts continually went back to the package and she just had to make sure that it was still there. She picked up her clipboard turned off the office lights, locked the door and strode down the corridor to do her daily checks before each performance. Going through each department of props, costume, stage management and front of house, everything in fact so that Mr. Reed could be kept informed of what was happening in his theatre.

Mr. Reed made the occasional visit just to check that the show was still in good running order but he was now so engrossed in preparing the next season's show that he left the daily running of the pantomime to Miss Plimple. Granny Probyn followed Miss Plimple through all the backstage areas but, seeing nothing untoward or suspicious she wondered if she should continue her pursuit. Then finally going under the stage she stopped and looked around. Luckily Granny Probyn knew the under stage area well, as it was from here Fluffy Yeomans made most of his entrances, so she could easily find an area where she wouldn't be seen. Miss Plimple checking that all was quiet and that she wasn't being overlooked, made her way to a dark corner where she had hidden the package she had been given. Granny Probyn held her breath, now it seemed she would find out what the letter to Miss de la Mouche was about when she heard a scream. A loud high pitched meow of a scream. Fluffy Yeomans ran from his hiding spot as Miss Plimple had inadvertently stepped on his tail. Both she and Granny Probyn held their breath while trying to recover their nerves.

Granny Probyn couldn't wait to escape the under stage area. Although she knew that she must let Miss Plimple leave or risk the chance of being discovered hiding in the dark. Fluffy Yeomans had fled the for the safety of the green room and a possible soothing chin rub from a sympathetic member of the chorus. He hadn't expected to see Miss Plimple and so when he saw her enter had hidden himself between some crates, unfortunately his tail was still exposed and Miss Plimple had accidentally stepped full force upon it causing his sudden outburst and Miss Plimple's heart to flutter alarmingly. Once Miss Plimple had left the under stage area, Granny Probyn waited for as long as she could before her curiosity finally got the better of her. Slowly she emerged from her hiding place and made her way across in the dark to where Miss Plimple had stopped. Looking around Granny Probyn couldn't make out anything that looked like it could be of interest to Miss Plimple then she realised where she was and the words of Ethel Dorfellwaffer came back to her, 'That it must have something to do with those hydraulics,' maybe Miss Plimple wasn't looking for something but at something.

Julian Pleach was just making himself comfortable, the afternoon performance had gone well with only one bum note in his song which nobody seemed to notice. He had checked his props for that evening's performance, met the most entrancing girl, finished his lunch, and was preparing his day bed for between show naps and was just about to settle down with thoughts of Miss Hetty Oppenheimer when Mr. von Stutlz interrupted him.

'Did you hear zat?' said von Stutlz. He and Julian Pleach shared the dressing room.

'What?' said Julian.

'Zat, Zat Screech!' Von Stutlz nearly screeched himself.

'Can't say I did,' Julian replied casually.

'Well go and have a look,' urged von Stutlz.

'At what?'

'Zat Screech! Zat's vot!' Von Stutlz although a large corpulent man was rather sensitive when it came to loud noises. 'I cannot go out into ze corridor dressed like zis,' he said pointing to his flannelette night gown.

Julian Pleach stuck his head around the door. The corridor was empty. Their dressing room was nearest the stairwell and noise from all over the theatre resonated up and down the stone steps. Nervously he stepped out into the corridor, von Stutlz bringing up the rear.

'Vat do you zink it vas?' whispered von Stutlz again.

'Hello,' Julian called out into the corridor and moving towards the stairwell. 'Hello,' he called again, at the silent urging of von Stutlz once he reached the handrail as he looked up the centre area of the steps.

'Maybe it was just the chorus girls in high spirits on the second floor?' he said at last as silence answered his call.

'It didn't zound like chorus girls to me,' said von Stutlz. 'Maybe you should call again.'

'Well,' said Julian turning again to face the stairwell. 'Hello, is there anybody there?'

'Yes,' came the answer which neither Julian Pleach nor Mr. Stutlz were prepared as they fled back to their dressing room slamming the door quickly behind them.

Granny Probyn reached the first floor landing and looked around. 'I wonder where Fluffy could be,' she thought, 'poor baby must have had a terrible fright.' And she started for the green room at the other end of the corridor in search of her charge.

The late afternoon light cast long shadows on the walls as it penetrated the dirty skylight above as Herr Delfger slowly descended the stone steps to the lower floors. Pausing on the steps, he could hear voices below him. A crowd of girls from the chorus made their noisy way down to the stage door and out into the pale wintery afternoon sun. Today was a matinee performance and most of the members of the cast would be staying in the theatre between shows. Steadily he made his way down to the second floor dressing rooms. Jimmy as call boy whose usual post was a stool by the stair well was on an errand for Mr. Maltravers making it easier for Herr Delfger to make his way to the dressing room of Miss de la Mouche.

He knocked quietly and waited. The door slowly opened to reveal Mr. Maltravers and Miss de la Mouche already in conference. Miss de la Mouche eyes opened wide in surprise as she looked hurriedly up and down the corridor.

'What are you doing here?' she enquired, 'it isn't safe, someone will see you.'

'It's all right,' said Maltravers, 'I've sent young Jimmy on an errand that will keep him out of the way most of the afternoon; now's our chance for taking a closer look under the stage.'

'No,' said Herr Delfger, 'Oppenheimer's, nephew is here. He's with Miss Plimple now I'm sure to drop off the package. I thought the old man had already done it but I must have been mistaken.'

'Even better,' said Miss de la Mouche, 'let's go down and get it, before it's too late.'

Maltravers put his hand across the doorway to bar Herr Delfger's exit. 'Not so fast, you know that neither Ashley nor I can compromise our cover here. We should just leave it as planned. Herr Hessen knows what he's doing.'

'Hessen is a fool,' spat Herr Delfger, 'von Marenbach should be leading the society, at least he is willing to take some action rather than have us sitting about like sitting ducks waiting.'

'Shh keep your voice down, that old interfering busybody next door will hear you.'

'She's out looking for that cat of hers, seems it's done a bunk,' said Herr Delfger, 'I could hear her calling for it as I came in.'

'So what do we do now?' asked Miss de la Mouche.

'We do nothing,' answered Maltravers. 'We know Miss Plimple has the package. We wait until she's contacted by her uncle and we get two birds with one stone.'

Herr Delfger sneered at them both. He wasn't interested in the party, he only wanted to make enough money to get out of his current situation. According to von Marenbach, Hessen was an incompetent fool, and as von Marenbach paid Herr Delfger, Herr Delfger wasn't one to argue. 'Cowards, you really think everybody is just going to sit around and wait? Well von Marenbach won't. Just wait when there's a new leader of the society.' And pushing Maltravers out of the way he opened the door and made his way back down the corridor to the stairwell.

Granny Probyn found fluffy curled up on the lap of Miss Plimple who was now sitting alone in the green room calming her nerves and drinking a cup of tea. Having made peace with Fluffy Yeomans he allowed her to tickle his chin, and finally settled down to sleep.

'There you are, you naughty boy, where have you been I've been searching everywhere.' Said Granny Probyn.

'Don't be too hard on him Mrs. Probyn,' said Miss Plimple, 'I'm afraid it's my fault, I trod on his tail earlier while I was doing my rounds. I think he was after a rat or something. He was down under the stage.'

Granny Probyn tried to sound nonchalant. 'What were you doing under the stage, you naughty boy,' she said picking Fluffy Yeomans off Miss Plimple's knee and making a fuss of him. 'Well I suppose I had better get back to my dressing room then,' Granny Probyn said, not knowing how to keep the conversation going, she slowly made her way to the green room door.

'Granny Probyn?' Miss Plimple called.

Granny Probyn turned back to the room, 'Yes, dear?'

Herr Hessen sat in his office studying the latest communication from Germany. Intelligence had found Professor von Meis in Greece and reports of his death had spread like wildfire throughout the scientific community. This was bad news, as the communiqué also instructed him to conclude business and retrieve the missing documents and return them to the Fatherland for analysis. He rang the bell and a few moments later Forsythe knocked at his door. 'Take this to Maltravers; tell him to report here as quickly as he can.' With which he handed Forsythe a folded note. Forsythe took the note without a word, bowed slightly and left. Herr Hessen now had to deal with von Marenbach. He had overstepped the mark too often and Hessen didn't want von Marenbach interfering, not now that he had clear instructions. He picked up the telephone and called a number taken from his pocket book. Whoever was on the other side of the line was obviously expecting this call as no pleasantries were exchanged Herr Hessen only said, 'tonight,' and hung up.

Scene 8

Karl and Professor Meis waited patiently in the dark, all had been arranged with Manoli that they would be transported to Gibraltar by a fishing boat and, as they waited on the beach, they could see in the distance a small boat coming ashore. This was going to take them out to the trawler where they would join with the boat.

Manoli had assured them all would be well. His first cousin and best man at his wedding had done all the arrangements. Nothing could go wrong.

They had left Athens that morning and made their way down to Piraeus. Careful not to draw too much attention to themselves they avoided the main bustling port and headed south for one of the smaller coves of the coast line. As clockwork the small row boat pulled ashore. Kostas, Manoli's cousin and best man was all smiles as he stepped from the small boat, but time was of the essence and only brief hello's were passed between friends before Karl and the professor were bundled into the boat and they were off again, pulling against the tide.

Water splashed over the side wetting Karl as he sat hunched down in the bottom of the rowing boat. Silently they rowed until suddenly they hit the hard metal hull of the trawler, which was lying at rest waiting for the passengers. The trawler in complete darkness was silhouetted against the weak moonlight as it shone through scudding clouds. Kostas called out and a rope ladder was thrown overboard so that Karl and the professor could climb up. Uneasy with having to climb, a rope was also lowered which was tied around the professor's waist as added protection in case he should loose his grip.

Karl followed the professor and as soon as they were on the ladder Kostas pulled away from the trawler and disappeared into the night.

Professor Meis hauled himself over the handrail of the trawler with the help of the man who pulled on the rope where he flopped onto the deck. Karl directly behind him was taken by surprise when his head appeared over the top of the rail to be confronted by a German pistol pointing directly into his face. Professor Meis was suddenly aware that all was not well with the plan.

Granny Probyn stood in the doorway. She didn't want to let this chance of talking to Miss Plimple go by. She might discover what it was that she was hiding and why the people who were blackmailing Miss de la Mouche wanted her out of the way. After calling Granny Probyn back and obviously wanting to talk Miss Plimple now didn't know where to begin. Granny Probyn broke the ice by asking if Miss Plimple had worked in the theatre for long.

'No,' she replied, this was her first engagement. She had got the job through a friend of her uncle's, and had so impressed Mr. Reed that she was immediately hired. In fact this was probably going to be the last time she would be doing it. 'I expect to be leaving for America shortly.'

'Oh,' was all Granny Probyn could come up with. Of all the things that Miss Plimple could have said, this was most definitely unexpected and asked, 'Why America?'

Miss Plimple caught her breathe before answering, 'My uncle is German, and wants to leave the country, it is also not safe here anymore. I have heard that the government here is actually sending Germans back, so when he arrives, we plan to go to America.'

'What about the rest of your family, what will they do?'

'I have no other family. My parents died in a car crash years ago. I was brought up by an aunt who lived here in Kent but she sadly passed away last year. So you see, I have no ties here, and maybe Uncle Oswald and I can start again in America.'

Just then the chorus girls returned giggling loudly amongst themselves, and seeing Fluffy Yeomans made a big fuss of him, after which Miss Plimple made her excuses and left for her office. Granny Probyn answered all the girls' questions about Fluffy, while Fluffy held up his chin to be tickled.

Napoleon Packard paced the living room, back and forward, back and forward. It was no use, he couldn't keep it to himself any longer, he had to tell his wife. How she was going to take the news he didn't know, but the second letter he received was certainly explicit in what would happen if he didn't do what was asked of him, and so there was nothing else for him to do but tell his wife.

Veronica Packard was a nervous woman with horsy features and an unhealthy disregard for anything other than her precious darling son. Beauregard Henry was her first thought in the morning and the last thing at night. At one time that affection had been laid at the feet of Napoleon but, since the birth of their only son it was clear that her husband now took a back seat and Beauregard Henry would be driving.

'Dear we have to erm… talk, erm…, I mean err… I have something ah… to erm… tell you, eh show you erm…,' stammered Napoleon. If the truth were known Napoleon Packard was afraid of his wife. Having plucked up the nerve he had found her sitting in the conservatory as she was contemplating what she could get for Beauregard's 10th birthday. A party of course was on the cards and was already organised and in hand along with his presents all neatly wrapped and sitting in the cupboard under the stairs, but Veronica thought that one more very special gift was in order and as she was ruminating on what it could be when Napoleon caught her unawares.

'Can't you see I'm busy,' replied his wife.

'Why yes, but dear, it is rather important, and I wouldn't erm... , I couldn't erm..., I wasn't sure whether...'

'Oh get on with it, what is so important that you have made me forget Beauregard's special birthday present?'

'Oh, I am sorry, I erm..., didn't realise that erm... well...' Napoleon couldn't think of anything to say so thrust the letter at his wife.

Veronica snatched the envelope from him.

'What's this? What have you done? Oh, my poor baby,' she said before even reading the letter. Convinced that her husband had done something scandalous, thoughts that Beauregard would become ostracised from society and his friends would abandon him flooded her brain.

'I er..., haven't done anything,' whimpered Napoleon. 'I er... think er... that you should read the letter.'

Veronica ripped open the envelope which was addressed to Napoleon Packard at the law firm's address and read the few lines written on the sheet of paper. Not wanting to believe what she was reading, she turned over the page to see if there was something on the other side. Finding that blank she then reread the short note.

As expected the parting of the news was not taken easily. And for an hour Napoleon tried to calm his wife's nerves, enough so that they could at least discuss the matter. Plainly put, the note had requested that Napoleon Packard was required to undertake a certain job which involved, as Napoleon put it, breaking the law, to acquire some information about which he and only he was privy too. If he didn't do this, then Beauregard Henry would befall the same fate as his school mate.

'Of course you should do it,' Veronica said, as if there wasn't anything to discuss. If her precious baby was in any danger whatsoever he simply had to do whatever was asked of him.

'But dear, you don't seem to understand. They want me to get rid of someone, and take a package back to Germany!'

'So?'

'Don't you err... realize what get rid of means? It means to err... to kill someone.'

'Oh,' she said, 'but Beauregard,' her thoughts returning immediately to her baby.

'And then how do I take this package or whatever it is back to Germany. Why me!'

Veronica sat for a while thinking. While Napoleon, who had been thinking a lot and not coming up with any answers gave up in exasperation and sat with a blank expression on his face.

To be confronted with a note that callously laid out what would befall precious Beauregard Henry if her husband didn't do exactly as ordered; there was nothing for it but to take charge.

After a while Veronica turned to her husband. 'You said that this Levi, has been killed and the police don't know who he is, correct? And that you think poor Mucus was murdered. Then what they are threatening is a real threat. Not just hot air.'

'Of course it is erm..., and that poor boy at err... Beauregard's school, maybe that was supposed to be err... Beauregard.'

'Oh,' Veronica, winced as she remembered the gruesome details. Details that Beauregard himself had delighted in telling his family. 'But then we must do as they say. Maybe we don't actually have to kill anybody.'

'Veronica, listen to what you are saying, this is crazy.'

'No, no wait,' she said suddenly putting her thoughts together. 'Think about what they want. Why did they pick you?'

'Weeeell,' answered Napoleon unsure what his wife was proposing.

'Think man,' said Veronica becoming exasperated. 'Isn't it obvious?'

'Weeeell,' answered Napoleon again. Nothing obvious came to

mind.

'Oh, you stupid man, think. Put two and two together. You and Mucus?'

'Yeees,' answered Napoleon again still unsure where this conversation was going.

'And your stupid hydraulics!' She almost screamed.

'Oh,' at last the penny dropped. For a solicitor Napoleon wasn't the brightest spark in the fire. In fact he only took the job at Veronica's insistence. He would have preferred to spend time pursuing his hobby of hydraulics.

'Who else knew about what Mucus was doing? That professor in Germany? Levi Oppenheimer? I'm not sure about that child at Beauregard's school, but it all fits. What did Mucus tell you?'

Scene 9

ueenie's café was opposite Shoreditch town hall. Everybody knew where Queenie's café was. Queenie herself had been around for so long that all of her regulars couldn't think of a time when they hadn't known Queenie or used Queenie's café.

Vincent, Queenie's son who was now forty and who still lived at home, had a flair for colour or so people told him. He had the shop along with its odd assortment of tables and chairs painted purple and pink. Queenie hated purple and pink, but, even she had to admit that Queenie's café stood out from the other shops around it.

Vincent also worked serving the patrons. While Queenie herself no longer did any of the cooking she surveyed her kingdom sitting by the cash register and talking to whomsoever took her fancy.

Vincent placed a cup of tea down on the table, wiped a crumb to the floor, and said, 'Ain't seen you around 'ere before?'

'No,' was the reply.

Obviously not wanting to talk, Vincent took the hint, wiped another rogue crumb to its demise and waltzed off to harangue his mother about buying some of those new Formica tables.

Von Marenbach took a sip of the tea, and turned up his nose. How could anyone drink this filth? He shuddered as he looked around the café. Full of local characters he could feel his skin crawl. Oh how he wished he was back in the Fatherland. He could do so much for the cause. Just because of one little mistake his father had sent him to this god-forsaken country. Well he would do what he had to do, then return the triumphant hero. Maybe even the Fuehrer himself would honour him.

His reverie was broken by Herr Delfger who had sat down opposite him. Catching Vincent's eye, Herr Delfger mimed a cup of tea and a piece of cake, and was rewarded by a nod and smile.

'Sorry I'm late, Herr von Marenbach, the wife isn't too good these days, she's taken a turn for the worse.'

'I'm not interested in your excuses or your wife,' snapped von Marenbach. 'I have another job for you.'

Vincent sashayed over carrying the tea in one hand and a piece of Russian cake in the other, placed them before Herr Delfger, smiled picked up the tuppence that Herr Delfger had left on the table, wiped another crumb, and sashayed away lamenting at his mother, 'Oh, If only we had those lovely wipe down Formica table tops.'

Queenie, ignoring all remarks rung up the cash register and the two pence disappeared from view.

Von Marenbach continued the conversation while Herr Delfger attacked his dry piece of Russian cake. 'I want you to follow a man named Napoleon Packard. It is important that nothing happens to him. Am I understood? Since we have lost the professor and our dear friend Mr. Oppenheimer,' Herr Delfger winced as von Marenbach continued, 'I need this man to decipher the papers when I get them. Am I understood?'

With a nod Herr Delfger finished his last piece of cake, drank his tea and rose to leave. 'Forgive me Herr von Marenbach,' he said, 'I shall not fail this time.'

Von Marenbach took another sip of tea, turned up his nose once again and rose to leave. With the sound of Queenie berating her son ringing in his ear, 'We 'aint gettin' no Formica tables you 'ears me?' He stepped out onto the street.

Ashley de la Mouche left the theatre later that evening after the performance, she had tried to talk to Granny Probyn but she had been rather vague in talking about her pursuit of Miss Plimple. Trying not to think on it, she waited at the bus stop for the number 38 to take her home. Rain had started to fall and by the time that she had reached her house door she was soaking wet.

Unlocking the front door to her tiny flat, she stood for a moment listening for her mother. She could hear the faint sounds of someone asleep in the front room. She slipped down the passageway into the dingy kitchen. Dishes were piled high in the sink, everywhere there was rubbish and food left out. Ashley looked around in despair. She desperately wanted a cup of tea to warm herself from the cold seeping through her bones. Slipping out of her mackintosh and placing it over the back of a chair she started to fill the old kettle at the stone sink moving dishes enough to be able to put the kettle under the tap. Then, turning on the gas, she placed the kettle on the ring and sat until it started to whistle.

Gerty was woken by the loud noise. 'Ashley is that you?' she called. 'Ashley?'

'Yes mother, I'm making a cup of tea, would you like one?'

'Tea, huh? You're becoming one of them, let's all drink tea,' she sneered entering the kitchen.

'Mother,' Ashley sighed, 'it's only a drink.'

'Why are you so late, von Marenbach was here and you missed him. He wants to take over the society, did you know?'

'It wouldn't surprise me,' replied Ashley.

'I said I couldn't support him openly, not yet, Hessen still has a lot of powerful friends. What about that bitch Plimple, there are reports that von Meis has been killed. We have to act now. We need those papers.'

'I'm trying my hardest; it's difficult to get that old woman to do something. You know I can't do it myself. People would ask too many questions.'

'It's always the same with you, excuses. You're no daughter of mine, you're a coward. You should be prepared to lay down your life for the cause. It's a great honour what you have been given to do and all you can do is cry into your teacup. Pah!' She snorted as she stormed from the room.

'Mother,' Ashley called to her mothers back, 'I will do it, its just difficult.'

Gerty turned at the door. 'If you don't then someone else will, and you'll be left out in the cold.'

'Mother, please promise me that you won't interfere. Promise me that you won't do anything stupid.'

'What's stupid about helping the cause?'

'The cause, the cause, that's all you ever talk about. Mother please, let me do this thing, then we'll get away. We'll go to America they can't touch us there.'

'You're a fool, Ashley. Do you really think that they would let us go? Even if I wanted to. Wake up. Open your eyes. This is a great opportunity. Grasp it!'

'I can't mother. I'm not like you. People are getting hurt.'

'What are the lives of a few Jews? Listen to me, Hessen has promised us that we can return to the Fatherland. He has already spoken to his superiors. We scratch his back he scratches our. What does it matter if a few people get hurt? As long as we are alright what does it matter? Once we are in Germany we can forget the past.'

'How can you say that? Mother! How can you forget what you did?'

'Very easily. The man deserved it. I was doing society a favour.'

'Mother, you killed a man! How can you stand there and behave as if nothing has happened?'

'I would do it again if I had to. If it would help the cause.'

'The cause! The cause! A bunch of mindless thugs who have taken control. Can't you see what they have done to us? What they have done to your beloved Fatherland? Mother please! Please don't do anything stupid. Promise me. These men are using you, me, they don't care what happens. As long as they get what they want. Where will you be when von Marenbach takes control? Hessen said he would protect you? What has he done for you? Nothing. I only agreed to get those papers so that we could be together, but Mother, look at what they want us to do? I can't do it.'

'Then I will.'

'No mother, no!'

Karl and the professor were manhandled down a companionway and bundled into a store room. The hatch bolted from outside was made of metal, in fact the whole room was made of metal. The only other opening was a small porthole which was rusted shut. Professor Meis sat on a pile of hessian sacking while Karl tried to find some method of escape.

'I'm sorry, my boy,' the professor said, 'I shouldn't have got you involved.'

'If I ever see that Greek again I'll kill him,' answered Karl.

'I thought we could trust him,' offered the professor, but it was clear he didn't hold out much hope of a future.

'So what do we do now?' Karl asked.

'We wait.'

'Wait? How can you be so calm? You know that they will kill us.'

'Karl my boy, they would have killed us if we had stayed in Germany. Once we had outgrown our usefulness they would have found a way to get rid of us. This way maybe it's for the better.'

Captain Kirby opened the storeroom hatch and stepped inside. Several hours had passed and both Karl and the professor had arranged the hessian sacks so that they could find some comfort from the cold metal floor.

The engines had started soon after their arrival on board and the lights had been turned on again so that the ship was now reflected in the dark waters.

The heavy rhythmic churning of the ships propeller had finally sent the couple into a fitful sleep which was interrupted by the captain.

'Professor Meis,' he said by way of introduction, 'my name is Captain Kirby, I do hope that you have not been too inconvenienced.'

'What do you mean by this? How dare you keep us locked up in this manner?' Karl shouted. He was about to continue with his tirade but was stopped by the arrival of a small man who had also entered the storeroom.

'May I present,' the captain continued, 'Mr. Smeeton of the British intelligence agency.'

'Gentlemen, please forgive the way that we have treated you, it seems our Greek friends were correct in who you are,' said Mr. Smeeton, 'You see we had reports of your death, you must understand that we have to be extremely careful in matters like these.'

'Your apology is accepted Mr. Smeeton, Captain, does this mean that we may move into more comfortable surroundings?' asked the professor.

'Of course, professor.'

Karl looked totally confused.

Captain Kirby led the party into the mess room. 'We can talk more comfortably in here while we await one of her majesties' ships,' he said.

'Forgive me captain; am I right in thinking that we won't be accompanying you to Gibraltar?' asked the professor.

'Correct,' said Mr. Smeeton. 'We shall chart a course to Malta and from there wait for HMS Cowslip to transfer us to Gibraltar then onto England. I have been in communication with London and they are expecting our arrival.'

'I wonder captain, is there any way that I can contact my niece in London to inform her of my safety?' asked the professor.

'Unfortunately not, the news of your disappearance and subsequent death has already been made public. If anyone suspects that you are still alive it will make our journey that much more difficult.'

'Professor, your niece is being carefully watched by our agency. She will be perfectly safe until we have a chance of reuniting you,' replied Mr. Smeeton.

Scene 10

Granny Probyn didn't sleep well that night. Thoughts of Miss Plimple and Miss de la Mouche kept crowding into her head so that she just couldn't seem to clear them. Perhaps, she thought she should go to the authorities. Although the note to Miss de la Mouche had expressly forbidden it. Granny Probyn had managed to avoid telling Miss de la Mouche of her conversation with Miss Plimple, but she also couldn't help wondering that Miss de la Mouche had something else to hide other than her mother.

Eventually she gave up trying to sleep and turned on the bedside lamp. Fluffy Yeomans, opened an eye, yawned, and tried to go back to sleep.

Picking up the novel Granny Probyn tried to concentrate on reading, but the words on the page swam before her eyes.

Closing the book with a snap, she decided to get herself a glass of water. Making her way to the bathroom at the end of the corridor, Granny Probyn, thought she heard a noise behind her. Turning to look back the way she had come the corridor was empty.

Having reached the bathroom she filled her glass and headed back to her room.

No sooner had she closed her bedroom door then she was hit from behind.

Fluffy Yeomans raised the alarm by meowing as loud as he could whilst clinging to the dark jacket of Granny Probyn's assailant. The commotion brought everybody out into the corridor of the hotel which finally brought the manager who opened the door with his pass key.

Finding Granny Probyn, slumped by the door, and Fluffy Yeomans standing guard over her, there was no sign of an assailant.

Inspector Ploddock sat in the hospital chair by Granny Probyn's bed. The doctors had informed him that they had given Granny Probyn a sedative, and that until she regained consciousness there was no way of knowing just how much damage had been caused by the blow to her head.

The hotel manager had told him that Fluffy Yeomans had put up a fight as the hotel staff tried to put him into his basket, but eventually cornered, he had been caught and taken to the theatre where he was left in the capable hands of the stage door keeper.

One of the chamber maids had packed a few of Granny Probyn's belongings which were sent along with her and these had been left in the bedside cabinet.

Inspector Ploddock, whilst waiting for Granny Probyn to regain consciousness, picked up her book and started to read. A great fan of crime writers he was soon engrossed in the novel.

Next day news of Granny Probyn's attack spread like wildfire throughout the theatre when the company turned up for the matinée. 'Who would do such a thing?' everybody asked.

Herbert von Stutlz seated at his makeup table broached the subject when Julian Pleach arrived.

'Do you tink it had zomtink to do wit zat scream we heard yesterday?' he enquired.

Julian Pleach was at a loss. Since his meeting with Miss Oppenheimer, Julian Pleach couldn't concentrate on anything. Even his mother had commented on it the previous evening when he returned home. With a glass of warm milk and a digestive biscuit, waiting as usual for her son's safe return but Julian had kissed his mother good night and almost waltzed off to bed without his usual regaling her of that evening's performance.

Julian shrugged his shoulders. 'Perhaps it was just a burglar,' he said. 'Maybe it was a robbery and she woke up to find a stranger in her bedroom and they hit her before escaping.' He suggested.

'Could be, could be,' replied von Stutlz. 'But what if Granny Probyn had zomtink to do with that scream?'

Determined as he was, von Stutlz had convinced himself that Granny Probyn had been up to something and this was her comeuppance.

'Ve should send her some flowers,' he added. 'Or ve could visit her betveen shows.'

Jimmy knocked calling the half hour. 'Tzank you!' Shouted von Stutlz to the closed door.

Ashley sat alone in her dressing room. Last night after their conversation, her mother had disappeared and Ashley was worried that she might do something violent. Knowing that Granny Probyn had followed Miss Plimple yesterday, had Granny Probyn found the package and not known what it was? Her mind was racing with all sorts of conjecture when Jimmy knocked the half hour which brought her back to the theatre. She had determined that she would confront Miss Plimple herself between shows and try to come to some sort of agreement. She knew of course that this was not what Hessen wanted. He wanted no witness to link the society with the papers but Ashley couldn't condone murder, not even to save her mother's life.

The cast seemed to be on edge during the performance. Fluffy had performed his role but had disappeared after his last scene when

Walter tried to put him back in his basket. Of course this meant that Walter wasn't at his desk at the stage door, which meant that anybody could, if they knew where to go get into the theatre.

Standing on the slated wooden boards that held the flying rig, from this position it was possible to look down and see the stage far, far below. The figure moved cautiously as there was a lot of dust which could easily be disturbed and sent floating down to the stage, just then the finale music started and the cast members, starting with the youngest dancers and members of the chorus came on to take their bows. Next came the principles each taking an individual bow and as the music segued into *The sun has got his hat on,* Julian Pleach and Miss de la Mouche in the guise of the Prince & Princess appeared at the top of their own staircase to descend and meet in the middle and take the last few steps onto the stage to take their bow.

As this happened upstage the figure could not see any of this but knew what was going to happen and sure enough the couple appeared below. Taking careful aim the figure lowered a barn door used for shuttering lamps between the slates of the floor. Set around a central hole which fitted to theatrical lamps, the barn door has four thin metal flaps which can open and close as needed to direct the light from the lamp. The couple below took a bow together, then Mr. Pleach stepped back a pace and indicated to Miss de la Mouche at which point the audience erupted into applause and Miss de la Mouche took another bow.

The barn door dropped like a guillotine completely severing her head which rolled to the front of the stage. Still with a smile on her face it came to rest just in front of the footlights in a ghoulish grin.

Many of the audience along with Julian Pleach fainted as the band continued to play the final refrain of *hip hip hip hooray*!

Scene 11

Inspector Ploddock walked the stage. The body of Miss de la Mouche had been taken to the mortuary. All the cast were in their dressing rooms. Some of the younger dancers were crying but generally there was a great silence which hung like a pall over the theatre. Nobody wanted to think on the tragedy. It was obvious that one of the electricians hadn't secured the barn door to the lamp and it had slowly worked its way loose over the weeks while the pantomime played. It was just bad luck that Miss de la Mouche was in the wrong place at the wrong time.

Or was it bad luck? Granny Probyn was still unconscious in hospital; were the two events related in some way? He had a sneaky feeling they were. But that's all he had and his chief was not known to work with sneaky feelings. 'Facts, boy, that's what makes good police work, facts,' was his chiefs mantra.

So Inspector Ploddock walked the stage. Hoping that something would come to light. Miss Plimple stood by in the wings waiting for the all clear. Someone had to clean the stage etcetera. There was a theatre to run. Mr. Reed had been telephoned. He was in Edinburgh doing research. Local legend had it that there were two children running wild in the Cairngorms, and he wanted them for the children in next years pantomime of *Babes in the Woods*.

'The show must go on,' Mr. Reed had boomed over the phone, and against her better judgement the house management agreed, so there was nothing for it but to get ready for the evening performance.

Julian Pleach lay on the day bed in his dressing room. Having disgraced himself on stage he was only glad that Miss Oppenheimer hadn't seen the terrible accident.

Mr. von Stutlz, plied him with smelling salts and cold water compresses for his forehead. 'Surely zey cannot be serious,' complained Mr. von Stutlz. 'Nobody vill come to ze theatre now, zis is a terrible tragedy. Ze poor girl who is ze understudy, has been told zat she vill go on tonight!'

Julian Pleach turned his head towards the wall, closed his eyes and tried to get rid of the image of what he had just witnessed but a warning kept coming back to him.

Thinking back to when he had just been told he had secured a part in this years pantomime he went to celebrate with a cream cake. So he took himself off to *Madam Valerie's* Patisserie in Frith Street. Unaware that he was being followed he had just made himself comfortable and started to look at the menu when a chap suddenly took the seat opposite him.

The man had introduced himself as Curruthers's and that he worked for the British Intelligence Agency. Taken slightly aback Julian asked if the man was a spy?

'In a round about way,' Curruthers answered. 'At the moment we are watching certain Germans, National Security and all that.'

The waitress interrupted the conversation, taking their orders, but once she had gone Curruthers continued. 'We want you to do a spot of work for us.'

Curruthers loved this part of his job, it made him feel special. He could tell by the look in the other person's eye that they thought he was some glamorous super agent fighting off adversity all in the name of Her Majesty's Government. The reality though was far from glamorous. Most nights Curruthers went home to his mother. His mother had henpecked his father until one day he had had enough, when he up and left never to be heard of again, leaving Curruthers alone with her. Now he was her only thing in life.

But Curruthers never divulged that part of his life. 'We want you in your normal activities at the theatre, to keep an eye on a certain person. We think she may be passing secrets to the Germans,' he continued.

'But what should I do?' Julian enquired.

'Only contact us if anything suspicious happens.'

'But who is it that I am supposed to be keeping an eye on?' he asked again.

'Your leading lady, Miss de la Mouche.'

Now Julian was in a quandary. Should he try and make contact with Curruthers? Surely they would know what happened. After the way that he had disgraced himself, he didn't think he should mention it. He was brought back from his reveries by Jimmy knocking at their door, wanting all cast and crew members in the auditorium.

Maltravers needed to talk to Hessen, but the police had ordered that nobody left the theatre until instructed to do so. He was convinced that he would be next and that von Marenbach was behind it. He paced his dressing room like a caged animal, trying to think how, and who was working with von Marenbach. He didn't think Herr Delfger had it in him to be a murderer, but he hadn't been seen since their argument in Ashley's dressing room and he did openly threaten him.

With the other members of the cast he made his way into the auditorium. Some of the chorus and dancers were still visibly shaken by what they had seen. The huge red velvet tabs had been drawn, so that the stage hands could get on with the job of cleaning while the inspector talked to the company.

Inspector Ploddock chose his words carefully. Having heard about Mucus Drillby and his suicide, Inspector Ploddock was even more convinced that his sneaky feeling was correct and that someone in the company knew more than they admitted. Everybody had already given statements to the other officers but what could they say about such a terrible accident? Julian Pleach hadn't mentioned Curruthers thinking that was what he would have wished and Maltravers had kept his mouth shut as to any friendliness towards Ashley.

'As you are all aware, Mrs. Probyn was viciously attacked last night and is lying unconscious in hospital as we speak.' At this some of the chorus girls gave little squeaks as they tried to hold back tears. Inspector Ploddock continued, 'I believe it was more than just a burglary gone wrong,' more squeaks from the girls, 'and I intend to find out what.'

Inspector Ploddock carefully ignored the fact the Miss de la Mouche, recently decapitated could not have had anything to do with Granny Probyn being in hospital and continued, 'In view of recent events,' he said, waving his hand in the general direction of the closed tabs, 'I would ask you all if you have any further information, no matter how small, please contact me or one of the officers who will be stationed here for the next couple of days.'

Inspector Ploddock had taken the executive decision to leave a PC on duty backstage at the theatre just in case. How he would okay it with his chief, he would cross that bridge etcetera, but for now, he felt it was imperative that he had a presence in the theatre.

Karl and the professor took to walking the deck for fresh air, the trawler was small and cramped and with the already full crew she was doubly stretched to accommodate them and Mr. Smeeton. Karl still had not forgiven either the Captain or Smeeton for the way that they had been treated, for letting them think that they had fallen in to the hands of the Germans.

'I don't trust that Smeeton,' he said to the professor, 'he gives me the creeps. He has predicted every question that we would ask and has an answer for it. And how long does it take to get to Malta from Greece? We seem to be forever stalling.'

'Calm yourself,' said the professor, 'I agree it does seem that we are travelling very slowly towards our goal, but at least we are going there.'

'And what of your research? Smeeton keeps avoiding the issue every time I ask the question.'

'Maybe then he doesn't have all the answers.'

They had finished a full circuit of the boat when the Captain came up behind them. 'Gentlemen, are you enjoying the view?' he asked.

'My young friend here would prefer a change of scenery,' answered the professor. 'Perhaps we may soon be in Malta?'

'I'm sorry professor, it seems that our bad seamanship hasn't gone unnoticed.' Clearly the Captain wanted to explain the situation to the professor, but merely said, 'I'm sure that land will be sighted shortly.'

'What did he mean by that?' Karl asked as soon as the Captain had taken his leave. 'I tell you that Smeeton has something up his sleeve and I don't like it.'

'Hush, Karl. Not too loud. This is a small boat, things can be overheard. I do think we need to watch Mr. Smeeton though, a little bit more closely.'

Fluffy Yeomans sat by the package that Miss Plimple had put under the stage. What could be inside it? Whatever it was he was now convinced that it had something to do with Granny Probyn being hurt. And that was another thing that was worrying him. He knew who had attacked Granny Probyn, but no one would believe him. Even Granny Probyn would have said that he'd had too much fish pate for tea and it had gone to his head. So what were his options? Chasing rats and mice, was a whole lot different than trying to catch murderers?

'Fluffy Yeomans, Fluffy Yeomans!' Called Jimmy. He had been sent by Walter to look for the cat. It wouldn't do if he couldn't be found. The theatre management were still adamant that the evening performance take place and hasty preparations were under way for Miss de la Mouche's understudy to take over. The only problem was that the unfortunate girl couldn't remember any of her lines and the one's she could remember were prefaced with a look up to the fly tower.

Fluffy Yeomans gave a soft, 'Meow.'

Espying Fluffy Yeomans in amongst the boxes he said, 'There you are. Old Walter's been doing 'is nut. 'E's got the 'hole backstage crew looking for yer. What yer doin' down 'ere any road? Eh?'

Fluffy Yeomans gave another 'Meow.'

'It's all right, I 'ear's that Granny Probyn, 'aint all that bad an' she'll soon be outa 'ospital.'

Fluffy Yeomans scratched at the wrapping of the package he was sitting on.

'Ere don't do that, you'll tear the paper.' Jimmy said.

Fluffy Yeomans scratched some more. 'Ere stop it,' he said again. Fluffy Yeomans was determined at all cost to open the package and discover what was inside.

'Naw look waht yer've done, gon' and ripped it wide open.'

'Meow,' replied Fluffy as the last of the wrapping was pulled back to reveal a bundle of papers all stamped in red with TOP SECRET across the top of each page.

'Ere what yer found ere then?' asked Jimmy. 'Yer shouldn't 'ave dun that.'

Jimmy bent down to pick up Fluffy Yeomans and in doing so read the first page. 'Blimey!' he said, and he gave a whistle like a ship blowing off steam.

'Naw look what yer's done? Yer've gone an got us all mixed up in summit that we aught not to be.'

Fluffy Yeomans meowed once more as Jimmy looked at him.

'Did you know that this was 'ere?' Jimmy asked.

Fluffy Yeomans meowed.

'Blimey!' Jimmy said again and once more let out a long low whistle.

Jimmy sat down on a nearby crate. The enormity of what Fluffy Yeomans had found suddenly hit him.

'If you knew that this was 'ere then you must know who put it 'ere in the first place?' Jimmy asked again.

Fluffy Yeomans meowed.

'Blimey!' Jimmy said again. He sat for a while contemplating what he should do. Then he had a sudden panic attack.

"Ere what if they knows that you knows then they'll know that I knows?' He suddenly said making a grab for the package and tried to repair the damage done to the wrapping.

Fluffy Yeomans meowed again trying to calm him.

'Alright, but what if they don't knows? Then we must hide it until we knows who they are?' Jimmy had said all this aloud although he was actually thinking to himself. 'So where do we hide it?' he asked Fluffy Yeomans.

Fluffy Yeomans jumped from the box he was sitting on and made his way back to the central staircase which led up to the dressing rooms.

"Ere we can't take it up there, someone 'll see us. No we'll 'ave to hide it 'ere.' At which point he looked around. Then he saw it, part of the scene of miller's store room was used on one of the hydraulic lifts, it contained the bench a couple of sacks and the safe. Perfect. Nobody ever went in there he thought to himself, it was only opened on stage. 'That's it, that's the place,' and without further ado he stepped onto the lift that held the safe, opened the door and hid the papers underneath all the fake money and jewels which were props for the pantomime.

'Well Fluffy Yeomans, I think its time we headed back upstairs or people 'ill start to wonder.'

Fluffy Yeomans meowed, and followed Jimmy up the stone steps that led to the stage. He now had to catch a murderer.

Hessen sat in his office. He needed to tie up a lot of loose ends. Far too many people had made mistakes and it made his operations look bad. So much so that Herr Tost had made it plainly clear that those in command were not happy with the way things were working out. Plainly if he didn't sort things out, and quickly, his neck was on the block.

The galling thing about it, he thought to himself was it was all the fault of von Marenbach, he was the thorn in his side. Without that upstart there would have been no other involvement and his plans would have been carried out. But no, von Marenbach had to get involved and muddy the waters. So much so that they had lost the papers. Or at least von Marenbach had lost the papers. No. Not even lost them but given them straight into the hands of the professor's niece. For all he knew she could have already handed them over to the British or, even worse, the Americans.

He looked down at his desk and list of names he had written. It couldn't be helped, it was either their necks or his, and he was more than partial to his.

Von Marenbach was at the top of the list, but he didn't quite know how to go about disposing of him. He had big connections back in Germany. He came from a wealthy family that had close ties with the party. He would have to play this one very carefully. As for the rest, they were all incompetent fools or dispensable pawns. It was just a matter of which one to lose first in this dangerous game of chess.

Forsythe knocked at his door.

'Come in,' he commanded. Forsythe opened the door to announce that Mr. Maltravers had arrived. 'Bring him up here,' he said, 'I don't want him socialising with my wife and her bunch of cronies.'

'Very good, Sir,' Forsythe said and closed the door after himself.

Hessen took another look at the list of names. He had carefully left off Maltravers.

Maltravers knocked at Hessen's door, 'Come in,' came the response. Maltravers could feel that cold sweat run down his back again. For the life of him he couldn't think why he had ever bothered with the party, it wasn't as if he was going to get much from it and, if he didn't play his cards right, it might just be his life. He opened the door and tried to put a confident smile on his face.

Hessen himself was all smiles. This was not what Maltravers had expected. So much so that Maltravers actually did smile.

'Come in, come in, take a seat, make yourself comfortable. Would you like a drink?' Before Maltravers had a chance to answer Hessen had already rung for Forsythe.

Forsythe must have been waiting outside the door as it immediately opened and he entered.

'What would you like?' asked Hessen.

Taken slightly off guard by the speed of the order Maltravers stumbled. 'Oh, erm scotch please, if you have it.'

'Of course, of course, two scotch please Forsythe,' with which Forsythe went to the sideboard and poured two large scotches into cut glass tumblers. He then placed them on a tray and delivered them to the desk of Hessen. 'Will there be anything else, Sir?' he enquired.

'No thank you.' Hessen answered. Forsythe bowed and left the room closing the door quietly behind him.

'Amazing service,' said Maltravers.

'Yes, I don't know what I would do without him. It is the one good thing that the English know how to do. Serve!' Hessen smiled, and continued, 'and I don't know what I would do without you.'

Caught off guard Maltravers spluttered into his drink, 'Oh, well I only do as I'm ordered. You know.'

'Indeed, we must all follow orders, even *I*,' Hessen emphasised the 'I', 'must follow orders. Which brings me to the point of our meeting.'

Maltravers, was becoming slightly nervous again. It seemed that Hessen's smile on closer inspection looked more like a shark about to take a bite out of its prey and that he was the prey. Maltravers suddenly felt that his trousers were sticking to the leather upholstered chair in which he sat. The shirt on his back was sticking as the sweat made its way between his shoulder blades.

Hessen continued, 'I have here a list. It seems we, and I do include myself in that, have been, how shall I put this? Somewhat careless of late. And I have had orders to clean up our act.' Hessen was still trying to be friendly towards Maltravers. 'So much so,' he continued, 'that I have decided to take drastic action.' With which he handed over the list to Maltravers.

'That list of names needs to be dealt with.'

'How do you mean dealt with?'

'Silenced. Permanently. If you get my meaning.' Hessen looked like he was going to bite at any moment. 'You may have noticed that your name is not on that list, but could quite easily be added if you don't want to undertake the job.'

'No, no, no, I'll do it.' Said Maltravers, whose trousers seemed to have glued him to the chair. 'Just how do you mean silenced?'

Hessen smiled.

Scene 12

Vincent loved the movies, ever since as a young boy, when Queenie and he would go to the Saturday afternoon matinees, he simply adored the movies. All the great stars, he had no particular favourite, but forced to make a decision, it might just be Janet Gaynor. No wait! There was also that newcomer, Veronica Lake. She hadn't made that many movies and she might not be as polished, but she still had class. Yes, Vincent adored the movies.

Most weeks he and Queenie would shut up shop, head up Kingsland Road to Dalston and join the queues outside the Kingsland Empire but today was a special day, and on special days they put on their glad rags and went to the Carlton.

Styled like an Egyptian temple, the facade of which, decorated by brightly coloured ceramic tiles in Art Deco style, was a film goers dream picture palace. The interior was if anything even more sumptuous than its exterior. Entering from the rear of the auditorium, three blocks of red velvet seats swept down to the stage while overhead the gallery and the upper gallery were decorated in neoclassical plaster work. The crowning glory was of course the ceiling, a huge oval of plaster work in relief and its central art deco chandelier surrounded by four smaller chandeliers.

Vincent and Queenie took their seats. The theatre was packed to suffocation. The audience gave off an expectant buzz as they waited for the main feature. This was the first showing of an MGM musical in Technicolour.

The house lights dimmed as the famous lion logo shone onto the tabs as they swished open. A hush fell over the audience. The lion roared. The movie began. Vincent was transported into another world, a world of swirling greys, hurricanes, munchkins, witches and ruby slippers.

'What do you mean. Gone!' Said a voice.

'Toto, I've a feeling we're not in Kansas anymore,' said Dorothy.

'But what do you mean, GONE!' Said the voice louder.

'Sssh.'

'You said that they were safe,' said the voice trying to keep as quiet as possible.

'We must be over the rainbow!' Exclaimed Dorothy.

'Well where are they,' said the voice becoming more agitated.

'Sssh,' said another.

'Are you a good witch or a bad witch?' asked Glenda.

'Then we'll have to go to the authorities,' said the voice, not trying to keep quiet this time.

'Sssh Odel, people are looking,' said another voice.

'Sssh.'

'Oh ssssh yourself,' said the voice.

'Who me? I'm not a witch at all, I'm Dorothy Gale from Kansas.' Said Dorothy.

'Well is that the witch?'

Odel, tried to sit still, but he couldn't. The news that the papers had been lost was too much. Ever since his Uncle Levi had disappeared he at least thought that what his Uncle had been prepared to die for had passed into the right hands. Now it was all gone.

'It's no use, I've got to get out of here!' Exclaimed Odel.

Vincent was brought back from Kansas with a bump.

Odel stood up and started to make his excuses. Unfortunately they were seated in the middle of the centre block of seats and whichever direction he chose to take meant disturbing a whole lot of people.

'Please Odel, just sit and wait,' said the other voice.

Vincent turned in his seat and glared. It would take more than a pair of ruby slippers to get back to Oz.

In the foyer of the theatre, Miss Plimple tried to console Odel.

'Please Odel, I told you. We cannot go to the authorities just yet. I haven't heard from my Uncle and he was supposed to be in London by now.'

'Then how are we to get the papers back?' asked Odel.

'I don't know,' replied Miss Plimple. 'If only I knew who took them.'

'When did you last see them?' asked Hetty.

'Well, after our last meeting I went to check that the package was still where I had hidden it. It was under the stage with a pile of boxes by the hydraulics unit. I didn't think that anybody would expect to find them there...'

'And were they there?' interrupted Odel.

'Why yes, erm no. I don't know, I was erm, Oh, I stood on Fluffy Yeomans tail and he made such a racket and frightened me so much that I rushed upstairs to the green room. But now thinking about it. I'm sure I was followed.'

'By who?' asked Odel & Hetty together.

'Granny Probyn.'

Act ii

Scene 1

Ethel Dorfellwaffer sat by Granny Probyn's bed. 'It's a good thing for you that your head is good and thick,' she was saying. 'Not many people could have survived what you have been though.'

'Yes, yes, yes, but Ethel dear,' said Granny Probyn. 'Tell me, what of the pantomime?'

'You've heard of the terrible accident?' Ethel asked.

'No, what accident?' cried Granny Probyn.

'Why Miss de la Mouche. The poor girl,' Ethel prevaricated, 'a terrible thing, terrible.'

'Ethel Dorfellwaffer if you don't tell me at once what has happened I swear there will be another terrible accident,' said Granny Probyn.

Ethel Dorfellwaffer bridled, unaccustomed as she was to being spoken too in that manner, but she didn't want to upset Granny Probyn any more than necessary. In fact she had meant to say nothing about the accident but a gossip's tongue was hard to hold when it was such a good story.

'Well,' she started, 'apparently they had just finished the show and were doing the walk downs,' Ethel Dorfellwaffer just had to drop in the occasional *in* word but seeing the menacing look on Granny Probyn's face she hastily continued, 'and then it happened. Oh the poor girl. One of the shutters of the big lights dropped. Killed the poor thing instantly.'

Ethel Dorfellwaffer decided to keep the really gory parts from Granny Probyn. It wasn't wise to strain her too much at the moment.

'Oh the poor, thing,' said Granny Probyn. She closed her eyes and tried to think. This was something out of a cheap novel, in fact

Granny Probyn was convinced that she had read this somewhere before, it seemed her life was becoming entangled in a book. Was it really an accident? But if it wasn't who could do such a thing? Did it have anything to do with the notes that Miss de la Mouche received? What about her mother?

That was it, 'What about her mother?' Granny Probyn almost shouted.

'Whose mother?' asked Ethel.

'Miss de la Mouche, what has happened to her mother?'

'I don't know, maybe the police have notified her.'

'Yes the police, we must go to the police. No, no we can't,' mumbled Granny Probyn.

Ethel Dorfellwaffer thought that she may have given Granny Probyn too much information and that she was on the verge of a breakdown. And she so wanted to tell her what she really had come to tell but, she would just have to keep it to herself even though it involved her precious grandson Beauregard Henry. So she sat quietly and fidgeted with the blankets and plumped up Granny Probyn's pillows so much so that Granny Probyn eventually asked, 'What is it Ethel? You have something else on your mind, so you might as well spit it out.'

'Well, now that you mention it, there is something else I've been meaning to say, but I didn't want to disturb you.'

'You've been doing nothing else since you arrived,' said Granny Probyn.

This remark put Ethel in high dudgeon, and she sat with her lips pouting and twiddling with her handkerchief. 'Oh stop that Ethel and get on with it, or you will put me back in a coma. You know I didn't mean it.'

'Well,' she eventually continued, 'as I said, there was something else, something very strange is going on. As you know my Napoleon was a friend of the poor poor man Mr. Drillby who killed himself. Well just the other day I heard Napoleon talking to Veronica.'

'That is strange,' said Granny Probyn.

'No I don't mean that it's strange that my son and his wife were talking, but now that you come to mention it. Hmn!' This was the first time that Ethel Dorfellwaffer actually thought about her son's relationship with his wife, 'Anyway, as I was saying,' she resumed, 'I overheard their conversation. Obviously Napoleon was unaware that I was in the house and ...!

At this point Granny Probyn switched off. As usual Ethel Dorfellwaffer would prattle away for at least another five minutes before finally getting to the crux of the matter. But it did seem strange now that Ethel had brought up poor Mr. Drillby's death. They say that things normally come in threes but so many deaths. Granny Probyn made a mental list and the order.

1. Mucus Drillby (friend of Napoleon Packard and person to arrange for Granny Probyn to be in Pantomime.)

2. That unfortunate boy at Beauregard Henry's school, (she couldn't remember his name, and didn't want to interrupt Ethel or she would never get to the point.)

3. Mr. Levi Oppenheimer, (he was Ethel Dorfellwaffer's charge when she was a young nanny in Germany)

4. Miss de la Mouche (she had received threatening letters and had to get Miss Plimple out of the way!)

Granny Probyn put a hold on her thoughts, and tried to concentrate on what Ethel was saying.

'... so as I was walking past the door I heard Napoleon say to Veronica, "that if he didn't do as he was asked somebody was going to get hurt." Of course not wishing to pry I continued down the passageway, but I couldn't help thinking ...'

'You mean to say that Napoleon has been receiving threatening letters?' asked Granny Probyn almost shouting.

'Well, yes,' replied Ethel, who had been cut off mid sentence.

'Oh dear, oh dear oh dear oh dear,' Granny Probyn said to herself.

'What? What is it?' Ethel asked in return.

'Ethel, dear,' Granny Probyn hesitated but decided to continue. 'I think all of us are in serious danger.'

'What do you mean, all of us?' Ethel asked shakily.

'Well, it seemed that Miss de la Mouche was also receiving threatening letters. Only I didn't expect them to take the threat so seriously.'

'You mean that Miss de la Mouche was...' Ethel Dorfellwaffer for once was speechless. She couldn't finish the sentence although Granny Probyn knew exactly what she was going to say.

'Yes,' Granny Probyn finished her sentence, 'murdered!'

'Oh!' Gasped Ethel Dorfellwaffer. 'But then if she was..., what about...? And poor Beauregard...,' Ethel couldn't keep her thoughts straight or finish any of her sentences.

She sat looking about the hospital room, allowing her thoughts to run wild. Granny Probyn on the other hand at last had an idea.

'Ethel,' she said. Ethel Dorfellwaffer, still looked glazed. 'Ethel,' she repeated, 'you've got to listen to me. What else did Napoleon say?'

Ethel tried to concentrate, but nothing would come. 'Ethel we must find out what these people want from Napoleon. Although I have a pretty good idea.'

'How do we do that? I can't exactly ask Napoleon can I? I wasn't supposed to know anything about it. Oh, how could he get himself mixed up in all of this?' she wailed.

'Ethel, get a grip on yourself,' said Granny Probyn, 'he is probably as confused as you. Now we have to come up with a plan.'

Karl Leibknecht walked the deck. He couldn't sleep so he decided to get some fresh air. Why were the British keeping him and the professor on this tiny fishing trawler? What was the point? Surely it would be best to get to Malta, then as quickly to Gibraltar. What was Smeeton up to? The professor had told Karl not to go asking too many questions but he couldn't keep back the nagging feeling that something was not as it seemed. There was a thick fog that surrounded the boat and shut out any starlight from the night sky. The moon probably, behind some cloud, was weak. The only sound was the throbbing of the engine and the churning of the propeller as the boat cut its way through the dark waters.

Having made a second circuit of the deck Karl stopped at the stern and looked over the rail at the churned up waters of the ship's wake below.

A light caught his eye as it flashed in the distance. Flash, flash, flash, flash it went. Then, from somewhere above him, from the bridge a light flashed in response. Karl quickly hid himself amongst some coils of rope. He had obviously not been seen by whoever was signalling but he didn't want to be caught either. Strange that Smeeton hadn't informed them that they would be intercepted by another vessel. He tried to make out who was signalling but the figure was a blur as the light from the torch filled his eyes.

Karl made his way as quietly as possible back to the cabin he shared with the professor. 'Professor get up,' he whispered as he nudged the professor awake.

'What is it?' asked the professor, slightly confused.

'Sssh,' said Karl. 'Something is happening, there's a boat, out in the fog, we signalled to it.' Karl stopped talking for a moment and stood listening. 'Do you hear that?' he asked .

'What?' the professor replied even more confused. 'I hear nothing.'

'Exactly,' said Karl the engines have stopped.

'Maybe it's the British boat that we have been waiting for.' The professor said.

'Maybe, maybe not.' Karl paused, 'Professor, this doesn't feel right. Don't you think that Smeeton would have told us if we were to be transferred tonight?'

'Why I suppose so,' said the professor trying desperately to think of other reasons.

Before he could come up with any plausible excuse, Karl decided on their next course of action. 'We have to get off this boat. Something is wrong.' He looked around the small cabin and found the professor's clothes. 'Get dressed, quick,' he ordered. 'I'll go and check above.'

The professor stumbled from his bunk and proceeded to dress. When Karl returned he started to object. 'Karl, where are we going to go? Have you forgotten that we are in the middle of the ocean? Even if we managed to get a lifeboat, where are we? We could be lost for days at sea with no compass or any idea of our position. Think about it. Karl.'

Karl spoke as if he hadn't heard a word the professor had said. 'There is definitely some sort of activity going on up there and they are doing it extremely quietly. That in itself is pretty odd don't you think?'

'Yes, yes I do,' replied the professor then added, 'but where do you expect us to go?'

'I don't know,' replied Karl. 'I just don't want us to be here when they make contact with that other boat.'

Karl looked at the professor who sat on his bunk. 'Maybe we could hide on this boat until we find out what exactly is going on.'

Just then there was a sharp rap at the door. 'Professor Meis, could you come up on deck please.'

'It seems, my dear boy, that we are too late.' The professor said as he got off the bunk and opened the door. Standing outside was a smiling Mr. Smeeton flanked by two men each holding a luger pistol.

'If you would follow me, Herr Professor.' Smeeton said indicating the upper deck.

The professor stepped out into the hallway closely followed by Karl. 'I'm afraid that this is a private party, Mr. Leibknecht.' Said Smeeton as he pushed him back into the cabin. Karl, taken by surprise, lost his footing and slipped, falling backwards onto the professor's bunk. 'Keep an eye on him, make sure he doesn't leave this room.'

One of the men nodded and closed the door. Karl could hear the key turn in the lock.

The SS Shattenberg stopped its engines as it drew near to the fishing trawler.

'Ahoy below,' came a shout from the fog. Professor Meis appeared on deck followed by Mr. Smeeton.

'Are we nearly prepared, captain?' asked Smeeton.

'Yes,' came the reply. The captain couldn't look Professor Meis in the eye. 'We should be ready to board in a few minutes,' he said and walked off to resume command of his men who were busy rigging a hoist to take the professor and Mr. Smeeton on board the battleship.

'Good.'

'What will happen to Karl?' the professor asked.

'He is of no concern to you now professor. I would imagine that after we have left, his body will be dumped into the ocean for the fish.'

'You realise that boy knows as much about my work as I do?' said the professor. 'If not more.' He added as an afterthought. 'He assisted me with all of my experiments.'

'My dear professor, are you trying to save the young man's life?' asked Smeeton.

'Mr. Smeeton, if that is your real name, I am an old man. I hardly have the strength to finish this journey, let alone do the work you will require me to. I will need my assistant.'

Smeeton thought about this for a moment. 'Captain,' he shouted.

The captain turned around, 'Radio the admiral and tell him that there will be three joining his party.' Then he turned to the man standing behind him. 'Fetch him.' He ordered, then as an after thought he added. 'If he gives you any trouble use your charms.'

The man smiled and walked back to the cabins below.

Herr Delfger whistled quietly to himself as he walked past St Pauls otherwise known as the actors Church in Covent Garden. He had been following Napoleon Packard since he left his home that morning. He crossed the square and followed Napoleon around the market itself on to James Street. After that he turned left in Floral Street and headed for the offices of the law firm of *Pritchett, Snickertt and Fox*. This was an old established family firm of solicitors that had been founded by the original Mr. Pritchett and Mr. Snickertt in 1810. Since then it had many generations of Pritchetts and Snickertts as its senior partners. Today, there was only one Mr. Snickertt left. Napoleon, after dropping off his hat and coat in his own office, knocked gently at Mr. Snickertt's door.

'Come in,' Mr. Snickertt shouted. It seemed of late that Mr. Snickertt shouted a lot. Most of the employees thought that he was getting grumpy in his old age, truth be known he was going a little deaf and couldn't tell his own level of voice. Of course this was all well and good when he was in court cross examining some rogue over insurance fraud or tax evasions.

'Well what is it, Packard? Time is money!' He exclaimed.

'Erm, yes, sir, I was wondering sir, if I erm could, erm....'

'Good God man spit it out! If I spoke like that I would bankrupt half my clients. Time is money,' he repeated.

'Yes Sir,' Napoleon said, even more nervous than before. 'I was wondering sir, if I might take a few days off work?'

'A few days off! Whatever for, man?' shouted old Mr. Snickertt. 'You haven't done anything stupid, have you?' Old Mr. Snickertt could never forgive his father for not allowing him to elope with the girl of his dreams when he was twenty two years old and had held a grudge ever since of anybody else doing anything he considered frivolous.

'No, Sir,' was Napoleon's reply.

'Then what is it?' asked old Mr. Snickertt.

'It's my wife Veronica; she hasn't been well lately and needs a short break.'

'I would have thought that she needed a break from you. Ha ha ha.' Old Mr. Snickertt laughed at his own joke.

Napoleon wasn't sure if he should laugh at the old man's joke or not so a small smile crossed his lips; but then he remembered what Veronica had said, and that he must play it seriously so he tried to put on a straight face. The effect was one of pained pleasure.

Snickertt looked at Napoleon who stood before his desk with this pained expression on his face. 'Oh get out and come back when you've got rid of that stupid grin,' the old man said.

Napoleon, was struck dumb, 'Thank you, thank you, thank you,' he burbled, as he made his way to the office door. 'Thank you.'

'Get out, man!' Shouted Mr. Snickertt, 'and split your current cases with Jennings and Fox. Tell them I said so.'

Napoleon almost ran down the corridor to his office, picked up his hat and coat, stuck his head around Mr. Jennings door and said, 'Sorry old boy, I have to be off for a couple of weeks. The old man says to split what I've got between you and Fox.'

'I say, Packard,' replied Mr. Jennings who was just about to have a cup of tea, 'it's a bit short notice what?'

'Sorry, old chap, can't be helped.' With which he donned his hat and headed out of the office to his appointment with the writer of the mysterious letters.

Odel sat in the easy chair in their apartment at the hotel. He had been wracking his brains as how to get back the missing documents his uncle had given Miss Plimple.

'It's obvious that that old woman has got something to do with it. She knows where they are,' he said to himself. Hetty had heard it all before now and it was beginning to get on her nerves.

'Odel, we've been over this a thousand times. Of course it's obvious that Mrs. Probyn knows where the papers are, otherwise she wouldn't have been attacked. It is only the police who seem to think that her attack was a mixed up robbery, so the only way to solve our question is to ask her outright.'

'How are we supposed to do that Hetty dear? "Excuse me Miss Probyn are you a German spy working for the NSDP?" Somehow I don't think she's going to be willing to talk to us.' Odel said. 'And how do we get into the theatre in the first place?' he asked, as the question suddenly came to mind.

'Well, that's easy,' Hetty said. 'Apart from Miss Plimple, there is also that nice young man Mr. Pleach. I think, correct me if I am wrong dear brother, that Mr. Pleach would like to get to know me a little better. What better excuse then for me to be in the theatre.'

'Hetty you're a genius, but no, this is far too dangerous. Uncle Levi knew what he was doing. We don't know what has happened to him. I can't let you do this.'

'And I can't sit around here all day doing nothing but listen to you prevaricate. We have to do something Odel. If for no other reason than this is what Uncle Levi wanted.'

'You're right, but I am coming with you.'

Scene 2

Inspector Ploddock sat at his desk. Sometimes he didn't like working for Scotland Yard. He was depressed. He couldn't help it. His job was depressing him. So why wasn't it like those Hollywood movies? Like Sherlock Holmes? No bad example, Inspector Lestrange was a nincompoop. Now he was even more depressed. Thinking of why wasn't it like all those crime thrillers by Miss Christie? She had a way of telling a story. Of course you never knew who it was who committed the murder. In fact, if the truth were known, he never could work out who did it. But still, her heroine Miss Marples, she always knew, right? So why not Inspector Ploddock? Because this wasn't fiction this was real life.

Then there was this open case of John Doe found floating in the canal. They still hadn't discovered who he was let alone solved the mystery of how he ended up, his body all broken, floating in the water. Ploddock was becoming even more depressed.

And all this came about because his chief had found out that he had left a police guard at the theatre for the last forty eight hours and his chief was not happy. Ergo, if the chief is not happy, then his minions aren't happy, especially if it were the minions who made the chief unhappy in the first place.

Oh this was getting him nowhere. He would just close the case on the unfortunate girl. How can you defy a theatre full of witnesses and say that the girl was murdered when clearly it was an accident? Why did he have to look for hidden meanings in everything around him? Why couldn't he just accept what everyone else saw? Why? Because he had a sneaky feeling in his stomach. But try telling that to the chief, "Hey, chief excuse me, Sir, I know that you're busy and all, so I just thought I'd waste forty eight man hours of police time on a sneaky feeling in my stomach." Depression.

No, this was too much. He had to get out of his office. He picked up his hat and coat, and walked to the main entrance. Sergeant Jones was on the main desk.

'Off early?' he asked.

'I'm off for a liquid lunch,' Ploddock said, 'if anyone asks, tell them I'm chasing up clues.'

'You're the boss,' Sergeant Jones laughed.

Outside on the street he couldn't decide whether to go across the street to the local pub or go a bit further afield.

"Oh this is ridiculous," he thought to himself, and took a taxi to Kingsland Road. 'I may's well take another look at the place where they fished out that John Doe. That at least was foul play and his report wasn't going to leave his desk until he had found out who it was.' He reasoned.

He walked a short way down the canal path, it didn't make him feel any better. No clues suddenly appeared out of the bushes which might have been overlooked by a junior officer. He was going to have to face it, this was going to be one case that would never get solved, unless he was extremely lucky, and today was not his lucky day.

Back on the main road, he decided to take a walk. He hadn't been to this part of town for so long. By the time he reached Shoreditch he was desperate for a cup of tea and a sit down; his feet were killing him. He was a martyr to his feet, always had been, always would be.

Across the road from the town hall he stopped outside Queenie's café. "Perfect" he thought, nothing like a good cup of tea and maybe even a piece of Russian cake.

Inside, Vincent was relating to a customer how inconsiderate some people can be. He was still incensed about that rude man at the cinema the other day. Really some people had no manners.

Now he would never know how Dorothy got those red slippers. It seemed that Queenie had fallen asleep during the first song, "Over the rainbow." 'It wasn't really her sort of movie he went on to explain.' But he! 'Oh it was magical, like the world sprinkled with fairy dust.' He loved it.

Inspector Ploddock sat down at a table near the window. Business wasn't very brisk at the moment. It could be the weather. It's not every January day that it doesn't rain and the sun actually shines, so people were making the most of it.

'What can I get you?' Vincent asked spying a crumb lodged on a chair opposite.

'A cup of tea, and a piece of cake if you have any.'

'Ha, that's a laugh. Of course we have cake, this *is* a café is it not?' he answered, 'what sort do you want, we got Battenberg, Eccles cakes, Russian cake, chocolate cake, and Victoria sponge. What d'yer fancy.' He flicked the crumb from the chair.

'Victoria sponge please,' he said.

'Oh we are pushing the boat out tonight,' Vincent replied and sashayed away between the tables. He carried on his former conversation with the other client who thought he had been rescued. 'So there we were in Oz and it was beautiful, and Glenda the good fairy comes down in this like soap bubble and what do I hear, "What do you mean the package has disappeared. How could it disappear from beneath the stage."'

At this point Inspector Ploddock pricked up his ears. Vincent continued his conversation whilst bringing Inspector Ploddock his Victoria sponge. 'So by now the whole theatre is telling him to shush, and what do you think he says, "Shush yourselves." I mean really some people!'

He placed the cake and a cup of tea in front of Inspector Ploddock. 'Aint seen you around these parts,' he said. Vincent was adept at having at least two or three conversations going at the same time, depending on who and where his customers were sitting.

'Did the man say which theatre the package was in?'

'How should I know I was engrossed in the lollypop guild by then.

No, wait, Drury Lane, I distinctly heard Drury Lane.'

'Can you remember what he looked like?' asked Inspector Ploddock.

'Too dark, I mean I wasn't really looking,' replied Vincent. Somehow, he had swapped conversations without realising.

'Who was he with?'

'Oh a girl, no wait, two girls, that was it. One must have told him that the package was missing, while the other was all like, "Shsss, don't do that, Odel, shush people are watching," that sort of thing. Probably his sister.' He added as an after thought.

'Odel, are you sure that she said Odel?'

'What's this, are you some copper or something?' asked Vincent. 'I didn't know it was a criminal offence to talk in the movies? I can always go back next week if I really want to you know. I don't want to press charges or anything like that.'

Inspector Ploddock was slightly confused. 'Press charges, against who?' he asked.

'The man who was making all that fuss during the film.'

Inspector Ploddock ignored the last remark. 'Can you describe either of the girls that were with him?'

'One was a bit quiet looking that was his sister, you know the fawning one, and the other she was a bit sort of jolly hockey sticks type, very efficient type of girl. Been to a proper school. If you get my meaning.'

Inspector Ploddock got his meaning. He knew exactly who Vincent was talking about. Now he had to prove that something sneaky was going on. He definitely had this funny feeling in his stomach. Or was it the Victoria sponge?

Maltravers paced his small bedsit. There was no need to look at the list that Hessen had given him he knew nearly all of the names on the list. The problem was how to do the job without ending up on the list himself. He mentally went through the list again, this time working through all the pros and cons.

1. Claude von Marenbach - He was going to be difficult to get rid of... at the moment he had no way of getting to or getting at von Marenbach. So he moved on to the next name.

2. Ashley de la Mouche - The poor stupid girl, always going on about that crazy mother of her's. Well she didn't have to worry any more. At least he was saved having to do the deed, after that fortunate accident.

3. Herr Delfger and his wife - Hmm he thought, these would be the easiest targets at present. Maybe he should go for these. It would also mean that Herr Delfger was out of the way and make his getting to Marenbach easier.

4. Miss Plimple - Easy to get at, difficult to dispose of. Also she had or knew of the whereabouts of the papers. If he got rid of her too soon the papers could be lost. Tricky.

5. Granny Probyn - That interfering old bat. Ashley should never have tried to coax her into getting Plimple to talk. Now she was another problem. Probably the easiest to get rid of. Except she was in hospital, and if anything happened to her now it would raise suspicions.

6. Napoleon Packard - Poor sod, didn't know anything. His name was only on the list in case Drillby had passed over any information. He would have to go.

7. Odel & Hetty Oppenheimer - He knew nothing about. Maybe he should try and find out who, what, and why their names were added to list.

That was it. He needed to find these Oppenheimer's. The name of a hotel was next to their name. At least Hessen knew that and that was where he was going to start.

Napoleon Packard sat opposite this very educated German gentleman. He had followed the instructions in the note which had been delivered to his home that morning coming to this grotty café and taking a seat by the window. The café seemed to be quite busy so nobody took much notice of him as he entered or as he took his seat and waited for something to happen. He was unsure of exactly what. The waiter arrived swishing his tea towel at a patch of spilt milk on the table before him; then gave a terrific wail and sobbed into his tea towel, as a look of terror crossed Napoleon's face.

'It's no use! No,' Vincent wailed, 'it's no use crying over spilt milk,' then burst out laughing at his own joke. Napoleon sat horrified, unsure what to expect.

The rest of the café used to Vincent's antics ignored him and the unknown man, smiling to themselves that Vincent had pulled off another prank and they got on with their own lives. Eventually Napoleon ordered a cup of sweet tea to calm his nerves. Vincent returned to the counter, laughing to himself all the way. After a few minutes von Marenbach eased himself into the chair opposite and introduced himself.

'Mr. Packard, I am aware that you are in no way responsible for the death of Mr. Drillby, but I believe that you may have some information regarding his death and the work he was undertaking.'

'I er... well er... hmm.' Was all he got out of Napoleon.

'Mr. Packard,' von Marenbach started again, 'let me put it to you this way.' He smiled. 'If you do not co-operate with us I will have no further use for you, or your family. Is that understood?'

Napoleon nodded.

'Good, I see that we are going to get along famously,' von

Marenbach said. 'Now this is what I want you to do,' and proceeded to explain in great detail what was required of him.

Von Marenbach stood to leave, 'I take it that you are in agreement?' he asked.

Napoleon, sat with his head bowed. Then slowly nodded.

'Good,' said von Marenbach. 'I shall be in contact again soon and you shall have some good news, I hope.' And he left the café.

On his way to the door von Marenbach stopped at a table. 'Keep an eye on him.' He said, and walked out of the café into the busy street.

Napoleon, unaware that he had spoken to anyone else, was in his own world. How was he supposed to do what he had just been ordered? He needed to talk to somebody but who. Veronica would only say, 'do it,' so alas, she was not an impartial agent, especially as it had been reinforced that not only Napoleon but his whole family was in danger. No, he needed to talk to somebody and get their advice.

Napoleon got up, left money on the table for his tea and walked out the café trying all the while to gather his thoughts.

After a while he found himself outside the great stone arch and ornate iron gateway of St Bart's hospital. What had brought him to this spot he was unsure but, remembering that Granny Probyn was in the hospital, he went in to the reception and asked which ward she was in.

Five minutes later Napoleon Packard sat by Granny Probyn's bed.

'My dear boy,' she said, 'I was talking to your mother about you just the other day.' Granny Probyn wasn't sure if Ethel had managed to talk to Napoleon or not so decided that he had best make the first move.

'I was just passing,' he said, 'and so I thought I'd pop in and see how you're getting along?'

'Couldn't be better,' she replied, 'Walter and Jimmy from the theatre came this morning. They are looking after Fluffy Yeomans for me while I'm in here. And the doctors say I should be able to go home soon, so all will be back to normal.'

Granny Probyn smiled. For the first time in her life she had run out of things to say.

Napoleon sat with a faraway look in his eye. The silence stretched on. Granny Probyn smiled some more.

Unable to bear it any longer she eventually broached the subject that had been on her mind.

'Napoleon dear, as I was saying I was speaking to Ethel the other day and she seemed to think that there was something amiss with you. You seemed sort of distant.'

'Distant?'

'Strange?'

'Strange?'

'Yes, you know different?'

'Different?'

This conversation was going nowhere. Granny Probyn took a deep breath and bit the bullet.

'Napoleon dear, Ethel tells me that you have been receiving threatening letters?' She let out the last of the air expecting Napoleon to tell her to mind her own business.

'That's right.' He said.

'Oh,' replied Granny Probyn. This was definitely not the response she had expected. But now that she had got over the first hurdle she decided to press her case. 'Do you know who from?' she asked.

'Yes,' he said, 'I met the chap this morning, nice fellow, in different circumstances of course. German I think. Certainly had a bit of an accent even though he spoke impeccable English.'

'And what does he want, this German?'

'Oh, to get rid of a girl and retrieve some top secret papers which her uncle smuggled out of Germany. She apparently has them. I then have to take them to Germany.'

'To Germany!' Granny Probyn exclaimed, 'Whatever for?'

'It's something that Mucus was working on and I it seems am the only person who can understand them. They want me to continue

Mucus's work.'

'But this is preposterous, what about Veronica and Beauregard Henry? What about your mother Ethel? She swore that neither she nor any of her family would ever return to Germany. Especially now with the current situation. Napoleon?'

Napoleon by the look of his face had made up his mind.

'Can't you see what an exciting proposition this is, I can get out of that terrible law firm and actually do what I've always dreamed of doing.'

'Napoleon,' said Granny Probyn, 'stop and listen to yourself. You simply cannot leave everything you have worked for to help a bunch of thugs and murderers. What about the poor girl you have to get rid of?'

Napoleon came down to earth with a bump. His dream had been shattered, even if he *could* kill someone his dream would be forever marred by the guilt. 'You're right,' he said, 'but what am I to do?'

'I take it that the girl in question is Miss Plimple, Mr. Reed's secretary at the theatre.'

'Why yes, how did you know?' asked an astonished Napoleon.

'You are not the first to have been forced into doing these people's dirty work, poor Miss de la Mouche was also being threatened,' explained Granny Probyn.

'So what do we do?'

'We have to help poor Miss Plimple. It seems these people will stop at nothing to get these papers.'

'If Mucus was right in what he was telling me before he...' Napoleon suddenly stopped. 'Do you think that Mucus was murdered? And what about Mr. Oppenheimer? Did my mother tell you about him? He was the owner of the factory where Professor Meis was conducting experiments. Mucus was telling me about his correspondence with the professor.'

'Yes, it's all fitting together. And it looks like they won't stop until they get those papers back so we'll have to be very careful and watch our backs as they say.'

Scene 3

Odel and Hetty arrived at the theatre just before the matinee. They had decided to leave a note for Mr. Pleach with Walter at the stage door before watching the performance again. Odel thought it best not to ask for Miss Plimple as it might seem to anyone interested that they'd been seen a lot together.

Jimmy delivered the note to Mr. Pleach and Stutlz's dressing room. He knocked on the door.

'Come!' Cried Mr. Stutlz.

Jimmy opened the door. 'Got a letter for you, Mr. Pleach,' he said.

Mr. Pleach was in the middle of making up, 'A letter? For me?' he said.

'Juszt leave it tzere.' Said Mr. Stutlz pointing to the edge of the dressing table and handing Jimmy a half penny. 'Now be hoff wiz you, we av to be ready for ze performance.'

'I wonder who it could be from,' said Julian once Jimmy had closed the door behind him. Wiping his hand on his makeup towel before he picked up the letter to look at the writing on the envelope. 'I must say I don't recognise the writing but it is a beautiful hand.' He turned the envelope over and slipped the edge of his makeup pencil knife under the flap and ripped the top off the envelope.

The note had a slight hint of perfume. 'It's from Miss Oppenheimer,' he said excitedly reading the note, 'she wants to see me after the performance this afternoon. She says she will be in the audience for the matinee.'

'Zen we had better make sure zat today's performance is extra spezial,' said Stutlz.

'Oh, how could it be anything but!' Exclaimed Julian.

Granny Probyn got out of the taxi by herself as the taxi driver fumbled with the handle of his cab door, 'Oh, don't bother about that young man,' she said to the taxi driver as she handed him her fare, 'I can sort myself out, I'm fit as a fiddle.'

She had just been released from the hospital and rather than go back to the hotel she decided to go to the theatre and see Fluffy Yeomans. Oh how she had missed him.

'Hello Walter.' She said as she walked into the stage door.

'Mrs. Probyn,' said Walter, 'glad to see's yer back in the land of the living.'

'I'm glad to be back,' she replied, then asked, 'where's Fluffy Yeomans?'

"E's wiv Jimmy at the moment, we're abaht to start the show any minute so 'e'll be waiting under the stage for 'is first entrance.'

Thanking Walter, Granny Probyn made her way down the central stone steps to the under stage area. There was lots of comings and goings by stage hands and chorus members in preparation for the show. Looking around she saw on the hydraulic lift various parts of the different sets that were used, some waiting off to the side to be changed during the performance. Jimmy was sitting on the bench which is used in the miller's store room. Fluffy Yeomans was curled on his lap waiting for his chin to be tickled.

'Mrs. Probyn!' Jimmy almost shouted, then remembered where he was and managed a loud whisper. 'You're outta the 'ospital? I told yer Fluffy that she wouldn't be long.' Fluffy Yeomans purred and jumped from Jimmy's lap and rubbed himself around Granny Probyn's legs.

'Oh, give over, you silly thing otherwise you'll trip me up and I'll be back in hospital with a broken leg.' But there was no denying she was so pleased to see Fluffy Yeomans.

Granny Probyn laid a hand on Jimmy's head and gave his scalp a scratch, 'and as for you, young man I have a little something to say thank you for looking after my Fluffy.' Saying which she delved into her large hand bag and brought out a bag of barley sugar twists. 'Don't eat them all at once. Now run off with you, you have other jobs to do as well as look after my Fluffy.'

Karl and the professor had found themselves taken aboard a German warship. After a brief introduction to the captain, they were taken to a cabin and locked in. Shortly afterwards they could feel the ship moving.

'Where do you think that they will take us, professor?' asked Karl.

'Back to Berlin I suppose,' he said.

There was a knock at the door. Smeeton entered followed by a couple of seamen.

'Good afternoon, gentlemen. I hope you slept well after our late transfer.'

'Where do you plan to take us?' asked Karl, impatient with all these false pleasantries.

'I am afraid that you will be going back to the Fatherland. All being well, we should be in Berlin this time next week. So I suggest, gentlemen, that you relax and if I may say so don't try anything stupid. Oh, and by the way, Herr Professor, by the time we return, your notes will be waiting for you on your desk.'

'What about my niece?' asked the professor.

'Ah, yes, well, lets just say, Herr Professor that if you do not do anything stupid she will be perfectly safe.' With which Smeeton turned and walked out of the cabin.

Karl and the professor heard the sound of the key locking the door again.

'What do we do now?' Karl snapped.

'As long as I do as they tell me, both you and my niece are safe. If I don't then they will kill us all.'

'They will kill us once they have what they want anyway, so why give it to them?'

'We have to buy ourselves some time. Who knows what may turn up. In the meantime I agree with our friend Smeeton we should just relax and not do anything stupid. After all we can't run anywhere. Once in Germany of course that is another matter.'

Odel and Hetty presented themselves at the stage door at the end of the matinee performance. Julian Pleach, had sent word that they were to be escorted up to his dressing room. All during the performance when he wasn't on stage and during the interval he had tried to make the dressing room more presentable. Mr. Stutlz complained bitterly.

'Vot do you mean I can't take my nap between ze shows?' he snapped, 'I alvays have my nap, just because you ave a pretty young lady coming to see you.'

'My dear Herbert, it's only for a short while,' Julian said as he stuffed the bedding which was lying around behind a curtain. 'We have to make the place a bit more, you know?'

'No, I don't know.'

'Presentable.'

'Vat is wrong wiz it? If it's good enuff for the great Henry Irving, it's good enuff for me!' Said Stultz and started to sulk into his makeup mirror.

A knock at the door ended their conversation. Herbert sulked even more. Julian lunged for the door and opened it with a flourish, 'Oh, how wonderful to see you again,' he gushed.

'Oh my!' Said Hetty, overwhelmed by his response. 'I was just commenting to my brother, Odel,' who she indicted with her fan, 'that it's a wonderful atmosphere backstage. So warm and friendly.'

Herbert von Stultz huffed into his mirror.

'Yes,' said Julian. 'We are one big happy family. Won't you come in, Miss Oppenheimer?' with which he opened the door as wide as it could go to allow them to enter. 'Welcome to our little world of make believe.'

'My dear brother Odel,' Odel nodded by way of introduction, 'doesn't believe that a cat would be able to act, do you Odel?' Hetty continued, 'surely you Mr. Pleach with your great charisma must be doing something truly magical.'

Julian Pleach blushed, 'Well I must say that if it wasn't for me he wouldn't have got his start in the business.'

Herbert von Stutlz umphed into his mirror and started to remove his makeup by applying a liberal amount of cold cream to his face and vigorously rubbing it in.

'Oh do forgive me,' said Julian, 'this is Herbert von Stutlz.'

'Ow do you do,' said Herbert and without looking away from the mirror continued to remove his makeup.

'Can I offer you a drink Miss Oppenheimer, or a seat maybe?' he said, indicating a chair.

'No thank you Mr. Pleach, we must be off, we have taken up so much of your time already. Really it was just to say thank you for your kind words the other day and how wonderful the performance was.'

'Oh but you've only just got here, surely you don't have to leave straight away,' said Julian. 'Maybe I could show you around backstage.'

'That would be delightful,' said Hetty, 'where shall we start? I know I would love to meet that wonderful cat, I know Odel would to, wouldn't you, Odel?' Odel nodded.

'Then you are in luck,' said Julian, 'as Mrs. Probyn's dressing room is just down the corridor.'

'What an extraordinary name for a cat,' Hetty said, 'whoever calls a cat Mrs. Probyn?'

'Oh no, that's not the name of the cat,' said Julian blushing at his mistake, 'the cats name is Fluffy, Fluffy Yeomans. Mrs. Probyn is the sweet old lady whose cat he is.'

'Oh, I see, how silly of me,' said Hetty and Odel obliged with a laugh.

Maltravers had just finished changing out of his costume and makeup, having decided to try and find these Oppenheimer's during the break between shows. At least he would be one step further forward, and also he could report some good news to Hessen.

On his way down the corridor he passed Julian Pleach talking to some guests. 'What a ridiculous fool,' he thought. Pleach was obviously trying to impress the girl. He smiled at Hetty and continued on his way to the stairs.

Mr. Pleach knocked on Granny Probyn's door. 'Mrs. Probyn, may I introduce Miss Hetty Oppenheimer and her brother Odel,' said Julian Pleach.

Maltravers stopped in his tracks, what incredible luck, here they were served on a plate as it where. Granny Probyn was also taken by surprise. Why would Mr. Pleach be introducing relations of the dead man whom the police couldn't identify?

'How lovely to meet you,' Maltravers heard Granny Probyn say. 'Do come in.'

Maltravers made his way back to his dressing room to wait.

Veronica Packard wailed into her large handkerchief. Ethel Dorfellwaffer sniffed into her small lace handkerchief. Napoleon stood his ground. 'No, my dear, I have talked it through with Mrs. Probyn and we have decided on a course of action.'

'Oh, my poor baby, my poor poor baby!' She wailed. 'How can

you contemplate anything so hideous?' she said.

Napoleon still stood his ground.

'You're a beast, a monster, oh, my poor baby!' She wailed again.

The poor baby in question, Beauregard Henry was at that moment totally unawares that his future was in the hands of such a monster. He was happily pursuing his favourite sport, bullying. Even after the untimely death of Edward Cebris Jones there were still plenty of other smaller boys whom he and his gang could pick on. The school bell rang for lunch.

Madam Delfger climbed the steps to the school. She opened the large wooden door and stepped into a whirlwind of children all running hither and thither, up the stairs to the dining room and the playground above. She stopped one small girl.

'Can you show me to the headmaster please?' she asked trying to be nice. It was difficult enough having to talk to the brats but with this cacophonous racket, they were like rats. She would quite happily have them all exterminated.

'His office is down the corridor, ma'am,' said the child through buck teeth, curtsied, and ran off squealing after her friends.

Madam Delfger barged her way through the throng of children like a ship breaking its way through an ice flow. The bodies of children littered the corridor in her wake.

Sybil Cumstance typed with an attitude as sharp as her elbows. Everything about Sybil Cumstance was sharp. As school secretary she held a position of authority and she meant to keep it. Children quaked at her sight. To be sent to the head master was as cruel a torture as any that a sadistic Chinaman could come up with. Sybil Cumstance loathed children.

Madam Delfger knocked on the door to the Headmaster's office.

'Come!' Barked Sybil Cumstance expecting some wretch of a child. A look of surprise then disappointment fell across her pointed features. She had just thought of a new punishment and was eager to try it out on the next reprobate that crossed her sacred portal.

'Oh, I do beg your pardon,' she simpered. That was the other odd trait in one so sharp. Sybil Cumstance oozed obsequiousness.

'Not at all,' said Madam Delfger noticing Sybil's crestfallen face, 'children,' she almost spat out the word, 'children,' she continued, 'should know their place and be quiet.'

The two women hit it off immediately and within minutes were as thick as thieves.

'So tell me, Madam Delfger.' Sybil whimpered.

'Do call me Lottie.'

'Lottie, what can I do for you today?'

'Vell I hav zis note from Mr. Packard. I am to collect his boy from school and to take him home. His poor muzzer is not well.'

'I am sorry to hear that. What name did you say?'

'Packard, the child is Beauregard Henry.'

'Oh,' said Sybil as if she had just thrown up her lunch, 'him.'

'Yes,' said Madam Delfger, 'it's no wonder ze poor woman has had a breakdown,' she added as if it were all Beauregard Henry's fault.

'Well let me have a word with the Headmaster, I'm sure everything will be in order.' She knocked at an adjoining door and walked in.

A few minutes later a large military looking man filled the doorway. 'Madam Delfger, how pleased to meet you, Sybil has told me everything. How unfortunate for the poor woman.' Major Thumbstanley was the exact opposite to his secretary. An ex Major in the Army he sported a huge moustache which quivered unnaturally when he spoke. 'Of course,' he continued, 'the little tyke must go home and see his beloved mother. I shall have someone bring him down. No doubt he'll be eating his lunch I shouldn't wonder.'

Madam Delfger didn't know where to look; the Major's moustache had a life of its own. 'Zank you,' she finally managed to say.

'Well I'll leave you two women to gossip,' said the Major and returned to his office.

A few minutes later Beauregard Henry presented himself at the office of Sybil Cumstance. Unsure of which prank he was being punished for, he had decided on his way down to the office just to accept whatever was coming to him. He had had a pretty full week of pranks and bullying. It was bound to catch up with him.

He knocked at Sybil's door.

'Come!' She barked.

Beauregard Henry opened the door nervously and stepped in.

'This,' barked Sybil Cumstance before Beauregard Henry had a chance to compose himself, 'is Madam Delfger. She is here to take you to your poor mother who has had a nervous breakdown. And no wonder I shouldn't think having spawned you,' she added. 'I want to hear of no nonsense. You are to do as you are told, or else. Am I understood?'

Beauregard Henry nodded.

'Then wait outside until called for,' she commanded. Beauregard Henry did as he was told and took one of the three seats outside Sybil's office.

'Oh I enjoyed that,' she said to Lottie, 'a firm hand that's what children need.'

'Indeed, indeed,' replied Lottie. 'Vell I must be going. Poor Mrs. Packard will be distraught.'

'Why yes indeed,' said Sybil and escorted her to the door.

Madam Delfger grabbed the boy's hand and marched down the corridor almost dragging Beauregard Henry to the heavy wooden front doors.

'Do call again,' Sybil called out to Madam Delfger's disappearing back.

Scene 4

Jimmy knocked at Granny Probyn's dressing room door. 'This is your half hour call, Mrs. Probyn.' He called 'Goodness gracious me,' she said as she looked at her watch. Julian Pleach was unaware that so much time had passed. He was in heaven and it went by the name of Hetty Oppenheimer.

'We simply must be going. We have taken up so much of your time,' said Hetty and made to leave.

'Must you go just yet?' Julian asked jumping to his feet. 'We haven't looked backstage, or seen the ponies in the stables, or taken a tour of the costumes and prop rooms.'

'I'm sure Miss Oppenheimer will be a frequent visitor if I'm not mistaken,' said Granny Probyn.

'Please do call me Hetty, Mrs. Probyn, everyone does.'

'May I call you Hetty?' whimpered a slushy Julian. 'That would be the icing on the cake.'

'Well,' Hetty teased, 'only if you promise to show me all those things you mentioned,' and she started to leave.

In the corridor Julian continued, 'If you'll permit me, I can arrange to have a full tour tomorrow if you would like?'

Odel finally said to Granny Probyn, 'It's been nice talking to you. I wonder, if I may come and visit you at your hotel. I have something very important I need to discuss.'

'By all means,' said Granny Probyn. 'Shall we say tomorrow at 12? There is no matinee so Fluffy Yeomans and I will be at home so to speak all day.'

'That will be perfect,' said Odel. He bowed and left.

Herr Delfger opened the front door. Madam Delfger was flushed in the face and had Beauregard Henry's right hand clamped firmly in her left. With his other hand he nursed a very red cheek where Madam Delfger had slapped him. Accustomed to getting his own way Beauregard Henry was in a state of shock.

'Welcome, my dear,' he said, 'and this must be young Beauregard.'

Beauregard Henry stared straight ahead.

'Come, my dear, let's not keep our young charge on the doorstep.'

Madam Delfger pushed her way passed her husband dragging Beauregard Henry behind her.

Herr Delfger looked up and down the road to make sure that no one had seen and if they did see anything that this was nothing out of the ordinary for the household. He closed the door and ran after his wife who had made her way to the small kitchen on a mezzanine level at the rear of the house.

The kitchen was a long galley affair with a window along the left-hand side above the sink which overlooked the landlady's small patio area below. At the far end of the room a door opened leading to six stone steps down into its own private garden.

'What's the matter with the boy?' asked Herr Delfger as he entered.

'He was acting up so I slapped him.' Madam Delfger replied. 'Little brat made such a scene on the bus it was the only way to keep him quiet.'

Beauregard Henry looked from one adult to the other. He had never been in a situation like this before. He had always got what he wanted when he threw a tantrum at home.

'I want to go home,' he said at last. 'I want my mummy.'

'I'll tell you what I want,' said Madam Delfger, 'it's that you shut your whinging mouth before I shut it for you.'

Madam Delfger looked in one of the cupboards and found the bottle of gin, poured herself a large shot and downed it in one.

'Now now, Lottie dear, we mustn't make Beauregard Henry unwelcome must we?' said Herr Delfger trying to smile. 'He may be staying with us for some time remember?'

'I want to go home,' said Beauregard Henry. 'I want my mummy.'

'Well you can't, see, cause they don't want you. They've had enough of you and your whinging, and so have I, so sit there and don't move.' She pushed Beauregard Henry onto a stool in the corner by the draining board, 'If I hears one more peek out of you, I'll lock you in the coal cellar.'

Normally a coal cellar wouldn't have frightened Beauregard Henry, in fact they were good places to explore. But the way Madam Delfger said it, made it seem there was something in the cellar, and it wouldn't be too happy to be sharing it.

'Now, now,' said Herr Delfger, 'why don't I put the kettle on and I'll make us all a nice cup of tea? I might even find a biscuit.'

'Who needs tea?' said Madam Delfger as she poured another two fingers of gin into her glass, 'this one's,' pointing the bottle at Beauregard Henry, 'is enough to drive anybody to drink.'

Beauregard Henry felt his cheek and kept quiet.

'Now what are we going to do with him?' Lottie asked her husband. 'How long have we got to put up with the brat?'

'You know what von Maren...' Herr Delfger stopped himself from saying the name. 'You know who said,' he continued, 'until a certain job has been done he stays with us.'

'Why couldn't Marenbach give you the job of getting back the papers instead we have to baby sit this... this...' Madam Delfger was at a loss for words.

'Sssh, Lottie please, we said no names remember. Just in case.' He nodded his head in the direction of Beauregard Henry. 'Little boys have big ears.'

'That still doesn't answer the question of what we are supposed to do with him,' she said and added another finger of gin to her glass.

'For starters, maybe we could lighten up on the gin for a while, you know what happened the last time.' Herr Delfger said. He liked to remind his wife of the accident with Mr. Oppenheimer. She suddenly sobered up. 'Next why don't you take the boy upstairs to the room we prepared?' he said, nudging his head for her to take the boy out, 'and I will prepare us all a nightcap.'

Taking a small white paper parcel from his waistcoat pocket he said, 'Then we'll have a nice quiet night,' and started to laugh. Lottie, looking at the packet, joined in the joke. Beauregard Henry started to cry.

Inspector Ploddock decided to visit Granny Probyn at her hotel. Having found out that she had been released from hospital and not having had a chance to talk to her while she was unconscious, he thought he had better tie up a few loose ends or the chief would be breathing down his neck. It seemed police work was becoming nothing but paperwork. Damn bureaucrats had to justify everything. He also had to return the book he had borrowed. Of course Granny Probyn was unaware that he had borrowed it, she being in a coma as she was, but he had got so engrossed in the plot, he did like a good mystery, that he had decided to take it away with him and return it at a later date. That date was now.

Inspector Ploddock asked at the reception desk if Granny Probyn was still in her room.

'I believe she is in the lounge sir,' came the supercilious reply from Cedric the hotel receptionist. 'Shall I have her paged?'

'No, that won't be necessary, just tell me which way to the lounge?'

'Through that archway and turn to your left,' said Cedric pointing the way.

'Much obliged I'm sure,' said Inspector Ploddock, and followed Cedric's instructions. He found Granny Probyn in a seat by a large bay window overlooking the gardens. The lounge faced away from the busy London traffic. One would think you were in the country.

'Mrs. Probyn?' asked Inspector Ploddock approaching her table.

Granny Probyn looked up from stroking Fluffy Yeomans who was curled on her lap, 'Yes?' she replied.

'Allow me to introduce myself, I'm Inspector Ploddock of Scotland Yard. We have met before at the hospital, except you weren't aware of it.'

'Indeed, inspector, please take a seat.' She indicated another place at the table.

Inspector Ploddock put down his hat and took of his coat. The book which he had taken was in the pocket. 'Oh before I forget, I borrowed this,' handing the volume across to Granny Probyn, 'I hope you don't mind, it's just I had to do something while waiting for you to wake, and I picked this up off your bedside cabinet, and when you didn't waken, I hadn't finished the book, so I thought, well...' For some reason Inspector Ploddock went all shy and confused and couldn't quite get out what he wanted to say.

'That's where it went to,' cried Granny Probyn, 'I thought the robber had taken it, although why a robber would want to break into my hotel room just to steal a copy of a novel they could buy at any kiosk, was beyond me.'

'Do forgive me,' said Inspector Ploddock.

'There's nothing to forgive, Inspector,' she replied. 'It's a rather silly book don't you think? I mean I can't believe that a sweet little old lady like that would commit murder just because she was jilted at the church. Can you?'

'They do say that truth is stranger than fiction, but I agree with you. However I did like the premise that Miss Christie's heroine goes to London to inform Scotland Yard that there have been five murders in her quiet little village, all made to look like accidents and gets herself killed before she has had a chance to reveal the murderer. It could quite easily fit your attack Mrs. Probyn.'

Fluffy Yeomans pricked up an ear and opened an eye.

'Really inspector in what way?'

'You come from your quiet little village, although this time the village is on stage at the theatre, and then there are all these accidental deaths surely some smart old bird sees that all might not be as it seems and makes a few enquiries, surreptitiously of course, and stumbles upon the real murderer. She then becomes a target for the murderer herself.' Inspector Ploddock was actually fishing, the thought had only just occurred to him.

'Meow,' said Fluffy Yeomans.

'Oh, I see,' said Granny Probyn, stroking Fluffy who had started to knead her lap. 'Then if that is the case and real life resembles Miss Christies book, the murderer must be obvious, except there isn't a sweet little old lady in the pantomime, or backstage except me,' Granny Probyn said with a smile, 'and I'm afraid I was not jilted at the church. So where does that leave us now inspector?'

'Meow,' said Fluffy Yeomans again and kneed harder.

'It was only a theory,' Inspector Ploddock laughed. 'Well perhaps I had best be going. I only wanted to return the book and to make sure that you are all right, and to reassure you that we are doing everything we can to find out who it was robbed you.'

'But inspector, apart from the book, which you have kindly returned, nothing else is missing.'

'Then can you think of any reason why anybody would want to attack you?' asked Inspector Ploddock.

Granny Probyn blushed slightly. Unused to lying she desperately wanted to tell all she knew, but she couldn't reveal anything that had happened at the theatre, somebody would be hurt if they suspected that the police were informed. She just had to believe that all would work itself out in the end.

'Inspector Ploddock, I err... you must excuse me there is a young man over there with whom I have an appointment. It seems he is a great fan of Fluffy Yeomans.' Granny Probyn smiled in the direction of Odel Oppenheimer.

'Forgive me once again,' said Inspector Ploddock and got up to leave. 'If you can think of anything that would help us in our enquiries, please do contact me.' He held out a hand.

Granny Probyn took it and gave a warm shake.

'Thank you inspector, if I think of anything, you will be the first to know.'

Inspector Ploddock bowed and left, smiling at Odel as he passed by.

Odel took the seat vacated by Inspector Ploddock, 'Thank you Mr. Oppenheimer, you arrived at a very opportune moment,' said Granny Probyn.

'Oh, I'm sorry, I thought, well you looked like you wanted to get rid of the man, that's why I attracted your attention.'

'It's quite all right. Now what can I do for you? You sounded so serious yesterday. Is it about Hetty you wanted to talk? She's obviously well smitten with Mr. Pleach and I'm afraid it's equally obvious that he is smitten back,' she said.

'Yes and no, Mrs. Probyn. Please don't be offended but I have to ask you, what do you know about the disappearance of my Uncle?' Odel looked at Granny Probyn with tears in his eyes.

Granny Probyn played with Fluffy Yeoman's ear for a while before she spoke.

'I have it on good authority,' she said, 'I am sorry to say, that your uncle is dead and the police are at a loss as to identifying the body. Now may I ask you a question?'

Odel nodded, he was trying desperately to hold back the tears.

'Did your uncle give Miss Plimple a package to look after?'

Odel nodded again.

'Can you tell me what was in the package?'

'Papers,' Odel sniffed. 'Top Secret. My uncle owned laboratories in Berlin. He knew it was unsafe in Germany. That's why he brought us here. He brought those papers to hand over to his friend, Professor Meis, he's Miss Plimple's uncle. She was to keep them safe and hand them to Professor Meis. We were all meant to meet up in America.'

'Then we had better find Miss Plimple as she is in very grave danger.'

'Mrs. Probyn, Miss Plimple, she doesn't have the package any more. It was taken from the theatre. Forgive me but at first we thought... I thought that you had taken it. Hetty and I used Mr. Pleach to arrange to meet you yesterday to see if we could try and find out where you had taken the package. Of course...' He stopped unable to keep up the pretence. 'Well it now all seems rather silly doesn't it, trying to act like international spies! It's blatantly obvious after your attack you don't have the package.'

'But I didn't take the package. It's true I did follow Miss Plimple to try and discover why Miss de la Mouche was being threatened, but I never found out. We were disturbed before I could ask Miss Plimple, and then someone attacked me and I've not had an opportunity to talk to her since.'

'Then if you didn't take it,' said Odel, 'obviously someone else did. But who?'

'There were two people in the dressing room, Miss de la Mouche had an accomplice. He must have taken it,' said Granny Probyn.

'I'm sorry I don't follow you.'

'Our first night at the theatre, Fluffy Yeomans and I heard talking in the dressing room next door, being new to the cast we didn't know who's dressing room it was. We found out later that it was Miss de la Mouche. She was having a conversation with a man. We had met so many new people that day, it was so exciting for us, but he had said that "she'll have to go." At the time Fluffy and I didn't know what it could have been about. We found out later that they had meant Miss

Plimple. That was the reason why I was following Miss Plimple. Oh I have been such a fool. I see now that Miss de la Mouche was using me. Trying to get to Miss Plimple that way rather than having to...' Granny Probyn couldn't say it, 'poor Miss de la Mouche, whoever was threatening her must have got tired of waiting.'

'Then Miss Plimple is safe, they have what they want.'

'I think not, these people don't like loose ends, its clear now why I was attacked.'

'So you think that Miss Plimple is still in danger?'

'Not just Miss Plimple, anybody who has had any dealings with those papers, whether they realize it or not they are in grave danger.'

'But that could be you, me, Miss Plimple, Hetty!'

'Exactly, we have to locate those missing papers, quickly, before someone else gets hurt.'

Scene 5

*J*ulian Pleach called early for Miss Hetty Oppenheimer. Julian had planned the whole day in his head. As there was no matinee this day, they would start by going to see Buckingham Palace, then a stroll down to The Houses of Parliament, on to The Embankment and back along the Thames. Lunch in a nice restaurant, and then escort her back to her hotel in time for him to make the evening show.

Herbert von Stutlz had advised against it. 'You'll be exhausted, my boy, think of your performance.'

But Julian couldn't think of anything other than Miss Hetty Oppenheimer.

Hetty kissed her brother on the cheek. 'Now you be nice to the old lady,' she joked as she left the hotel with Mr. Pleach on her arm. Odel smiled to himself. At last Hetty had found some happiness, but he was determined to find out what had happened to his uncle and so set off to keep his appointment with Granny Probyn.

Hetty and Julian were enjoying themselves immensely.

They both liked each others company so much that it was easy to forget the outside world. They walked and talked and walked some more.

Maltravers waited in the lobby of the hotel careful that he shouldn't be seen by either Pleach or the girl or her brother. Once he was sure that they had gone he made his way to the second floor and the suite that the Oppenheimer's occupied. The maid was just finishing servicing the room when he made to open the door.

'Oh excuse me sir, I thought that you had left for the day,' the girl said.

'Yes, I just meant to leave these for my sister. It's her birthday you see I want it as a surprise when she returns.' Maltravers held up a large bunch of flowers.

Not questioning the gentleman, the maid curtsied and left the room door open. Maltravers entered and closed the door behind him. There was a private lounge, sitting area with large soft sofas, sideboard and drinks cabinet etcetera. Two doors at opposite sides of the room led to the bedrooms. Maltravers chose the door to his left, only because it was nearest. Inside was a large double bed under a heavy canopy of drapes, a bedside table on either side. A large chest of drawers, wardrobe, and dressing table finished off the suite of furniture. Maltravers opened the wardrobe door. Inside hung Hetty's dresses. Maltravers laid the flowers on the bottom of the bed, and removed a square gold box wrapped with a red ribbon from the paper bag he was carrying and put it with the flowers.

Closing the door behind him he quickly made his way out of the hotel in case she or Odel should return early.

'Yers cutting it a bit fine aint yer Mrs. Probyn?' said Walter. Granny Probyn with Fluffy Yeomans in his basket hurried to her dressing room.

'Sorry, Walter,' was all she managed to say as she raced through the stage door. Miss Plimple was waiting for her at the end of the corridor.

'I'm sorry, Jane,' she said to Miss Plimple as she passed her, 'there's been an unfortunate complication; I'll tell you all about it later. Is everything all right with you, since our meeting this morning?'

'Yes,' said Miss Plimple, 'Odel stayed with me the whole afternoon until Mr. Pleach arrived. When he found out that he had left Hetty alone at the hotel he rushed back there. That was just before the half hour call.'

'Yes I'm terribly late, but at last I'm here,' apologised Granny Probyn again.

'Don't worry I've delayed the curtain by five minutes so you can get yourself and Fluffy Yeomans ready.'

'Thank you my dear, I'll speak to you later.'

'Vots zat?' said Mr. Stutlz coming out of his dressing room and overhearing the end of their conversation. 'Zis is very unprofessional, Never! Never hav I been late for a performance.' And stormed off back to his dressing room to await the call for beginners.

Beauregard Henry woke up in a small bedroom. He glanced around from the single bed upon which he lay. He shivered. He looked over to the small fireplace. There was a large wooden table placed in front of it; there was going to be no fire to keep him warm. He wrapped the thin blanket closer around himself. The walls, papered only with lining paper, were a dull tobacco stained yellow dotted about with a few cheap prints in frames. On the ceiling a large water stain, enough to make a dozen Rorschach tests, filled half the room. Above the table a single gas bracket popped and hissed giving a dull light to the room. The window was covered by a heavy brown serge material which had been nailed to the top of the window frame. Beauregard Henry wanted his mother.

Light streamed in from the landing as Madam Delfger opened the door. She carried a small tray and placed it on the table. Stretching across she turned up the gas mantle to brighten the room slightly. 'Your tea's here,' she said and walked out of the room closing the door behind her. Beauregard Henry could hear the lock being turned.

He crossed to the table. On the plate in front of him was a congealed mass of white jelly. He picked a small piece with his fingers and gingerly put it to his mouth. It was cold, wet, horrible, and chewy. He spat it out onto the wooden floor. Surely his mother was wondering where he was and was now calling for him? Where was he? He couldn't quite remember as his hand went to his cheek. He remembered a slap, that was it, a slap on the bus. Then brought here to this house. Where?

He needed to go to the loo.

He walked across the room to the door and banged. Nothing. He banged again. Nothing. He shouted. Nothing. He banged and shouted. Nothing. He looked around the room again. Then he saw it under the bed. A little chinky, as his father called them. He was desperate and unless he wanted to wet his trousers which he didn't, and hadn't done since he was four years old he would just have to use it. He started to unbutton his trousers and was just about to let flow when the door opened.

Taken by surprise he turned rather too quickly and sprayed the room and door when Madam Delfger happened to walk in.

'You dirty little brat, you filthy disgusting dirty....' Such was her shock, Madam Delfger couldn't think of any suitable name to call the boy and stood with her arms held wide and the front of her skirts sprayed.

'I'm sorry,' Beauregard Henry tried to apologise and hide his willy at the same time. Unfortunately he was still mid stream and his trousers became soaked. 'I didn't think anybody was going to come, so I...' He trailed off as his trousers got wet. He started to cry.

'Stop your whinging you dirty little sod!' Madam Delfger screamed.

Beauregard Henry tried to stop and the more he tried the harder he cried. 'I'm sorry,' he said again through his tears.

'Sorry's not gonna clean my dress, sorry's not gonna clean these floors, sorry's not gonna do nothing,' shouted Madam Delfger. She just knew that this was a mistake. She had tried to tell her husband but he wouldn't listen, now look at the mess, and where was he? Out! 'Sorry.' She mumbled, 'not as sorry as I am, for marrying that good for nothing, my mother warned me against it, "you have a beautiful voice Muchen" she used to say, "don't waste it on this man." And what did I do?'

Beauregard Henry stopped crying, he was finding it difficult to keep up with Madam Delfger's mood swings. His trousers were becoming uncomfortable. Should he say something?

'Excuse me, madam,' he said, 'I need to change my trousers.'

'And what am I supposed to do about it?' she snapped back. She looked around the room and noticed that he hadn't touched the plate of tripe and onions. 'Can't even eat your supper. Well you'll get nothing else until that's eaten. I'm not wasting good food on the likes of you.' And she stormed out of the room locking the door again behind her.

Beauregard pulled off his wet trousers and sat on the bed, pulled his knees up to his shoulders and wrapped the blanket even more tightly around himself. He wanted his mummy quite desperately.

Hetty arrived at the hotel in high spirits. She had had a wonderful afternoon with Julian but the time had come when he was due at the theatre. Hetty had wanted to join him there but she needed to change for the evening. Besides they had arranged to meet each other again the next day. Oh, she was so happy. She burst into their apartment suite. Odel wasn't there. A little surprised, he might be asleep, she thought and crossed the room to his bedroom door. She knocked gently, 'Odel,' she whispered. She didn't want to wake him if he was asleep. 'Odel,' she said again as she opened the door an inch. She put her head around the door. The bedroom was empty. Where could he be? She wondered to herself.

She crossed the room to her own bedroom where she immediately noticed the flowers. Oh, how wonderful! Flowers from Julian. Hetty didn't stop to think who else the flowers could be from. In her state of euphoria she naturally assumed they were from Julian Pleach. If she had thought about it, she would have realised that he had been with her all day and had not the time or opportunity to leave flowers on her bed.

She picked up the bunch of roses and smelt their delicate aroma. Then she saw the golden box. Finding a vase from the other room she filled it with water from the bathroom, arranged the flowers and placed them on her dressing table. She then untied the ribbon of the gold cover box. Inside were was tray of four chocolates. By the size of the box, there must be three layers. Twelve beautiful chocolates. She took a chocolate and placed it to her lips. 'Thank you, sweet Julian,' she murmured as she kissed the chocolate. She then slipped it into her mouth and allowed it to melt. Hetty wanted to savour the taste. It had been a wonderful day.

Veronica Packard was beside herself with fear and panic about her baby, Beauregard Henry. When he didn't come home at his usual time she had assumed that he was with his school friends. She had waited a while before she telephoned the Spratts. Hugo and Lavinia Spratt lived two streets away on Mapledene Crescent, their son Winston and

Beauregard Henry would often walk to school together.

'I'm sorry Veronica, Winston returned home simply ages ago. Shall I ask him about Beauregard?' Lisped Lavinia Spratt. A large woman she insisted on wearing chintz dresses one size too small with the result that everything she wore made her look like an over stuffed easy armchair. 'He's in his bedroom doing his homework,' she said and put down the phone.

'Winston.' She called from the foot of the stairs, Lavinia tried not to climb the stairs unless it was absolutely necessary. Knee trouble she maintained. The doctors called it overweight.

'Winston,' she called again. 'Did Beauregard Henry walk home with you this evening?'

Winston stuck his head over the top of the banister. He was in the middle of a wrestle with his younger brother. 'What? No. He left school at lunch time. A big lady called for him said his mother was ill,' said Winston and resumed punching his brother.

Lavinia waddled back to the phone. 'Winston said that he left early because you were ill.' She paraphrased.

'What!' Screamed Veronica down the phone. 'Who said I was ill?'

'Tha's what Winston jus' told me,' lisped Lavinia, 'that Beauregard Henry left early with a large woman because you had been taken ill.'

'Oh my God!' Exclaimed Veronica dropping the phone. Her worst nightmare had just come true.

'Veronica,' lisped Lavinia, 'Veronica!'

But Veronica wasn't listening.

Napoleon found her slumped by the hall telephone table. Lavinia Spratt's voice somewhere in the background. Veronica's legs had given way. 'They've got him, they've got him, my poor baby, they've got him.'

Napoleon picked up the phone.

'Oh thank God you're there,' lisped Lavinia in a panic, 'is Veronica all right?'

'Yes, yes, she's just had a funny turn, she'll be all right, thank you, thank you,' said Napoleon and hung up the phone.

'They've got my baby, my poor baby, YOU!' Veronica Screamed, 'YOU! You are responsible for this! My poor baby, I told you, you should have done what they wanted, now they're going to kill my baby!' She wailed.

Napoleon was afraid that his wife was right. He hadn't done anything since his meeting with von Marenbach. In fact since his talk with Granny Probyn, he had positively stayed away from the theatre just in case he should be followed. Now what was he to do? They had kidnapped his child.

'It's all your fault and that stupid old woman, why did you ever listen to her?' wailed Veronica, 'now look at what's happened. They've taken my poor baby.' She burst into sobs again.

'We thought, I thought it was for the best.' Said Napoleon weakly.

'Since when have you ever had a sensible thought in your head? Always in that stupid shed of yours tinkering away with those stupid machines, now look what it's done. They've taken away my baby.'

Napoleon picked up the telephone.

'That's right, telephone that man and tell him you'll do whatever he asks only don't hurt poor Beauregard.'

'Operator could you get me the Excelsior Hotel please.'

'What hotel? Why is he staying in a hotel?' Veronica couldn't grasp that Napoleon wasn't ringing von Marenbach, but was in fact trying to contact Granny Probyn.

'Hotel Excelsior, how may I help?' said Cedric.

'Ah, yes, could you put me through to Mrs. Probyn's room please?' said Napoleon.

'What? No. Not her, not her,' wailed Veronica.

'I'm sorry, sir, is anything the matter? I can hear a rather distraught lady in the background.'

'Yes, no, yes, everything is fine. Could you just please put me through to Mrs. Probyn's room?'

'I'm afraid it wouldn't help, you see she isn't in the hotel, sir. She left a little while ago with a young gentleman. In rather a hurry if I may say so.'

'Give that to me, give it to me.' Veronica was now trying to wrench the telephone from Napoleon's hand, 'They've got my baby!' She was shouting down the phone.

'Are you sure everything is all right, sir?' Cedric asked again, 'only the lady does seem a bit distraught.'

'Oh, yes, everything is fine,' said Napoleon, trying to sound blasé, 'our son is staying with his friend, our neighbours don't you know, and my dear wife is at a loss.'

'They've got him, they've got him,' Veronica insisted.

'Oh, I see,' said Cedric, thinking they must have rang from the lunatic asylum. 'Is there anything else I can do for you?' he added trying to be nice.

'Yes, yes if you could, could you leave a message for Mrs. Probyn, and say that they've got him and she should come over as quickly as possible? Thank you.'

'Not at all, sir, I'll make sure she gets the note as soon as she arrives.' Cedric put the phone down and wiped his brow. You get all sorts he thought and returned to his work and the hotel ledger.

Napoleon put the phone on the hook. Now what was he going to do? Sitting on a small stool Veronica was sobbing quietly to herself.

The door bell rang. Oh, lor! Thought Napoleon, Lavinia Spratt. Veronica ignored the doorbell. Napoleon opened the door and to his surprise it wasn't a large woman dressed in chintz but a small man dressed in trilby and trench coat.

'Good afternoon, I wondered if I might have a word?' said Herr Delfger.

'I err... well that is... you see...' Napoleon was prevaricating because Veronica was sitting behind the door. It wouldn't do for strangers to see her in this condition.

'It won't take a moment of your time. May I come in?' Herr Delfger insisted and made to enter.

Napoleon Packard stood his ground and barred the small man

from entering.

'Might I just add,' continued Herr Delfger, 'that it concerns the welfare and safety of your son Beauregard Henry.'

At the sound of her son's name Veronica jumped from the stool sending it flying and snatched the door from Napoleon.

'Where is he? Where is he? Tell me he's safe!' Shouted Veronica.

'I think maybe we continue our discussion inside,' said Herr Delfger looking up and down the street.

'Yes, yes,' said Napoleon and stepped aside to let the man in. 'This way,' he said and he led him into the front room.

Herr Delfger stood by the door. The front room hardly used was neither comfortable nor suitable for holding an intimate interview. 'Please take a seat,' said Napoleon. There were eight chairs in the room, six dark brown leatherette dinning chairs arranged around a solid utilitarian dinning table to his left. The only concession to soft lines was a lace runner in the middle. Of the other two chairs one was a very low, soft, over stuffed arm chair complete with antimacassars and the other a Parker Knoll rocking chair. Both these were positioned either side of the fireplace. He decided to take a seat at the table. Napoleon stood in front of the fireplace while Veronica loitered behind him by the door.

Herr Delfger was feeling uncomfortable. This wasn't how it was supposed to be. He had imagined that he would squeeze a little money out of these people before he put the pressure on Packard to do the job. But here he was in a position of power and still feeling decidedly uncomfortable.

He cleared his throat. 'Achem.'

Napoleon waited. Unsure if he should start the conversation. Herr Delfger cleared his throat again and started. 'Achem, as you are no doubt aware, we have your son.'

Napoleon nodded.

Herr Delfger didn't quite know how to continue. 'So we have to come to some solution?' he tried to word the question so that he would get a response from Napoleon but he only nodded his assent.

'What I suggest is that you and your good lady wife,' Herr Delfger turned around to see if Veronica was still by the door.

She was, and holding a large cast iron frying pan. Before he had a chance to finish his sentence Veronica Packard had swung the pan like a baseball bat. It hit the side of his face sending him sprawling from the chair.

Napoleon jumped to the man's aid while the pan quivered in Veronica's hand.

'What have you done?'

'Isn't it obvious?' Veronica was very calm for someone who has just ploughed a frying pan into someone else's face. 'Is he alive?'

Napoleon felt the side of Herr Delfger's neck for a pulse.

'Yes.'

'Good, tie him up and take him upstairs to the back bedroom. He can sleep it off there.'

'Veronica what on earth are you thinking of?' asked Napoleon.

'They hurt Beauregard, let them see how much this hurts.'

Scene 6

Hessen didn't like it. He paced his study. That phone call had unsettled him. Maltravers was an incompetent fool. He should never have let him do his dirty work for him. Maltravers it seemed was avoiding his calls. Now the police were involved. How could he have been so stupid as to throw von Marenbach from his own window? Did he not think it would arouse suspicions? He said it again Maltravers was an incompetent fool.

He couldn't do anything about it now; he would just have to nerve it out with the police when they arrived.

Forsythe knocked at his door, 'Excuse me, Sir, the police are downstairs, shall I show them up?'

'If you would, Forsythe, thank you.' Hessen stopped pacing and seated himself behind his desk.

Forsythe knocked again at his door,

'The gentleman of the law,' he said and bowed to leave.

'Thank you, Forsythe, Gentleman,' Hessen said standing and stretching an open hand across his desk. 'Please be seated.'

'Thank you. I'm Inspector Ploddock, and this is Sergeant Wiggins,' indicating his partner. 'I'm sorry to intrude on you like this but we are trying to contact as many people as possible who may have known Mr. von Marenbach. I believe that you were good friends?'

'I wouldn't put it exactly like that, inspector. Would you like a drink?'

'No thank you not while we are on duty. Exactly how would you put it?' Inspector Ploddock asked.

'Well, we were business associates, that sort of thing.' Hessen made his way to the side cabinet and poured himself a large whiskey. 'Are you sure you wouldn't like a drink, gentleman?'

'Quite. What sort of business are you in Mr. Hessen?'

'Import, export, that sort of thing.' Hessen was making a fool of himself and he knew it. He took a large swig of whisky to steady his nerves. 'Von Marenbach helped me a couple of times with my import business.' Hessen suddenly sounded surer of himself.

'Would you have any idea why Mr. von Marenbach would want to take his own life?' asked Inspector Ploddock.

'Suicide?' Hessen nearly shouted. The tension in his shoulders evaporated. He became more effusive.

'Gentlemen, what can I say, he was a business partner, and one shouldn't speak ill of the dead as they say, but there were times when he didn't, how can I put this? He wasn't in complete control of his faculties.'

'So you are saying he was mentally unstable?'

'I didn't say that exactly, inspector, I'm not an expert in these matters but he was a very moody person. Mood swings from one extreme to the other.'

'I gather from Mr. von Marenbach's neighbours that he was unmarried. The only person other than himself coming and going to the flat was a middle aged woman presumed his cleaning lady, you wouldn't happen to know if there was some sort of personal relationship going on?' enquired the inspector.

'Alas, inspector, there I cannot help you.'

Once the inspector left Hessen picked up the telephone. He wanted to congratulate Maltravers on his successful attempt at getting rid of von Marenbach; maybe he wasn't such an incompetent fool after all.

'Who's it you want?' said the landlady. She was slightly hard of hearing and this new contraption in her hallway was the bane of her life. She didn't want it but her daughter had insisted. 'You can charge extra for the rooms, actors always need to have a telephone, put it on their weekly bill, they'll never notice.'

'Oh Mr. Maltravers, why didn't you say so?' said the landlady. She leaned forward so that she could look up the stairwell. Maltravers had a room on the third floor.

'Mr. Maltravers, there's a telephone call for you!' She shouted.

'Be right down Mrs. O,' he replied and rushed down the stairs.

'Nothing but a pain, having to answer that bell all day and night,' Mrs. O, grumbled and went back to her own apartment.

'Hello,' said Maltravers.

'Maltravers,' Hessen smiled into the telephone.

'Oh, it's you.' Maltravers was suddenly nervous. He didn't really have that much to tell Hessen.

'I just wanted to congratulate you. I didn't think you had it in you, but I was obviously mistaken. I should think that the rest of the list is easy.'

Maltravers was unsure to what Hessen referred. Although he had left the poisoned chocolates in the hotel of the Oppenheimer girl she could hardly have died already? Or could she? 'Thank you,' he said, 'I thought that Miss Oppenheimer was the easier... I mean the best target to go for first. That's why I chose her.'

'Oppenheimer?' Hessen asked.

'Yes, Hetty Oppenheimer, I left her a small gift,' Maltravers didn't want to say too much as he was standing in the hallway of his apartment house.

'I'm not talking about Oppenheimer, I'm talking about von Marenbach.' Hessen said.

'Von Marenbach?' asked Maltravers. 'I was leaving him till last. I wasn't sure... I don't know how to go about it. I thought...' Maltravers trailed off.

Silence.

Hessen finally asked. 'If you didn't kill von Marenbach then who did?'

The following day had been a busy day for all concerned. After Hetty was taken to hospital Granny Probyn asked Napoleon to arrange a meeting at his house later that afternoon.

Odel was the last to arrive, he had stayed with Hetty all day. Though quite ill the doctors said that she would improve in a couple of days.

They were also unsure how Hetty could have contracted such a virulent form of food poisoning, especially as Mr. Pleach, with whom she had lunch the previous day, was fit as a fiddle.

Julian Pleach was beside himself with guilt. 'Why couldn't it have been me?' he asked no one in particular.

Granny Probyn looked around the room at the strange assortment of people. Fluffy Yeomans in his cage, Odel, Mr. Pleach, Miss Plimple, Napoleon and Veronica, and Ethel Dorfellwaffer. All here because they had some contact with top secret German papers.

'Right,' said Granny Probyn to get things moving, 'as you all know Beauregard Henry has been kidnapped. Presumably to force Napoleon to extract the papers from Miss Plimple. But as we all know, Miss Plimple no longer has them. So where does that leave us? Our friends will undoubtedly miss that odious man upstairs, and so we can expect contact from some other source. You said, Napoleon, that you were given your instructions from a man named von Marenbach. Well all we can do on that point is wait.'

Veronica burst into sobs again. 'As for Beauregard Henry, we have to try and question the gentleman currently upstairs and see if we cannot get him to cooperate with us.'

'What about the papers?' asked Odel.

'They could be anywhere?' said Granny Probyn, 'we don't even know if they are still in the theatre. But, I do think there are spies still within the cast. We must be very careful what we say and to whom.'

Everyone nodded. 'We must try and piece together the trail of events from Mr. Oppenheimer giving those papers to Miss Plimple.'

'Shouldn't we go to the police?' asked Ethel at the mention of Mr.

Oppenheimer. Fluffy Yeomans meowed. She remembered him all those years ago as a small boy playing with her younger sister.

'You know very well, that we can't get the authorities involved at the moment. Beauregard Henry is in serious danger and we must do everything possible to make sure that nothing we do endangers him more.'

Ethel nodded her head in agreement. 'What about Hetty? Miss Oppenheimer I mean,' asked Julian Pleach. He wasn't really sure what was going on, only that Hetty was ill and her brother suspected foul play.

'The doctors say that she will be fine in a couple of days.' Odel said, 'she is very weak but in a stable condition.'

'Where do we go from here?' asked Napoleon.

'I think it's time to ask our new friend some questions. If you wouldn't mind bringing him downstairs Napoleon?'

Napoleon nudged Odel on the elbow. 'I could use a little help,' he said, 'ever since he has woken up he has been struggling to get free. Good job I was in the boy scouts.' They both left the room.

'Veronica dear, I think we may need the use of your lovely frying pan again. Not I hope that we have to use it,' said Granny Probyn. Veronica got up from her chair and silently went to the kitchen to fetch her frying pan. 'I think it might be best if we arrange the furniture a little better. Mr. Pleach, would you mind moving your chair a little closer to the window and pushing the table up against the wall? Miss Plimple would you be so kind as to place that chair in the centre of the room? There that's better,' she said.

Granny Probyn surveyed the room one more time. In the centre of the room stood a single dining room chair. The remaining chairs formed a circle around it. Veronica returned with the frying pan. 'Just place it on the table so that, when our friend is seated, he will be able to see it.'

Everyone was nervous as they each took a seat and waited for Napoleon and Odel to return. They could hear muffled bumps and groans as they manhandled Herr Delfger down the stairs.

Ethel Dorfellwaffer jumped from her seat as the door bell rang. They heard the thud and chomp of the letter box closing. Veronica looked out of the window. The paper boy was just closing the front gate.

'It's the evening paper,' she said and automatically went to the front door to get it. She returned just as Napoleon and Odel had placed Herr Delfger on the seat in the middle of the room.

Herr Delfger was unable to look at everyone in the room. He was especially nervous of Veronica who had dropped the newspaper onto the table and taken her place behind him.

'What do you want?' he asked looking from one face to the next.

Herr Delfger's face was bruised from where Veronica had lambasted him with the frying pan. He suspected that she might have broken his nose.

'We would like you to answer some questions,' said Granny Probyn. Herr Delfger spun around to look at who was talking.

'We are anxious to find the whereabouts of Beauregard Henry. I believe that you can tell us where he is?'

Veronica sniffled into her handkerchief.

'I don't know, I only came here to bargain, I don't know where he is,' said Herr Delfger.

'How can you bargain with something that you don't have?' Napoleon asked.

Herr Delfger swung around to look at who asked the question.

'I er, I don't know, I er...' he said.

'Surely you must know,' insisted Granny Probyn.

Herr Delfger turned again in her direction.

'I don't have... I only came to bargain,' he said again.

Veronica jumped from her seat and rushed passed Herr Delfger. He cowered as she passed, expecting to be hit again.

'I don't know where he his,' he insisted.

Veronica picked up the frying pan and stood over Herr Delfger.

'Please! Please!' Cried Herr Delfger.

Veronica raised her hand to swing the pan.

Granny Probyn jumped from her seat and put a steadying hand on Veronica's, 'That won't be necessary,' she said.

Veronica, sniffled. But her hand stayed.

'Please, Veronica, there are other ways.'

Veronica sniffled some more. Her hand slowly fell allowing the pan to fall onto the table.

Herr Delfger's eyes followed the frying pan. There he saw the newspaper lying on the table and its headline.

GERMAN DIPLOMAT TAKES OWN LIFE.

Claude von Marenbach was found this morning dead after...

Herr Delfger panicked; this was what the old woman meant.

'He's at my home, with my wife. She is looking after him, I only wanted to... please don't kill me.'

'Why should we want to do a thing like that Mister er... what is your name?' asked Miss Plimple.

Herr Delfger turned in his chair to look at Miss Plimple. 'I er...' he looked back at the paper.

Granny Probyn followed his eyes to the newspaper and scanned the headline. 'So, mister, what did you say your name was? If you don't want to end up like your friend here,' Granny Probyn tapped the paper, 'I suggest that you start talking.'

All eyes looked at Granny Probyn. What on earth was she talking about? What friend. She looked around the room at her companions' faces.

Herr Delfger looked at his lap. He had no other option. If von Marenbach was dead, what was he doing? Maybe he could negotiate his way out of this situation.

'Delfger,' said Herr Delfger, 'my name is Delfger.'

'There isn't that better Mr. Delfger? Now we can have a sensible conversation. So, where is Beauregard Henry?' Granny Probyn asked again.

'At home, with my wife. My wife took him there yesterday from school.'

'And just where is home?'

'Hackney.' Herr Delfger tried to give as little information as possible.

Veronica whimpered. 'I take it that he is being well looked after?' said Granny Probyn.

'My wife,' Herr Delfger began looking at Veronica, 'she loves children,' he lied.

'And where exactly in Hackney?'

'What are you going to do to me?' asked Herr Delfger.

'That depends on what you have done to the boy,' said Odel stepping closer to the chair.

'I haven't touched the boy my wife she's the one...' Herr Delfger bit his tongue.

Veronica stifled a cry.

Granny Probyn took a deep breath as if to summon up her courage, 'Mr. Delfger, I think it better that you tell us the whereabouts of Beauregard Henry, if not, I'm afraid I won't be able to stop my friends.'

On cue, Napoleon and the rest all gathered closer to Herr Delfger crowding the chair.

'Richmine Road,' said Herr Delfger quickly, '134 Richmine Road.'

'Thank you Mr. Delfger,' said Granny Probyn then turning to Odel asked, 'would you mind going with Mr. Pleach and Napoleon? While we stay here and keep Mr. Delfger company.'

'We'll be as quick as we can,' said Napoleon as he left the room.

'Take your time,' said Granny Probyn, 'Herr Delfger and I are just starting to get to know each other.'

'I told you never to contact me here.' Hessen said into the phone. 'I know you did it? I thought we agreed to let me deal with any outstanding problems.'

'If we wait for you the problems will only multiply. I am only making your job easier.'

'Once Maltravers has done his work, then I promise, you'll get your chance to prove your loyalty.'

'My loyalty has never been questioned. Unlike some.'

'Why did you do it?'

'It just happened. Von Marenbach told me he wanted to take over the order, he said there was no place in it for me. He was standing by the open window. I took an opportunity that might never present itself again.'

'Luckily the police are convinced it's a suicide. Hopefully after my little chat I convinced them even more, so we should hear no more about it. As for you let Maltravers finish the job.' Hessen hung up the phone.

On their way to Hackney the three men decided that it was best to confront Madam Delfger straight away. If she put up any resistance, well it was three men against one woman.

The taxi dropped them off outside the house. Napoleon paid the driver before they entered the small garden. They climbed the four steps to the front door. Napoleon knocked. Napoleon knocked again.

'She aint in,' said a voice.

'Excuse me?' said Napoleon unsure from where the sound had come.

'I said she aint in.' Napoleon looked down into the area below the steps.

'She left abhat alf an hour ago,' said an old woman. 'In a terrible state she was.'

'Did she have a small boy with her?' Napoleon asked.

'Nar, they don't have kids, not them, stage folks, she gave herself all sorts of hairs and graces.'

'Do you know when she'll be back?' asked Napoleon again.

"Ard to say, aint it. I mean her husbands been out all night, reckon he's left her. Don't blame 'im either,' offered the old woman.

'I wonder if you could do me a great favour,' said Napoleon, 'I believe that my son, is...' He couldn't continue, the strain was just too much. He started to cry.

The old woman looked up at the three men.

"Ere, what's the matter wiv 'im?' she said.

'You'll have to forgive my friend,' said Odel. 'We believe that his son has been kidnapped by this couple and he is being held here.' Odel thought honesty was the best policy.

'Get away wiv, yer,' said the old woman, 'whys don't yer calls the police.'

'We were told that if we went to the police that the boy would be hurt. Please we need to know if the boy is in there,' Odel said.

'What's it ter me?' the old woman asked. 'Supposing I might have a pass key, I could get into trouble. Once they pays the rent I got no reason to be in there.'

'Should anybody ask you could say that you heard running water and you were afraid that a pipe had burst. Like any responsible landlord, you were just making sure. And I'm sure my friend here will make sure that you are equally compensated,' said Odel, looking through his pocket book and finding only small change.

'Yes, yes, indeed,' said Napoleon, 'here take my wallet.' He said fishing into his jacket and pulling out his wallet.

'I don't know about that but a few bob wouldn't come amiss if yer knows what I mean. I'll just get that key.' And she disappeared into her flat.

Within minutes they were in the hallway.

'You'se gentleman can go in, I'll stay here thank you very much,' said the old woman.

Unsure of what they would find, the three men walked slowly throughout the house checking every room and cupboard. Napoleon took the top floor.

'I've found him,' he shouted to the others after a few minutes search.

Beauregard Henry was too much in shock to register that his father had come to rescue him. He sat in a daze.

The others ran upstairs. Beauregard Henry looked from one to the other then recognised his father and wailed.

Back home, before they could enter the front door Veronica enveloped Beauregard Henry. She would have smothered him if he hadn't been grabbed by everyone and congratulated. Ethel Dorfellwaffer over come by emotion had to take a seat. It was then that she remembered Herr Delfger and rushed back to the living room. Frantic her eyes roamed the room. Herr Delfger was gone.

Scene 7

Two days later, just before dawn, the SS Shattenberg slipped in to the great man-made harbour at Wilhelmshaven. Karl was already awake and dressed when Smeeton knocked on the door.

'Wake up professor,' Karl said as he gently shook the professor's shoulder.

Smeeton opened the door and stepped into the cabin. 'Ah, good dressed already,' he said to Karl, 'I thought I would give you a few moments notice to get yourselves ready. professor?' He bowed and left the cabin locking the door behind him.

'Well, we're here wherever here is,' Karl said. 'Did you sleep alright?'

'Why do you ask?' replied the professor.

'You look a little pale, that's all.'

'It's probably this cold dawn light. Come, my boy, help me get dressed.'

Half an hour later Smeeton knocked again. They could hear lots of noise going on around the boat as it prepared to dock.

'I have just come to tell you, professor, that we shall be leaving shortly. I don't have to remind you that it would be unwise to try anything silly.'

'Can you tell us where we are?' asked the professor.

'Of course. We are at this moment docking at the navel base in Wilhelmshaven. From here we shall drive to Berlin. I'm sorry it's going to be a long journey but, I have my orders to have you in Berlin as soon as possible.'

'What will happen when we reach Berlin?' Karl asked.

'That depends on you. If you co-operate, there is no reason why you should not be well looked after. After all, professor, Germany needs great minds like yours to build its empire.'

'And if we don't?' Karl asked again.

'You already know the answer to that, my boy. I just hope that you are not stupid enough to think you can disobey the party.'

Again he bowed and closed the door.

'Karl, listen to me, whatever happens, we cannot continue our work here in Germany. It will be used for evil. Those in charge will stop at nothing until they have fulfilled their own lustful desires. If we must, we must sabotage our own research, but, we must give the impression always of cooperating. Until I know that Levi, his family and my niece are safe. Then, well it doesn't matter what happens to me.'

Karl nodded. He knew the professor was right. He just didn't want to think about the future. He had closed his eyes to what was happening before, he could do it again. He decided, as long as he and the professor were all right, the others could look out for themselves.

Smeeton knocked a third time that morning.

'Gentlemen, if you would care to come this way? Our transport has arrived.'

The professor and Karl were taken up on deck. The air was cold and sharp. It was threatening to rain. Smeeton stayed behind them, flanked by two armed guards. They stopped by the rail. A set of steps had been placed alongside the ship, and a ramp took them to the dock side.

Below them a car, and behind a lorry with tarpaulin, sat waiting.

'Gentlemen, our carriage awaits,' said Smeeton then laughed at his own joke.

The captain was waiting by the steps to say goodbye. Slowly the professor made his way down the steps. Eventually they had all descended to the dock.

'Professor, this way if you please.' Smeeton indicated the car. 'Your assistant can travel in the lorry.'

Karl moved towards the lorry. He took one last look at the professor who nodded his head in assent. Karl climbed into the lorry and was followed by the two guards who sat either side of the open end. Smeeton opened the car door for the professor, 'This way if you please, professor,' he said.

Silently Professor Meis got into the back seat of the car. Smeeton closed the door and went to the opposite side and settled in beside the professor. 'Drive on,' he said and the car slowly pulled away from the dockside.

'As I said earlier, professor, it is going to be a very long journey so just say if you need to stop.'

The professor nodded his head, the only indication that he had heard the man.

The small convoy was soon out of Wilhelmshaven and on its way travelling through open countryside to one of the new autobahns.

It then made its way through the small village of Schortens, no more than a hamlet. Reaching the last house overlooked by a large barn, the convoy turned left to take the slip road which led to the autobahn. Suddenly there was an explosion in front of the car which swerved off the road and stopped on the grass verge at the side. The lorry came to a halt behind and the guards jumped out. No sooner had they landed on the ground then they were attacked from behind by two men.

The first guard had his throat cut with a swift movement while the other assailant snapped the second man's neck. Karl moved further back into the lorry hoping that he would not be seen. The two assailants both turned to look into the rear of the truck.

At the same time another assailant had dragged the driver off the lorry from the cab and had him on his knees by the roadside held under guard.

The driver of the car had smashed his head against the windscreen and was lying dead half in and out of the car as Captain Porfrey held a gun at Smeeton.

Karl put his hands in the air.

'Don't shoot,' he said, 'please, don't shoot.'

One of the attackers motioned with his gun for Karl to move towards the rear of the lorry. Slowly Karl made his way to the edge of the truck.

The two assailants were standing over the bodies of the guards.

'Get down from the truck,' ordered one of the attackers.

Karl couldn't see any space where he could jump without landing on one of the bodies.

'Down,' shouted the other man. Eventually he tried to climb down the edge of the truck using the mudguard of a rear wheel. Karl's foot slipped the last few inches and he lost his grip on the cold metal of the edge of the lorry and went sprawling in the dust of the road.

'Bring him over here,' said Captain Porfrey who had by now motioned to Smeeton to get out of the car. Smeeton slowly crawled from the car taking care that his pistol was hidden from sight.

One of the assailants grabbed Karl by the shoulder of his jacket and half dragged him to the side of the road where the lorry driver shivered on his knees.

'On your knees.' Karl was ordered.

Smeeton walked over to join them.

'On your knees,' the assailant said again.

Smeeton slowly sank to his knees on the other side of the lorry driver.

'That all?' said Captain Porfrey to his men.

'Yes,' said the first attacker, 'two guards. Quoooic!' He ran his finger across his throat.

Captain Porfrey nodded. He lent into the back of the car, 'Professor Meis, allow me to introduce myself. Captain Porfrey, special operations.'

Professor Meis was slightly dazed. He had hit his head against the front seat as the car had skidded to a halt.

'Please allow me to help you, sir.'

'Thank you, thank you,' said the professor. 'What happened?'

'We unfortunately don't have time to discuss that at the moment. Once we are on our way I can explain everything. First I need to deal with our three remaining prisoners,' said Captain Porfrey as he helped the professor from the car.

'Jenkins,' he called over to the man who had dragged the lorry driver from his seat, 'take the professor to the cars, we'll join you in a moment.'

Jenkins nodded, and took of the professor's arm and without saying a word helped him to walk across the junction in the road to a barn next to the last house.

Captain Porfrey stood in front of the three men as they knelt. The other two assailants behind them.

'Gentleman, I have a problem, and that problem is you. You see I only have enough space to take the professor and my men. So I am afraid I am going to have to leave you behind.'

'Wait,' shouted Karl, 'you can't leave me, the professor needs me.' One of the men behind hit Karl with the butt of his gun. Karl slumped forward to the ground.

'Excuse me, sir,' said Smeeton, and put his hand up to speak. The lorry driver was shivering with fear.

Captain Porfrey looked at Smeeton, 'Yes what is it?' he asked.

'Just how do you intend to leave us?' Smeeton asked lowering his hand. This movement gave him the opportunity of passing it in front of the pistol he had tucked into his coat and taking hold of the grip.

Karl groaned, 'The professor needs me.'

'Unfortunately there can be no witnesses,' said the Captain. He gave a small nod. A gun appeared at the head of the lorry driver. 'No please, No!' He screamed.

Smeeton decided to act. He pulled the gun from his pocket and fired once at the captain and turned to fire on the men behind.

Before he had a chance of firing a second bullet, the first assailant fired a shot. A look of horror crossed Smeeton's face as he realised that he had been hit. He fell back with his arms outstretched the gun still in his hand.

'Tie, up this man,' ordered the captain indicating the lorry driver, 'and get those vehicles off the road.'

The two men immediately jumped to do his bidding. The captain bent down to help Karl to his feet.

'I'm sorry we had to put you through that, it's just we didn't know who was his assistant. We only got word that the professor was travelling with a companion. It could have been either of you.'

Karl put his hand to the spot where he had been hit.

'Come along, we need to get away from here as quickly as possible,' said the Captain and escorted Karl across the road to the barn.

He opened wide the large door. Inside were two cars. Jenkins was already sitting in the drivers seat of the first with the professor in the back.

The captain opened the car door and helped Karl in to sit next to the professor.

'Karl my boy, are you alright?' the professor asked. 'Did the lorry crash as well?'

'No, professor,' said the Captain, 'we needed to be sure that we got the right man.'

'Karl, speak to me, are you all right?'

'Yes, professor, I'll just have one hell of a headache for a day or so.'

'I'm afraid that Hopkins can be a bit enthusiastic at times. Here drink this,' and he handed Karl his hip flask. 'You too, professor.'

Shortly after, Hopkins, and the other man whose name was Fletcher entered the barn. 'You two take the other car. I will travel with the professor, and debrief him.' The two men nodded, and silently moved to the second car. Meanwhile the captain jumped into the front seat with Jenkins as he started the engine.

'Okay, Jenkins, get us there as quickly as possible. The convoy will be missed when it doesn't reach Oldenburg. That should give us enough time to get across the border.'

Madam Delfger sat in the dark drinking, this was the third time that she had sat through the film. The films credits rolled again.

CONFESSIONS OF A NAZI SPY.
staring Edward G. Robinson.

She groaned to herself. Why had she chosen this place? The theatre was practically empty. Only a few people with nothing to do on a Saturday afternoon. The doors at the rear of the auditorium opened. Even though there was a curtain it didn't stop a stream of light flooding the aisle.

Vincent entered. The door closed sending the theatre back to semi darkness. The titles still rolled, the music building in intensity. The usherette shone her torch to look at Vincent's ticket then wearily lit his way down the isle. Luckily Vincent knew where he was going. He took his seat. Queenie wasn't too well today. She also didn't want to see this particular movie, Edward G wasn't a favourite of hers, so she used her illness to stay at home.

Vincent was engrossed in the plot.

'Rubbish.' He heard a voice from behind him.

Really people didn't know how to behave in a movie theatre.

'It's not like that, it's not like that at all,' said the voice.

Vincent looked over his shoulder.

'Do you mind?' he said to a rather large German lady, 'I want to listen to the film.'

'What for? Utter rubbish,' said Madam Delfger. 'I can tell you a real confession of a Nazi Spy.'

Madam Delfger was also slightly inebriated. The packet of sweets she had bought had been finished ages ago. Only her bottle of gin had sustained her through the second showing of the movie.

'Oh yes,' said Vincent, thinking, I've got a right one here. He wondered if he should call for the usherette but gave up on that idea as he saw her snoring away in her seat by the door.

'Rubbish,' said Madam Delfger again. 'Real spies don't go about like that all cloak and dagger. I should know. I know a thing or two.'

'Oh, yes,' said Vincent again wondering if he should move a few seats further forward. He wanted to watch the movie.

'I killed a man horrible man he was. Came into my house accusing me of kidnapping his niece. As if I ever would.'

Vincent tried hard to concentrate on the movie.

Madam Delfger took the last swig of gin from the bottle.

'It's all his fault. Weasly little man, I don't know what I ever saw in him. Last time we did the act was months ago. "Don't worry" he said "they'll be hammering at the door." He said, "why don't we go to England? Make a change" he said. What change?'

Vincent tried even harder to ignore her.

Madam Delfger threw the empty gin bottle at the screen. It landed a few seats away from Vincent.

'Rubbish,' she said again. 'If you want a real spy story, I'll tell you one.'

Vincent was obviously not going to be able to watch the movie, not while this drunk was here. The Kingsland Empire was becoming a real flea pit. 'This is the last time I'm coming here,' he said to himself.

He got up and made his way back to where Madam Delfger was sitting. The usherette was now slumped in a heap in her chair. It would take an explosion to waken her.

'Why don't we go and have a nice cup of tea?' said Vincent.

Being brought up in a café, tea was the world's best remedy for any and all of life's problems.

'Tea, tea, always drinking tea. Leave me alone.'

'But you were going to tell me a real spy story,' said Vincent.

'You wouldn't believe it. It's not like a movie.'

'Why not try me, I'll tell you if it will make a good movie. I come to the movies a lot. I can spot a good one a mile away. How does it start? Your story,' Vincent encouraged her.

'With a murder. I murdered a man, a horrible man. He came to the house screaming and yelling. My husband he brought him. Tried to get some extra money. He was trying to squeeze him. Well why shouldn't he? Why should he have it all living in a swanky hotel when we were in that rat house? We couldn't leave, couldn't pay the rent.' Madam Delfger continued. Once she had started the flood gates had opened and she couldn't stop herself. She had to get it off her chest. 'We hadn't done the act in over a month. Last time was at Colin's Music Hall. And then we didn't finish the week, the manager said we weren't putting bums on seats. That's when Heinz, he started talking to some friends. An old pal from before we met he introduced him to von Marenbach, Harve Boulc'h, a real bag of wind.' Madam Delfger belched loudly. 'Von Marenbach paid Heinz little bits and pieces. To do odd jobs. Dirty jobs he didn't want to do himself. Didn't want to get his hands dirty. They never do, sit in their posh apartments letting the little people take the blame. Well Heinz got a little money from the man. He wanted more. When we got that brat he thought he might be able to squeeze a bit out of them.'

Vincent was having trouble keeping up. There were too many he's and them's without any clarification but he got the gist.

'So you tried to blackmail the boy's parents?' he asked, trying to clarify it slightly.

'Not me, Heinz, I didn't want to do it. But he said it would be our big chance. He said that if I didn't and the police found out about Oppenheimer well, I would be in prison. He blackmailed me, Me! His own wife.' She almost screamed.

'Sssh!' Came a disgruntled voice from the front row.

'Keep it down,' said Vincent, 'or they'll throw us both out. So the boy belonged to the man that you killed.' Vincent was still unsure who she was talking about or what relationship they had to each other.

'No, no, no, I didn't kill him, I murdered him, threw him down stairs,' said Madam Delfger. She was becoming slightly confused. The gin was taking it course.

'So, you murdered a man then kidnapped his son.' Vincent was determined to straighten out this story, 'and tried to blackmail...' He trailed off. Who where they trying to blackmail? It didn't make sense. This woman was obviously drunk as a skunk.

'Von Marenbach, he made Heinz get the boy, said he was to watch this man Packard, he had the papers or he had to get the papers. But he wouldn't do it. So we got the boy. Dirty little thing peed all over the room. Nothing but a whinging brat.' Madam Delfger was slipping away from the plot once again.

Vincent tried to put her back on track. 'So you kidnapped the boy and tried to blackmail him to get the papers?' he asked helpfully.

'No he didn't have the papers, von Marenbach needed those, and he needed Packard to decipher them. So we got to do the dirty job. Heinz thought he might make some extra money. Give them an extra squeeze, went to see them, and called at the house...'

Madam Delfger stopped.

Vincent was on the edge of his seat now, waiting.

Edward G Robinson up on the screen was waffling on about Hitler and how he must be stopped.

The silence grew longer. Madam Delfger had got it off her chest. Vincent was hooked he wanted more.

'What happened to your husband?' Vincent finally asked.

Madam Delfger only sniffed.

'Did you get the money?' Vincent tried again with a different tack.

Madam Delfger burst into tears, 'Gone he has, gone, never even thought about me, my mother was right, always said he was no good, that I would regret the day. Well she was right. Gone and left me he has and now what am I to do? Can't go home, can't go to the police. ohhhh!' Madam Delfger burst into more tears.

The usherette wakened by the noise shone her torch, 'Sssh,' she

175

snapped. 'Keep it down or you'll be out,' she threatened.

Vincent got out his hanky and gave it to Madam Delfger her own was already sodden.

'What am I to do?' she wailed and sobbed at the same time.

'Come luv,' said Vincent, 'let's have a nice cup of tea.'

Scene 8

Granny Probyn had called an emergency meeting for after that evening's performance. Napoleon and Veronica had taken Beauregard Henry off to a distant aunt on Veronica's side of the family, somewhere in the wilds of the Scottish mountains. It wasn't exactly the best time of year to see the Caingorms but Napoleon and Veronica didn't want, for the sake of their son, to be in harm's way any longer.

Napoleon had identified von Marenbach as the man who had approached him at the café in Shoreditch. According to the paper he had taken his own life. Unsure as to who else might be waiting in the background, the Packard's weren't going to take any chances and had left early the next day.

The small group had quickly searched the theatre. Each had taken a different area. While Granny Probyn checked the foyers she left Fluffy Yeomans in the dressing but, along with the rest, had been unable to find out anything more about the whereabouts of the papers. It seemed like a hopeless cause.

Odel spoke first. 'I know that most of you have been thrown into this situation. My uncle Levi was determined that we...' He looked at Hetty who was sitting on the couch tickling Fluffy Yeoman's chin, '... should not be involved. That we should be at all cost shielded from these people. But I feel that we owe it to his memory that we finish what he tried to do. I think that it is time to go to the authorities.'

Granny Probyn, had been thinking along the same lines. Now that Beauregard Henry was safe, what harm could come from going to the police? They had far more experience at dealing with this sort of thing. The tricky thing was who to contact. Granny Probyn looked around the dressing room at the faces of her comrades, Miss Plimple, Hetty and Odel, Julian Pleach, even Ethel Dorfellwaffer.

'In that case,' she finally said, 'I suggest that I contact the police tomorrow and present our case.'

The following morning, Granny Probyn left her hotel early and made her way to Scotland Yard. Slightly apprehensive she made her way to the reception desk. Sergeant Jones looked up over his half moon glasses and gave a reassuring smile.

'What can I do for you?' he asked still smiling.

'I'd like to see Inspector Ploddock if I may?' Granny Probyn said.

'Of course you may. Just take a seat and I'll have word sent up.' Sergeant Jones pointed to a row of chairs on the opposite side of the reception.

'Thank you,' Granny Probyn said and made her way across the room to sit down.

Sergeant Jones picked up the telephone receiver from behind the counter and spoke softly into it. 'He's on the loo,' was the reply. Sergeant Jones looked over at Granny Probyn and smiled again replacing the receiver. She smiled back.

'He'll be right down,' he shouted across to Granny Probyn, 'just finishing off some paperwork.'

'Oh, I can come back later if...' she started to say, but Sergeant Jones had gone back to his own work behind the counter.

Granny Probyn sat quietly for a moment or so.

Just then the front doors burst open. Constable Jenkins was grappling with a rather large lady and trying to steer her towards the counter.

'Alright George?' asked Sergeant Jones.

Constable Jenkins nodded and adjusted his helmet.

'What have we got here?' Sergeant Jones asked again.

'Drunk and disorderly.' Said Constable Jenkins. 'Sat outside the Carlton causing a disturbance'

'What's your name?' asked Sergeant Jones.

'What?' replied the woman trying to focus her eyes on the person asking her questions.

'Name?'

'Name what?' she responded and burst into a fit of girlish giggles.

Just then Vincent walked into the foyer holding a rather bloody handkerchief to his nose.

'What's wrong with you?' asked Sergeant Jones.

'Isn't it rather obvious?' mumbled Vincent through his hanky.

Constable Jenkins was holding up the large woman, 'these come as a pair.'

'Name?' asked Sergeant Jones to Vincent.

'Vincent.' Vincent replied.

'Vincent what?' asked Sergeant Jones again. These two were going to be hard work.

'He did it,' yelled the woman. 'It's his fault. I didn't want to do it, he made me.'

'Oh I never did,' replied Vincent, 'you were the one to start it. I only wanted to see how Dorothy got her red slippers.'

The couple started to argue again.

'All right George, take them through to the cells, let them sleep it off a bit and then maybe we can get some sense from the pair of them. And you better get the doctor to look over this one just in case.'

Constable George Jenkins manhandled the woman through the inner door followed closely by Vincent.

Granny Probyn sat transfixed as the small scene played out in front of her. She looked up at Sergeant Jones after the couple had left. Sergeant Jones smiled again and went back to his paperwork.

Inspector Ploddock came rushing through the inner doors. 'I'm sorry to keep you waiting,' he said, 'unfinished paperwork, and the boss being a stickler always wants it done. This way,' he said. And he led Granny Probyn through the inner door and down a corridor to a small interview room. 'Would you like a drink of water or a cup of tea perhaps?'

'No thank you,' replied Granny Probyn looking around the room.

'Please take a seat and tell me what this is all about. Is my theory correct and you have found some little old lady with a rather large chip on her shoulder?'

'Inspector, I haven't been entirely honest with you,' Granny Probyn began, 'you see… well it's rather difficult you see, we don't have any proof and it all sounds a bit fantastical, more than Miss Christie would put in a book and what with being in the theatre you might think that we have overwrought imaginations, but…' Granny Probyn couldn't get her thoughts into a coherent form.

'Why don't we start at the beginning,' said Inspector Ploddock. 'My mother always said it's a very good place to start.'

'That's just the point, I don't know were it began or how,' said Granny Probyn slightly at a loss.

'Well how about when you got involved. Is this anything to do with why you were attacked?'

Granny Probyn nodded her head. 'I think so.' She added.

'Does it have anything to do with the unfortunate accident of Miss de la Mouche?

Granny Probyn nodded again.

'Then why don't you tell me the whole story and I'll worry if it's too fantastical.'

As Granny Probyn related her story to Inspector Ploddock he had a very very sneaky feeling.

The end of the pantomime was looming with only four more performances to go. Normally a time of excitement would be in the air but today an unexpected lull hung like a pall over the backstage areas. There had been many happy memories which the company would take with them when they left the theatre for the last time, new friends made but, there were also many unhappy memories.

Maltravers was a very worried man. Hessen knew who killed von Marenbach but he had said nothing. Maltravers was convinced that his name had been added to the list. What was he to do? Run? Where? Eventually he would be found. If not by the party then by the police. He wasn't sure which if any was the better option. Either way it meant loss of life, either in a prison cell or a coffin.

'Act one beginners standby,' called Jimmy as he knocked on the dressing room door. Maltravers gave a grunt in reply but Jimmy was already halfway down the corridor knocking at each door on his way. How was he to get out of this situation? If he could only recover the papers, that would surely solve his problems. He decided he had to act tonight.

The show that evening was like a lead balloon. Everybody was on edge. The police had interviewed everybody again about the deaths of Miss de la Mouche and Mucus Drillby and it was difficult for much of the cast to forget what had happened. Miss de la Mouche's understudy had a sudden attack of nerves before the walk down so that she had missed her entrance, leaving Mr. Pleach standing alone centre stage. Nervous and unsure of what to do he hesitated for a moment before resolutely walking into the wings and grabbing the understudy by the hands and dragging her back on stage to take her final bow. News of Miss de la Mouche's tragedy had of course made the papers.

PANTOMIME TAKES A HEAD DIVE screamed the headlines of one of the more scandal mongering papers, which only increased interest in the show. As box office sales soared, Miss Plimple looked with disgust when she saw the house manager rubbing his hands together. Business was booming with half of the audience waiting for some other ghoulish thing to happen.

At the end of the performance Maltravers made his way slowly from the stage back to the dressing room, he was still unsure as to how he was going to get close to Miss Plimple but he had to question her. He had to make her talk. As luck would have it as he reached the top step to the second floor who should he see but Miss Plimple coming down the corridor. Now was his chance.

'I'm going to have words with Mr. Reed tomorrow when he arrives,' said Miss Plimple as she neared the top step. 'Tonight's performance was not good.' Although she, like the rest of the cast, had a lot on her mind she was still a professional and work took her mind off what was happening. It was something she could concentrate her energies on.

'I er… I wonder if I could have a private word,' said Maltravers. Miss Plimple gave him a quizzical look. 'It's rather personal…' Maltravers seemed slightly embarrassed. He looked around not wanting to be heard. 'Perhaps it would be better to talk in my dressing room.'

Miss Plimple nodded her head and followed Maltravers to his room expecting him to ask for a loan on his wages. He did seem the type that liked to spend money. He closed the door behind them.

After a short silence Miss Plimple's curiosity was slightly piqued, she asked, 'What did you want to tell me?'

Maltravers sat at his dressing room mirror and looked at his reflection and that of Miss Plimple behind him. 'I think,' he began, 'that the death of poor Ashley wasn't an accident,' he said in a matter of fact sort of way. He started to take off his makeup. He opened a bottle of liquid and poured it onto a cloth before stoppering the bottle again. He turned to look at Miss Plimple.

Miss Plimple stood slightly taken aback. This wasn't what she had expected. She sat on a chaise lounge against the wall beneath the costume rail.

Maltravers crossed the room quickly and sat next to her. He made to comfort Miss Plimple as he continued. 'I didn't mean to frighten you but you see I have to do something.' With which he grabbed Miss

Plimple and forced the cloth over her mouth. Miss Plimple struggled for a while but Maltravers was too strong for her. The chloroform quickly worked its magic and soon Miss Plimple was like a rag doll in his arms. He tied her hands and feet together, placed a strip of tape across her mouth, then covered her in a blanket and returned to his mirror to remove his makeup. He estimated that Miss Plimple would sleep like a babe until the cast had left. Then he could get to work. He smiled to himself as he rubbed cold cream on his face.

Karl and the professor sat in silence as Captain Porfrey debriefed them as to their situation. How counter-intelligence had received word from some Greeks to say that they had boarded a fishing vessel and were safely on their way to Malta and then more reports of Germans kidnapping the wife and children of Captain Kirby of the fishing trawler they were aboard. Using the captain's family as hostages so that Smeeton could hold them safely aboard while waiting to transfer them too a German Ship. Intelligence had confirmed this when it had deciphered coded transmissions to warships currently patrolling the Mediterranean. It was then a simple waiting game to see which German ships suddenly altered course and to plot its progress.

'Where are you taking us now?' asked the professor.

'We are on our way to the border, to the Netherlands from there, we shall take a boat and we will be in Harwich tomorrow morning.'

'Captain, may I also ask? Do you have any news of my niece or of my friend Levi Oppenheimer and his family?'

'Our man Curruthers has been keeping an eye on your niece I believe. As to your friends. I'm sorry I don't know.'

Professor Meis nodded his head.

'What will happen to us when we get to England?' Karl wanted

183

to know.

'That is for you to decide,' replied Captain Porfrey.

Sergeant Wiggins walked down the white tiled corridor that held the prisoners cells. He passed the first stopping only to look through the spy hole. Madam Delfger lay sprawled across her bunk lying on her back snoring loudly. Next door Vincent groaned to himself as he sat in his prison cell. What was Queenie going to say when she found out? She must be beside herself with worry not knowing of the prisoner's whereabouts. He hadn't returned home last night. It was all coming back to him now that his head was clearing of the gin fumes.

He held his head. It was pounding out a rhythm not unlike a kettle drum. Vincent was nursing a hangover and headache he had never experienced before.

He looked up as the door to his cell opened and Sergeant Wiggins walked in.

'Now then, me boy,' Wiggins said in a thick welsh accent, 'lets see if we can't make some sense out of the fog shall we?'

Vincent nodded.

Sergeant Wiggins pulled up an old wooden chair from the corner of the room and sat opposite Vincent as he sat on the edge of his bunk.

'Look you, supposing you'd like to tell me what's all this is about?'

Vincent looked at him in some confusion through a fog of gin fumes.

'Supposing we start with that, my boyo?' said the sergeant seeing the confused look on his face.

His question only confused Vincent all the more as he was uncertain to what the sergeant was referring.

'That, look you,' Wiggins said pointing, 'blood all over the place, chief's going to have a fit I can tell you.'

Vincent looked down his shirt front covered in blood from his nose bleed.

'Nose bleed,' mumbled Vincent.

'I know's that, I can see that, don't need to be a chief inspector to work that out.' Wiggins said. 'What I want's to know is how it got there?'

'Oh,' said Vincent, 'she hit me, punched me.'

'I take it you had a bit of a lovers tiff then?' asked Wiggins winking conspiratorially.

'What! Never!' Exclaimed Vincent highly offended.

'I takes it then that you and the er ... young lady don't know each then?' asked Wiggins.

'Never met her before.' Replied Vincent, 'not 'til last night.'

'I see. Thought you'd try it on did you, and she give you one for it?' Wiggins said, nudging Vincent with his elbow a couple of times.

'Certainly not,' Vincent answered primly. 'I met her in the movies, and she, ... well she...'

'This was at the Carlton then,' Wiggins cut in. Not being a picture goer himself he continued, 'funny sort of picture they've got showing for a grown man to watch?'

'Not at all,' replied Vincent slipping from one conversation to another, 'not if you are a true friend of Dorothy's.'

'An' you're a friend of this Dorothy are you?'

'Well,' said Vincent waving his hand rather noncommittally, his wrist had a decided limp to it.

'And you saw her at the pictures?'

'Where else.'

'Tell me about this Dorothy, where's she from like?'

'Kansas.'

'There's a thing. Foreign is she?'

That's a bit rich thought Vincent coming from a man of the valleys. 'From America,' he said, 'but she's travelled a lot.'

'Look you now, how did she get here?'

'She followed the yellow brick road.'

'Yellowbrick Road, Yellowbrick Road.' Sergeant Wiggins thought for a moment. He couldn't place it. He made a note to look up Yellowbrick Road on the station map.

'But she wants to get back to Kansas. As Dorothy says, there's no place like home,' Vincent said to fill in the silence.

'Look you, there's the truth,' said Sergeant Wiggins as his eyes filled with tears for the green valleys of home.

'So let me get this straight,' Wiggins said bringing his mind back to work. 'You met this Dorothy at the pictures last night and she hit you?'

'No.' Vincent said flatly.

Sergeant Wiggins wasn't sure if the gin fog had actually lifted. 'I'm not following you, boyo.' He said. 'Tell me again who hit you?'

'She did.' Vincent said jumping conversations again without realising it.

Wiggins seemed to be going around in circles with this line of questioning, so he decided to change tack.

'Look, lovely boy,' he said, 'you went to the pictures to see Dorothy.'

'No,' Vincent said. He looked at Sergeant Wiggins. All this questioning was making his headache worse. 'I went to the pictures to see Edward G. Robinson.'

Wiggins sat nodding his head, 'and he introduced you to her did he?'

'She threw her bottle at him. Said he wasn't a proper spy.'

'This Edward Robinson,' Wiggins looked down at his notebook to check the name, 'he's a spy is he?'

'Sometimes.' Answered Vincent. 'Queenie doesn't like him. That's why she didn't go. Every time she goes to the movies she says he's the same.'

'Look you, this Edward likes movies?'

'Suppose so.'

Sergeant Wiggins looked at his notes. He didn't seem to be any clearer than when he started, he was wondering if Vincent's gin fumes had affected him. He tried to clear his mind and arrange the facts that had been presented.

'Look, lad,' he started again. 'Let's go back to the top shall we? You went to the pictures to see this Edward, who's a spy, and he introduced you to Dorothy who then threw a bottle at him because Queenie doesn't like him.' Yes, that was making a bit of sense. 'Who's Queenie?' he asked.

Vincent wasn't really following anything that the sergeant was talking about. He tried hard to concentrate but the pounding in his head just wouldn't go away.

The sound of Queenie's names got passed the drums.

'What's that?' asked Vincent.

'I said who's Queenie?'

'Me mum.' Mumbled Vincent feeling guilty. Oh, she will kill me when she finds out about this, he thought.

Sergeant Wiggins nodded and wrote in his note book.

'There's a thing. And when did you first see this Edward,' he looked at his notes, 'G Robinson?'

'Oh years ago, it was probably his first or second film he'd made. Queenie didn't like him then. She'd prefer Spencer Tracy, or Clarke Gable.'

'Look you, you're telling me this spy Edward G Robinson's an actor?'

Vincent gave Sergeant Wiggins a look of incredulity that he didn't know who Edward G Robinson. 'One of the greats.'

'There's a thing.' Sergeant Wiggins knew all about actors or so he thought. Funny bunch. Take that lot down at the theatre. Inspector said it was murder. More like attention seeking to him. Yes funny bunch. 'And Dorothy how does she know this Mr. Robinson?'

'Oh they work for the same company.'

Vincent was brightening up. The conversation was of his favourite subject, Hollywood gossip. 'She's been making movies for ages. Started off singing with her sisters, she's not as young as she looks.'

Sergeant Wiggins nodded in agreement as he jotted down his notes. By the look of the woman lying on the bunk next door he'd say she was definitely past it.

'This is her first starring part though,' Vincent continued.

'Ah, thought she'd celebrate a bit then did she?'

'Suppose so.' Vincent said. Thinking the question was a bit strange.

'And no doubt had a bit too much to drink then she hit you,' concluded Sergeant Wiggins.

Vincent looked at Sergeant Wiggins. 'The man's an idiot,' he thought.

Sergeant Wiggins had finally managed to make some sense of Vincent's story.

'Tell me why she threw her bottle at er...,' he looked at his scribbling in his note book, 'Edward G Robinson.' He looked up.

'Said he wasn't a real spy, real spies didn't act like him. She said she had killed a man. She and her husband. He did some jobs for a man, Marentrapp, Marenshafft, can't think of his name.' The gin fumes were finally lifting. 'Tried to blackmail him and he refused. Threw him down the stairs and dumped the body in the canal.' Vincent had confused the stories.

Sergeant Wiggins looked up from his note taking.

'Look you, you're telling me that she,' he flicked his thumb in the general direction of the cell next door, 'killed a man?'

Vincent nodded. He was sure that was how it had happened.

'What was the man's name.' Enquired Sergeant Wiggins.

Vincent finally remembered. He smiled at Sergeant Wiggins and said, 'Marenbach!'

188

Inspector Ploddock sat behind his desk thinking. Should he go to the chief? His sneaky feeling was no longer a sneaky feeling but it wasn't solid fact either. True, thanks to Granny Probyn, he had solved the problem of who the body was in the canal. But why? That was a different matter. Of course it added more credence to Granny Probyn's story. He decided he would tackle the chief.

Having come to the momentous decision he took a deep breath and stood up. Now was the time to do it.

Wiggins knocked at his door.

'Come,' he barked all resolve draining from his body as he slumped back into his chair.

'Look you, inspector,' Wiggins said. 'I've got a funny thing downstairs.'

'If it's another of your exploding leeks I'm not in the mood,' he snapped.

Wiggins was known in the station as Wagger Wiggins for his propensity for practical jokes.

'Nothing like that. A couple just come in this morning drunk and disorderly. They are now in the cells.'

'Yes, yes, I heard the woman while I was trying to conduct an interview. Got the lungs of a harridan. Book her and charge her and don't bother me with it,' he snapped testily.

'No, no, look you,' eager to get out his news. 'I interviewed the man who was with her. Slightly less inebriated. There's the thing turns out he met her at the cinema. Said he was going to meet a friend, Edward G Robinson. Said he was a spy.'

At the name of Edward G Robinson Inspector Ploddock started to smile. 'I am not falling for any more of your practical jokes. I've had a shitty morning and I have to face the chief…'

'No, you don't understand,' interrupted Wiggins. 'He says she threw a bottle at this Edward chap. He also said that she and her husband had tried a spot of blackmail.'

Inspector Ploddock was half listening. The story was getting more and more outrageous. This sort of thing might work on a younger inspector but he wasn't going to fall for it. The station would be laughing at him for weeks.

'There's the thing,' continued Wiggins. 'This Vincent down in the cells said that when the blackmail didn't work they killed the man threw him down the stairs. But hear look see this is the best bit.' Wiggins was positively aglow with excitement. 'Turns out he said they dumped the body in the canal.'

The smile fell from the inspectors face. 'What did you say his name was?'

'Well, see, he couldn't remember at first, and then he said it. Marenbach!'

'But that's not right, Marenbach wasn't found in the canal.' Inspector Ploddock said. In one fell swoop all the cases on his desk had been somehow linked. He tried to see the connection.

Marenbach, ok he was German but did he have anything to do with Levi Oppenheimer's death? Plausible. From his meeting with Hessen he had been informed he did import/export business. What better cover for smuggling information. The documents delivered by Oppenheimer were top secret all to do with work in his laboratories back in Berlin. The death of Ashley de la Mouche, again according to Granny Probyn, was blackmail, something about her mother being German, blackmailing by parties unknown working to retrieve those papers. Mucus Drillby was known to be working on a project with a professor from those very laboratories who had also disappeared in Germany. The professor himself was supposed to arrange a collection of the documents from his niece Miss Plimple. It was all there, like a large spider's web slowly coming towards the centre. If he could only follow one of those threads he would surely find the killer.

'Are they still in the cells?' he asked the waiting Wiggins who was bouncing slightly on the balls of his feet. 'I had better have a word with them.'

'She's still out cold.' Wiggins answered.

'Well never mind, take me to him. What was his name again?'

'Vincent. Vincent Blotcher. Lives with his mum. Has a café up in Shoreditch.'

'I know the one,' he said, 'Okay let's have a little word shall we?'

Inspector Ploddock walked down the corridor to the cells. As they passed the first door Wiggins said, 'Look see, she's in there, snoring fit to bust.'

Inspector Ploddock stopped at the door and lifted the spy hole cover. Still in the same position when Wiggins had looked in on her earlier, she was happily sleeping off the gin.

'Let her sleep,' said the inspector. 'Where's Vincent?'

'Next one down,' said Wiggins nodding in the direction.

Inspector Ploddock moved to the next cell and lifted the spy hole cover. Vincent was now prowling around the tiny cell. He looked around as he heard the cover snap up. The inspector nodded to the jailer who unlocked the door.

Vincent stood with his back to the barred window looking at all the police blocking the door. Should he try and make a run for it like Jimmy Cagney in *Angels with dirty faces*?

Inspector Ploddock and Sergeant Wiggins entered, the door slammed shut behind them with a bang which echoed through the old brick walls of the police station.

Vincent sat on his bunk and lowered his head in shame.

Before the inspector could introduce himself Vincent raised his head and asked, 'Am I going to prison?'

'Well that depends on you,' answered the inspector. He took Sergeant Wiggins's notebook and looked at the spidery scrawl across its pages.

'Oh, me mum'll kill me when she finds out, oh the shame,' said Vincent, and buried his head in his hands.

'I wonder if you wouldn't mind answering some questions for me?' asked the inspector. He thought that Vincent needed gentle treatment; no need to get heavy, Vincent was scared and he would answer truthfully if he could.

Vincent nodded his head and looked at the inspector. He had rings around his red bloodshot eyes.

'You went to the pictures to see an Edward G Robinson movie, correct?'

Vincent nodded. 'At the Kingsland Empire.'

'And you met this woman Dorothy there?'

'Who's Dorothy?' asked Vincent.

Inspector Ploddock looked down at Wiggins's notes and looked at Wiggins who shrugged his shoulders, he continued, 'the woman you were arrested with. The one who punched you.'

'She's not Dorothy she's Lottie. Lottie Delfger. Her husband's just left her. Poor thing had no where to go.'

'It says here she lives in,' Ploddock flipped a page, 'Yellowbrick Road.'

Vincent looked puzzled for a moment then giggled nervously.

'Look you, what so funny?' interrupted Sergeant Wiggins who felt that his policing skills had been called into question. 'You told me Dorothy lives in Kansas and she followed the Yellowbrick Road.'

'Well she does.' Vincent answered. 'Any one who's seen the movie will tell you that. 'There's no place like home and all that,' quoted Vincent.

Inspector Ploddock closed the note book and handed it back to a rather red faced Wiggins.

'Why don't we start at the beginning again,' said the inspector patiently. 'You went to the pictures to see a gangster movie which starred Edward G Robinson.'

Vincent nodded. 'At the Kingsland Empire.'

'And while you were there you met this Lottie Delf... what did you say her name was?'

'Delfger.' Vincent said.

'Delfger,' the inspector repeated, 'and she told you that she and her husband tried to blackmail somebody and he wouldn't pay so they killed him?'

Vincent nodded again but added quickly, 'But Lottie said it was an accident. He fell down the stairs.'

'And the name of the man that they had killed is Marenbach?'

'Yes…, no…, erm…,' Vincent thought. 'No he was the man that Lottie's husband was doing some work. Small jobs she said "doing his dirty work."'

'Did she tell you the name of the man that they killed?'

'Erm,' Vincent thought again. Finally he shook his head. 'Only that they put him in the canal.'

'And you believed her?'

'Well, no, not really. I mean she was drunk when I got to the theatre, been in there all day, drinking. She shouted at the screen, threw her empty gin bottle at it. Said she was a better spy than Edward G any day.'

'She admitted she was a spy?'

Vincent nodded again.

'Who did she spy for?'

'The Germans, I suppose.'

'And you believed her?'

'Weeeell,' Vincent said again, 'not really, I mean she wasn't acting all suspicious and furtive like was she? I mean if you're going to be a spy you don't go shouting about it to a cinema screen do you? Kept on about kidnapping some kid. Said her husband went off to squeeze a bit of money off the kid's parents but didn't return. He did a bunk if you ask's me. Took the money and ran. Mind you I'm not surprised, but still, she was lonely and needed a shoulder to cry on.'

'Then what happened?' asked the inspector trying to keep Vincent on track before he went off on a tangent.

'Well,' Vincent thought for a minute. 'She was making so much noise; I thought that Beryl would chuck her out.'

'Beryl?'

'The usherette. Works at the Kingsland Empire, been there years.

But she just slept through it all. I mean there weren't that many people in there just two or three. Don't know why I go, it's become a real fleapit. Queenie prefers the Rio now, and for an extra special treat, the Carlton.' Vincent was on a roll.

'What about Mrs. Delfger?' urged the inspector.

'Oh, well, like I said she was making such a racket I thought I'd better go and shut her up or I'll never be able to hear the movie. And that's when she said, "it's not like that in real life and that she was a spy," and stuff and started crying. Well, I said, "I'm good at spotting a good story line so why not tell me..."'

'What time did you leave the Cinema?' cut in the inspector. He could see a rather large tangent coming, and wanted to distract Vincent from it.

'Oh, let me think, it must have been a little before elevenish, we sat halfway through the next film as well you see. *Look Ma I'm no Angel*? Set in a borstal institution about a young boy who grew up to be a whistling sensation, bit silly really I thought, but Lottie loved it. Said it reminded her of her own career, she and her husband had a variety act apparently, I don't think it was any good though, they couldn't get any bookings.'

Inspector Ploddock changed questions. 'Where did you go after you left the cinema?'

'Well, eventually I said we should go and have a nice cup of tea so we went to Bert's Bangers on Dalstan Junction. Not very good tea. Queenie always said "that a good cup of tea can solve all the world's problems." Lottie didn't drink her tea, said it was English muck, well I couldn't argue with her could I, we were in Bert's Bangers. Like limp dishwater it was. Queenie always makes a good strong brew.'

Inspector Ploddock was on tangent alert and changed the subject yet again. 'How did you end up outside the Carlton?'

'She wanted something stronger. Said if we'd hurry we could make closing time at the Strangled Parrot. She bought a couple of bottles of gin; I got a bottle of stout. After that I tried to get her home somewhere in Hackney I think on Richmine Road. It was quite close. She didn't want to. I think she was locked out if you asked me. Made any excuse not to go back home, said that kid was there whinging all the time. I don't think she likes children. So we sat on a bench in De Beauvoir Square. I said I was tired and wanted to go home. I knew that Queenie would be worried about me. I'd only gone to see Edward G, so she would have been waiting for me to return. But Lottie just kept on drinking and offering me one. I had finished my stout by then, I thought if I have a drink with her I could get her to go home. Well one swig led to another...'

'The Carlton?' cut in the inspector.

'I'm getting to that, you see, drink and me don't really mix. One port and lemon with Queenie's my limit, well I started to tell Lottie about all sorts of things. We ended up arguing about the way people behave in public, especially at the movies. Like that man last week at the Carlton.' A look of recognition dawned on Vincent's face, 'you're that man in the café the other day.'

Inspector Ploddock nodded. 'Go on.'

'Well I suppose it was my fault, by then I had had quite a bit to drink. I said it was disgraceful that the management should let people into the cinema just to create a nuisance of themselves. I mean we're all paying customers aren't we? All I wanted to see was how Dorothy got the ruby slippers. Missed it you see when they were arguing behind. Queenie had fallen asleep. So Lottie decided that we should go and demand our money back. But when we got there the cinema was closed. So we banged on the doors trying to get them to open up. Lottie was shouting at the top of her voice that they were all thieves and tea drinkers and that they should be locked up for putting Dorothy in ruby slippers.' Vincent smiled. He looked at the stern face of the inspector watching him and immediately assumed he'd be back in prison. 'I suppose it was quite funny at the time,' he mumbled.

'And that is when the Constable Jenkins turned up?' the inspector asked.

Vincent nodded again. 'He tried to calm us down but Lottie was in full flow. A sort of tussle broke out and Lottie made a swing to hit the police man. I guess I got in the way.' He shrugged and fell silent.

'Thank you, Mr. Blotcher,' said the inspector rising to leave.

'Am I going to prison now?' asked a rather deflated Vincent.

Inspector Ploddock had acted swiftly wasting no time in talking to his chief. He needed the release of Madam Delfger in the hope that she would lead him to the murderer. Convinced as he was about Vincent's story which corroborated everything that Granny Probyn had told him.

Although still only circumstantial evidence, and against his better judgement, the chief grudgingly allowed for Madam Delfger to be released, on the strict understanding that she was to be watched at all times and so, a few hours later, she and Vincent were in the dock before The Hon. Mr. Eustace Puckering 12th Baronet known in the criminal fraternity as Useless Puckering and both released with a fine of 3 shillings and sixpence.

Inspector Ploddock had re-interviewed everybody at the theatre, but their stories remained unchanged. As far as the general consensus was concerned the deaths of Mucus Drillby and Ashley de la Mouche were tragic accidents. But that sneaky feeling continued. He had ordered a search of the theatre for the missing documents but as Granny Probyn had already told him, she, Miss Plimple and the others had already searched and had all drawn a blank. At least he was able to close the John Doe file which sat on his desk but this only confirmed even more that his sneaky feeling was correct. But the facts didn't add up.

Going to the morgue with Inspector Ploddock, Odel was able to identify the body of his uncle. 'Why didn't your uncle come to us first?' he asked the boy as they waited for an assistant to bring out the body. 'None of this would have happened.'

'I think that my uncle was afraid of the authorities. He didn't want to jeopardise the escape of Professor Meis, but I think that may have already happened. His niece has not heard from him and she fears the worst,' Odel answered.

The assistant wheeled into the large room a trolley on which lay a body covered in a sheet.

Odel blanched slightly.

'Are you alright?' asked the inspector. 'Would you like to sit down?'

'I'm fine. Please lets just get this over with.'

Inspector Ploddock nodded to the assistant who uncovered the head of the body.

The waxen face of Levi Oppenheimer stared at them. Odel put his hand to his mouth. Unable to speak he gulped then nodded his head in answer to the inspectors question. It was unmistakably his uncle.

'How did he... how did he die?' Odel asked in a whisper.

'The coroners report says that he suffered from a number of contusions and fractures, possibly as a result from falling down stairs. As you know we pulled his body from the canal. But it is believed that he died before being put into the canal as no water was found in his lungs.'

Inspector Ploddock nodded to the assistant again who covered up the body. Odel watched as he wheeled the trolley and his uncle from the room.

'What will happen to him now?' asked Odel.

'Now that we have found out his identity and discovered his next of kin, there is no reason why he cannot be buried.'

Odel nodded, 'I'll make the necessary arrangements.'

'I shall get the assistant to fill out the necessary forms.' Again, thought the inspector, this job is nothing but paperwork.

Odel left the mortuary and made his way back to the hotel to break the news to his sister who was under the tender ministrations of Julian Pleach.

Inspector Ploddock had also contacted Napoleon Packard asking that he return to London and was expecting a reply to his telegram at any moment.

Vincent & Lottie stood on the steps of the court house in a daze. Although she had been questioned it seemed that the police weren't interested and decided to get rid of the problem of what to do with the couple as quickly as possible. Of course she was unawares that she was being used as bait to catch a killer.

Vincent looked at Lottie. It was a very awkward moment. Neither of them knew what to say to each other. Vincent needed to get home to Queenie who he knew would be beside herself with worry. But he just couldn't leave Lottie by herself. Where would she go? Eventually he asked the question.

'I suppose back to the house and vait for my husband.' She replied.

'And if he doesn't turn up what then?'

'He'll come home,' she said.

'Was it true?' Vincent asked. 'You know about the murder and everything?'

'Yes.' She answered simply. 'I suppose that brat is still at the house. I had better return him to his mother.'

'Shall I help? I mean can I help? I have to go home first to mother. She'll be terribly worried but I can't leave you like this.'

'Thank you.' She said as they started to walk home.

Having locked his dressing room door before leaving the theatre Maltravers waited outside the stage door out of sight until Walter had gone to the loo before he slipped back unseen into the theatre. He was determined to find the papers as they were his only means of surviving. He looked at his watch by the dim emergency lights as he climbed the stairs. The chloroform should be wearing off by now. It was best to get Miss Plimple to talk while she was still drowsy.

As he unlocked his dressing room door he could hear her stirring. Perfect timing. He crossed the room quickly.

'Miss Plimple? Miss Plimple?' he said softly.

'Hmmm,' groaned Miss Plimple not fully awake.

'Miss Plimple, I need to ask you something, can you hear me?'

Miss Plimple nodded her head and tried to speak. 'Hmmmm,' she groaned again.

'Miss Plimple,' Maltravers asked again quietly. 'Do you have the papers; you were given a package by Mr. Oppenheimer. Do you have your uncle's papers?'

Miss Plimple groaned again.

'Miss Plimple, I'm going to take off the tape covering your mouth. Do you understand?'

Miss Plimple groaned and still groggy nodded her head.

Maltravers grabbed the edge of the surgical tape. 'This may hurt.' He pulled the tape off in one swift movement.

The shock brought Miss Plimple back to consciousness. She starred at Maltravers for a second before realising what had happened to her. She tried to scream but Maltravers quickly covered her mouth with his hand. She stared at him with terror in her eyes.

He looked at her and said, 'I do not wish to hurt you, Miss Plimple, please believe me, but do not try to scream. There is nobody in the theatre except you and me. There is nobody around to hear you. There is nobody here to help you.' This of course wasn't true. The police had been all over the building that day and were still stationed at various points, put Maltravers was desperate and he needed something with which he could use as leverage with Hessen to keep his name from being added to that list.

'I repeat, I do not want to hurt you, but if you force me to I will take measures. Do you understand?'

Miss Plimple nodded.

Maltravers took his hand away.

Miss Plimple took a deep breath.

'Good,' said Maltravers. 'I see that you are going to be reasonable so I ask you again, where are the papers that Levi Oppenheimer gave you?'

'I don't have them.' She answered quickly.

'Please be reasonable Miss Plimple, I know that Levi Oppenheimer gave you certain documents, important documents, plans and experiments of your uncle's work. Please don't play games. Tell me where they are?'

'I don't have them,' she repeated. 'They have been stolen.'

'Don't take me for a fool, Miss Plimple, I am deadly serious. Where are those papers?' his voice was hardening.

'I told you, I don't have them.' A steely look in Miss Plimple's eyes told Maltravers that this was not going to be easy.

'I warn you Miss Plimple I have some very effective methods of getting information all of which are highly unpleasant, and it will be a long time before we are disturbed by which time I doubt that you would care. So I ask you one more time. Where are the papers?'

'Are you going to kill me the way you did, Mucus & Ashley?' she asked defiantly.

Maltravers shrugged his shoulders. 'There is a possibility you may suffer the same fate as the others.' Not knowing who killed Mucus

Drillby or Ashley he didn't want to disillusion her. If she thought that he had killed before (which he had) it might persuade her to talk. He continued, 'That depends on your answers. I will ask you once more. Where are the papers?'

Miss Plimple looked away. It was a hopeless situation, how could she have been so stupid, after all that Inspector Ploddock and Granny Probyn had said about being vigilant? Whichever way she looked at it she was trapped, even if she knew where the papers were and told Maltravers, she would end up the same as Mucus and Ashley. Discovered dead and made to look like an accident.

'I don't know, I don't know, I don't know. I'm telling you the truth, the papers were stolen. I took them from Mr. Oppenheimer and hid them under the stage in amongst the hydraulics; it seemed the best place for them. There were plenty of other boxes down there. Who would notice another package?' Miss Plimple knew her words were not having any effect on Maltravers.

'You leave me no alternative,' said Maltravers. Crossing the room to his make-up box he removed the bottle of chloroform and a handkerchief. 'This will make it a little easier,' he said. 'For me,' he added seeing the look of surprise on her face.

Scene 9

Karl and Professor Meis descended the gang plank from HMS Cowslip onto the container dock in Harwich. Having said farewell to Captain Porfrey and his men they had boarded the corvette, HMS Cowslip at Amsterdam later that night, and now the cold grey light of a British winter morning gave them a cheery welcome.

Curruthers introduced himself.

'Gentlemen, if you would.' He indicated the waiting car. 'I have orders to take you to your hotel today so that you may rest.'

'Please, before we go any further, have you any news of my niece?' asked the professor.

'She's fine. Although there have been lots of strange going on at the theatre I am assured that she is okay.' Answered Curruthers. 'Now gentlemen,' and again he waved his hand in the direction of the car, 'we have a long journey before us.'

Augustus Reed bounded into the theatre. After catching the overnight train from Edinburgh, he had in tow two of the most miserable looking scabby kneed street urchins imaginable. The twins Mac and Morag could not have been more than seven, but had the capacity for creating havoc given the slightest chance. Mac wiped his ever snotty nose upon his sleeve which was already stiff from the constant wipes across his face.

Augustus Reed boomed at Walter that a room must be found to accommodate his latest protégés. 'And I want a full company call before this afternoon's performance. I received a telegram from Miss Plimple saying that certain standards had dropped. Won't do, won't do at all,' he boomed as he strode off into the theatre.

The twins stared at each other, then a feral grin possessed both of them and they ran after Mr. Reed.

Granny Probyn awoke after a night of fitful dreams. She looked down and felt the comforting warmth of Fluffy Yeomans as he lay curled up beside her. She withdrew her arm from under the eiderdown and proceeded to tickle his chin. Without any hesitation he raised his head a little higher for a good effective tickle.

'Come along, lazy bones, today are the last two performances,' with which she pulled back the covers and sat, 'but we still haven't found the papers,' Granny Probyn said as if continuing a conversation in her head.

The Papers! Thought Fluffy Yeomans. He knew where the papers where, but how to get this information across to her was going to be difficult. Fluffy Yeomans sat bolt upright and gave Granny Probyn his paw.

'Yes, my dear, what is it?' she asked.

'Meow.' He said.

'And meow to you tooo-ooo,' sang Granny Probyn gaily on her way to the bath room.

She returned some twenty minutes later looking spick and span, as her father would have said. 'Come along Fluffy no time to dawdle, we've just got time for a good breakfast and then we can be at the theatre in good time. And no more than an hour later she found herself in such upheaval at the stage door. Not only were people bringing things but also taking away personal possessions which they had acquired over the length of the run. It was easier in some cases if the lodgings were close by.

Apparently in the short space of time from Mr. Reed's arrival at the theatre, 'Them devil twins have turned the bleeding paint frame room into a jungle, they've tied ropes between the four frames and are now flicking paint at anyone who approaches. Poor Ernie, I didn't have a chance to tell him before he walked in "and there they were" he said "two chimpanzees in the paint room." Poor sod copped a whole 5 gallons. There's gonna be hell to pay,' said Walter.

Granny Probyn couldn't help smile to herself though reproached herself quickly, about the poor unfortunate man.

'Anyway's,' continued Walter, 'it's given the stagehands a terrible time as some of the set pieces are being stored in there. They don't know what to do what wiv paint flying around. Little monsters.'

Inspector Ploddock was a worried man. As soon as he'd heard that Miss Plimple was missing he immediately set up a search party in the theatre. He sent someone to her home but all had come up negative. He feared that she might be the next victim. He wasn't alone in that assumption. Granny Probyn also knew what great danger Miss Plimple was in.

Shortly before the theatre opened to the public Mr. Reed addressed the entire company. Well not the entire company as Miss Plimple couldn't be found.

He was not a happy man. 'Thoroughly unprofessional what was happening in his theatre,' he said. 'Just because there had been a couple of slight accidents was no excuse for not giving your best on stage.'

Some of the younger dancers and chorus members started to cry. Granny Probyn sat tight lipped. She was scanning the faces of all the members of the cast and crew. Which one of these people had kidnapped Miss Plimple? She looked from face to face.

Her gaze stopped at Maltravers. She remembered the look that he had given Miss de la Mouche that afternoon in the corridor. He was the man in Miss de la Mouche's dressing room, he was the other person. Aware that he was being watched he looked at Granny Probyn. She quickly looked away but she knew that he had noticed.

Augustus Reed ploughed on, unaware of any dangers, '...and so I want each of you to give your all for the last two performances.' He finished with a flourish.

Everybody got up from their seats and made to go back to the dressing rooms more depressed then when they had arrived at the theatre.

Granny Probyn tried to make sure that she was surrounded by lots of members of the cast away from Maltravers. Once through the pass door she quickly went to the stage door.

'Walter, do you know where Inspector Ploddock is?' she asked as soon as she entered the vestibule.

"E was here abhat 'alf an hour ago. Aint seen him since. Far too much goings on for my liking, never in my thirty years has anyfink like this 'appened,' he continued.

'If you see him, can you give him a message? Tell him I've found Miss Christies's little old lady. Now I must go and get ready for this afternoon's performance.' But her mind was churning as she turned away to return to her dressing room, muttering to herself as she went.

Maltravers made his way slowly back to his dressing room. Granny Probyn had just jumped to the top of Hessen's list. It had to be done as quickly as possible, before she had a chance to talk to that incompetent police inspector. But how was he going to get at her? He loitered at the top of the stairwell. His dressing room was a floor above hers. He heard her muttering as she climbed the steps. Jimmy was in his usual place on his stool at the beginning of the corridor.

'Is everyfing all right?' he asked Granny Probyn as she passed him, seemingly unawares of his presence.

The question brought Granny Probyn back to herself. 'Yes, yes, dear,' she said. Then it finally hit her. How could she have been so stupid? 'Fluffy Yeomans,' she said, and rushed to her dressing room.

'Yes,' Maltravers thought to himself, 'Fluffy Yeomans, that's how.'

The afternoon performance went without a hitch. Whether it was because of the police presence in the theatre or because Augustus Reed was watching from the wings everything seemed to go smoothly.

All during the performance Granny Probyn had a chance to search again under the stage. She was convinced that the package was somewhere there, but again she came up with nothing. She had begun by searching the spot where Miss Plimple had stepped on Fluffy Yeomans tail. But nothing that looked remotely suspicious stood out from the other boxes and crates.

As she waited for Fluffy Yeomans to finish his scene with Mr. Pleach in the miller's shop, Granny Probyn racked her brain as she scanned the under stage area. Where would be a safe place to hide secret documents? She could hear the applause as the scene came to an end and she waited for the scene change. "Where would be safe?" she asked herself again. "Where would be safe?" Then, as if by magic, Fluffy Yeomans descended on the stage hydraulics along with the set pieces of the miller's shop. There, in front of Granny Probyn's eyes, she saw, the bags of flour stacked up against the counter with it's weights and measures and there was Fluffy Yeomans in his final pose, on top of the safe standing on his hind legs, holding Mr. Pleach's hat.

Granny Probyn almost cried out in disbelieve. Of course it was obvious; whoever had found the papers had put them there. Where better to hide papers than in a safe? Especially one that was only opened once during a performance and nothing ever taken from it. How could they all have been so blind?

As soon as the lift came to a stand still Fluffy Yeomans jumped from the top of the safe and through the safety cages to the waiting lap of Granny Probyn. Above them they could hear the chorus doing their next number.

'Oh you clever boy,' she whispered to Fluffy Yeomans, 'it was you wasn't it? But how did you get the papers in there?'

In her excitement she almost forgot that there was a performance going on and that there were far too many people milling about, so she had to bide her time until the moment she could tell Inspector Ploddock.

Queenie was in a right old state; she had opened up the café that morning and her early morning regulars found her crying over her first cuppa.

'Me Vincent's dun a bunk,' she told anyone and everyone who cared to hear. 'What's to become of me?' she wailed into her already sodden cup of tea.

For the rest of the day she was inconsolable, so much so that most of the customers just left their money on the counter where it lay untouched.

Vincent finally walked in with a sheepish countenance. He wasn't sure of the reaction he was going to receive. Behind him loitered Madam Delfger in the doorway. Queenie looked up when the figure of Madam Delfger cast a shadow over the counter blotting out the pale winter afternoon sun. At first Queenie didn't recognise the shape of Vincent standing before her then she wailed with relief, that her baby had come home. She almost jumped the counter in her haste to grab him to her ample bosom. 'Where've you been, me darlin'?' she cried, 'Oh, I's bin so worried, I thought all sorts of calamities.' She held him at arms length and looked at him. She then noticed the dried blood down his shirt front. 'Oh, me baby,' she wailed again, 'what's they dun to yer? Have yer been to 'ospital? What happened to my precious?'

Vincent tried to answer but couldn't catch his breath, a lump had formed in his throat as he fought back the tears.

'It vas my vault,' said Madam Delfger, from the doorway. 'I hit him, we vas, how do you say? Drunk.'

'Drunk!' Queenie almost burst Vincent's ear drum. She held him at arms length again. 'Yer mean to tell me yer've been out whoring and drinking, while I've been worried sick to death about yer?' She grabbed Vincent by the ear about to drag him upstairs like she used to do when he was a small boy.

'Please,' said Madam Delfger. 'Please don't hurt him. He has been so good to me, so helpful.'

'An' who are you?' Queenie snapped, still holding Vincent's ear in her vice like grip.

'I vas the one who started it. It was not Vincent's fault. He saved me.'

'Oh,' said Queenie, now unsure what to do. 'Well in that case...' she trailed off. She finally let go of Vincent's very red and painful ear. 'But why is 'e covered in blood?' she asked again, 'where've yer bin?'

'We vere at the cinema, then ve went for a drink and then...' Madam Delfger couldn't contain her tears anymore, she rubbed her nose with the back of her hand as she dropped into the nearest chair.

Queenie immediately grabbed a cup from the counter, poured a good strong cup of tea and took it to the woman. 'There, there,' Queenie said. 'Don't take on, it can't be all that bad, have a nice cup of tea.'

Madam Delfger sniffed. 'My husband's left me...' she said as she sipped the dark brown liquid. She screwed up her face as she tasted the bitter tea that had been stewing all day and, picking up the sugar dispenser, proceeded to sweeten it. 'Gone he has, just left me, with no money, no nothing. Not a vord. Vincent had been so good. He helped me last night. It vasn't his vault.'

'Well, I always said my Vince, was a gem.' Said Queenie as she cast him a glance that said, just wait till I get you upstairs.

Vincent, knowing the look on his mothers face, took the plunge. 'I said I would walk Madam Delfger home. Make sure she was alright and all that…' he paled under the stare Queenie gave him.

'Yes, my landlady, she's not a nice woman. I expect all my things to be in the street.'

'Well, in that case, I suppose…' Queenie herself couldn't come up with a retort that meant she didn't want her son helping her. That's what people did. Help their friends and neighbours. 'But you make sure that you come home this evening,' she looked at Vincent, 'or woe betide I'll skin yer alive. Giving me a fright like that.' Queenie got up from the table and made her way behind the counter. Staring at all the coins left, she immediately started cashing up.

Vincent, taking his chance, took Madam Delfger by the arm. 'I won't be long, I promise,' he said as they left the café.

Maltravers was feeling trapped. He sat in his dressing room unsure of how to proceed. All during the matinee performance he had tried to get close to Granny Probyn but she had managed to avoid him. There were too many people hanging around, and, what with that police constable at the stage door, he was more insecure than ever. He also had the problem of Miss Plimple, who must have woken from her dose of morphine which he had given her the previous night, and now he had no way of getting to her, being as she was locked in a wicker basket in the paint frame room. Those two brats that

Mr. Reed had brought had put paid to his plans to have her taken to his apartment earlier that morning. So now what was he to do? Should he try and make a run for it? Sooner or later one of Hessen's henchmen or the police were bound to find him, but where would he go? Back to Germany? Too risky. How would he get to America if he did a bunk now. The police would be on to him. Maybe if he just finished the last show, made as if nothing was wrong, and left at the earliest opportunity. He was sure he couldn't go back to his room. His landlady, Mrs. O, was too big a gossip. Who knows what she had told any passing stranger? It was all too dangerous. And what of Miss Plimple? If she hadn't been discovered by now, well, he could live with her death on his conscience. A horrible way to die he had to admit, starving to death, but it wasn't as if he hadn't killed before. No if it was his neck or somebody else's his neck always came first.

He started to pack the few essentials that he would take with him. He would leave everything else. May as well travel as light as possible. As for money, he had a bit stashed away. It would see him to America and then, well, he could take care of himself.

Curruthers took the professor and Karl to a hotel in the centre of London. When they were safely deposited he went back to his office. Only then did he find out that Miss Plimple had disappeared. A note had come through the normal police channels. This was not good news. He immediately set off for the theatre. Meanwhile the professor and Karl freshened themselves up and ate the meal that Curruthers had room service deliver.

'I know we shouldn't leave,' said the professor, 'but I do feel I should see my niece as soon as possible. What do you think?'

'It's alright, by me, professor,' taking another bite of his pork chop, 'but do we have any money? I mean how do we get to the theatre from here? We could be miles away.'

'You're right, my boy,' said the professor, thinking, 'but we could always ask at reception. There's no harm in trying.'

Karl gave a shrug as he finished his meal. 'You should eat, professor,' said Karl as he looked across at the professor's plate which he had hardly touched.

'I can't,' he said, 'until I know that Jane is safe.'

'Then I suggest we leave as quickly as possible,' Karl said.

Inspector Ploddock had had a busy day. It seemed there were a thousand and one things to arrange, and all the time he had this feeling in his stomach that he should be at the theatre. So when he discovered that Miss Plimple had gone missing he knew that she had to be found and quickly, he had set up a huge manhunt for her. Apart from the theatre which had been searched, and her apartment, he really didn't have a clue as to where she could have been taken.

He had also arranged that Napoleon Packard, Veronica and Beauregard Henry be escorted to London for their safety and had finally managed to get seats on the day train from Edinburgh. They were due to arrive that evening and Inspector Ploddock left instructions that they be taken straight to the theatre just in time for that evening performance.

He was also co-ordinating the men to follow Madam Delfger. He was convinced that she was the link that would bring all the loose ends of his tangled web together and lead to the discovery as to who the murderer was.

Herr Delfger finally could feel his face coming back to life. Every time he looked in the mirror a stranger looked back. He had tried to whistle, whistling always seemed to relax him, but the pain of pursing his lips was too much. The bruising had gone from bloody red to dark purple and now it had a yellowish greeny tinge. He had spent the last couple of days since his escape from the house of Napoleon Packard sleeping on the couch of an old music hall friend.

Harve Boulc'h was professional paper tearer and flatulist, known within the business, as "a song, a smile, and a stain." He and Herr Delfger at one time had a double act under the name of "Harve & Heinz blowing your way" which they toured around Bavaria, but the act had drifted apart when one hall manager suggested they do a love duet cheek to cheek. Then fate intervened when Heinz met and married Lottie, and their paths never crossed again until they both tried their luck in Britain with its variety shows.

After two days without a breath of fresh air and Harve rehearsing his act Herr Delfger finally decided he should go home.

When he arrived, he found that the house was empty. He made himself something to eat and slept in the fireside chair waiting for Lottie to come home. The next morning after she didn't arrive he was fraught with anxiety. The boy was gone which he knew but had something terrible happened to Lottie. Had she been here when Napoleon and the others arrived? Was she now in prison? And what of himself? Were the police after him? What of Marenbach? A hundred and one scenarios ran through his mind. He decided to see Maltravers. He would leave Lottie a note, if she returned she would find it and meet him, if not well he had to think of himself now.

It seemed like Napoleon Packard, Veronica and Beauregard Henry had done nothing but travel, which was true. They had no sooner arrived in Edinburgh when they received the telegram from Inspector Ploddock asking them to return to London. Against Veronica's wish he had consented. Inspector Ploddock wanted to confirm that the man who had been blackmailing him was Marenbach.

Veronica was slightly pacified when she found out that they would be accompanied by the police. Beauregard Henry had said nothing of his ordeal in two days. He stared out of the window on their journey northwards, and showed no sign of recognition as they travelled back to London.

Granny Probyn was anxiously waiting for news, in her dressing room, afraid that Maltravers had realised that she had made the connection between him, Miss de la Mouche and Miss Plimple, she had decided after the performance to await the arrival of Inspector Ploddock and locked herself and Fluffy Yeomans in their dressing room .

Maltravers in his dressing room was also in a state of nervous tension. Afraid at any moment that the police would knock on his door, he knew that the interfering Granny Probyn had finally pieced together what had happened. It was only a matter of time.

The suspense in waiting was agony.

The knock finally came. Maltravers jumped. Slowly he got up from his dressing table. Another knock came from the door more insistent this time. Maltravers made his way across the room, unlocked the door and opened it expecting the police. Instead he was faced with a baboon's bottom. Or so he thought.

Herr Delfger pushed passed into the dressing room as Maltravers looked up and down the corridor outside before closing the door.

'What are you doing here?' he finally asked, 'and what has happened to your face?'

'Marenbach is dead,' said Herr Delfger. 'They know all about us. They were waiting for me. That old woman with the cat. She's the leader.'

'What are you talking about, leader?' asked Maltravers.

'They know all about Oppenheimer, they were waiting for me,' said Delfger, 'Lottie's gone. I said to meet me here.'

'You can't stay here,' said Maltravers trying to make sense of Herr Delfger, 'it's far too dangerous, there are police everywhere. I'm stuck here myself until this stupid show is finished then I'm off.'

'But you have to help me,' cried Herr Delfger. 'Hessen has to protect me. I was only doing what I was asked.'

'Hessen won't protect you, he would rather give up his precious butler than protect you, he's a ruthless killer. He might not do the deed himself, oh, no he gets some other idiot to do the dirty work, but make no mistake, he'll find you.' Maltravers handed over the list that Hessen had given him.

Herr Delfger looked at the list and scanned the names.

'You mean he plans to...' he couldn't finish the sentence.

Maltravers nodded. 'You can add my name to that list as well. It seems I didn't do quite as good a job as he thought I would. Somebody else killed von Marenbach.'

'It's that interfering old woman I tell you, and her gang. She's responsible. Look what they did to my face. Who would suspect a sweet little old lady killing off her enemies. Who would believe it, but I tell you it's her.'

'Maybe I've misread the signs, maybe you're right,' said Maltravers, 'but then what's her game? Why would she want top secret German papers? It just doesn't make sense.'

'Look at Hessen's list, every one of them is associated with her. That Napoleon and his wife, don't you think it's too much of a coincidence that they just happen to be friends of the family? Look what happened to Drillby? The Oppenheimer's how did she ever get to meet them? Who knew they were in England? Think about it, she's had everybody running around after each other and there she is right in the centre of things. Like a great big spider waiting for her prey to get caught in her web.'

'You're still suffering from concussion,' Maltravers said. 'It's preposterous. Who could she be working for?'

'Isn't it obvious? She's with British Intelligence. They even staged her own attack, saying she was robbed in her hotel room. Why were no other rooms robbed that night and what was taken? Nothing. Look at the facts. Plain as the nose on my face.'

'It's a very bad simile, your nose being the way it is, but I do get your meaning. And if what you say is true then we need to leave now. I thought this afternoon she had figured something out. I'm sure she's made the connection between me and Miss Plimple.'

'Miss Plimple?'

'Yes, I er... decided to take matters into my own hands. To keep my name off that list you understand. Unfortunately things didn't work out the way they should have done.'

'You mean you've killed her?'

'No, not quite, but if I do nothing, she will die. Very slowly.'

'Did she have the papers?'

'I see you're thinking what I was thinking. Even if I did find out anything, I wouldn't be telling you now would I?'

'But we need to help each other, or we both go down. I mean Lottie's bounds to inform the police at some point where I am. If I'm found, well...' Herr Delfger left the threat hanging in mid air.

'You can save your threats. I don't have the papers. Some one else has got them. And I can only assume that you are correct in your assumptions and that old Granny P is playing a game of double dealing.'

'Why? What makes you say that?'

'Just a look she gave me this afternoon while old man Reed was prattling on I knew she had made the connection, but...' Maltravers fell silent for a moment. 'I think it's time we paid old Granny P a visit.'

'What? Now?'

'No time like to present, besides we have to get out of here and she could be our means of escape. Maybe she hasn't informed the authorities yet. There may still be a chance. Come on.'

Dark clouds were hanging overhead and they were threatening a downpour when Vincent and Lottie finally reached Richmine Road. It felt as if they had walked all over London.

'We'd best get inside quick,' said Vincent, 'or we'll be soaked. I thought it was too much to be true. We've had four glorious days of sunshine. Better than some summers if you ask me.'

They made their way up the steps and as Lottie fumbled with the keys she heard the familiar bark of her landlady.

"Ere, what's going on that's what I'd like to know. Strangers ringing my bell day and night. And what was that boy doing here? Said you had kidnapped him, well I knew you wouldn't want the police so I let 'em in nice and quiet like, but it's difficult to keep something like that quiet.'

'I haven't got any money so you keep your mouth shut.' Shouted Madam Delfger and proceeded to open the door dragging Vincent in with her and slamming it behind them.

The landlady gave a shrug of her shoulders. 'I'll have her yet.' She mumbled to herself.

'Interfering old bag,' said Lottie.

'So is it true, you did kidnap a boy?' Vincent asked. He was convinced that the police hadn't believed his story, something he

216

hadn't really believed himself which was why they had been released.

'I told you,' she said flatly.

'And you killed that man, then you and your husband dumped him in the canal?'

Madam Delfger only shrugged her shoulders.

Vincent gulped. He was alone in a strange house with a murderer. 'I promised Queenie I wouldn't be long,' he said trying to sound more confident that he was.

'Relax,' said Madam Delfger, aware that Vincent's attitude had changed. 'I told you it vas an accident. He fell down the stairs. What would you do?'

She walked off down the corridor into the kitchen. Vincent stood for a moment looking at the stairs and realised he was standing at the bottom, presumably where the body of Mr. Oppenheimer had landed. He quickly followed Madam Delfger into the kitchen.

Madam Delfger was standing over the sink with her head in her hands sobbing to herself. 'I should have come home last evening. Heinz was here waiting for me. He has left a message telling me what I should do.' She handed Vincent a note which she held in her hands. Vincent put an arm around her shoulders and read the note. He didn't understand a word as it was written in German, but to console the poor woman muttered, 'There, there. We'll do as he says.'

'Ve need to go to ze theatre tonight. He says he vill be there.'

'Tonight!' Vincent almost screamed. 'I can't go to the theatre tonight! Look at me! And what about Queenie? She'll kill me!'

Madam Delfger only sobbed into her hands.

'Oh, all right. But I need to change and… and… I don't have any clean clothes. I can't go to the theatre looking like this, neither can you.'

'My husband, you should fit his clothes,' she said.

217

Miss Plimple was awakened by the ache in her arms. She tried to move but her hands were tied behind her back. She could feel her mouth had been taped, forcing her to breathe through her nose, her ankles were also fastened.

A weight of material was almost smothering her, as she slowly opened her eyes. She tried to think where she could be. Her knees were bent in front of her, she tried to stretch her legs but her feet immediately came into contact with an obstacle.

She closed her eyes and tried to fight the fear that was welling up inside her. Was she buried alive?

Her mind raced as she tried hard to remember what had happened. Maltravers, came into view. Maltravers had what? She tried to concentrate harder. That was it Maltravers had drugged her. But then how did she end up here? She opened her eyes again. Although it was dark, through the small patch of free space she could see light through wicker work.

That was it, she thought, she was inside a costume basket, hence the material which pressed down on her. Her arms ached again. She tried to move her position. She could hear the basket creak as she moved.

Curruthers had a wasted journey out to the theatre. He questioned Walter and the police constable stationed at the stage door, but could get no coherent information from either of them, only that Miss Plimple hadn't turned up for work and couldn't be found at home. Nor could Inspector Ploddock be traced anywhere at police headquarters. 'He is a busy man,' Sergeant Jones informed him at the desk, 'especially today. It seems he's out to catch a murderer. Off to somewhere in Hackney.'

Curruthers wrote down the address. 'Is he still going to be there?' Curruthers asked. Sergeant Jones shrugged. 'Can't help you there, that address is the only information I have.'

Curruthers decided to travel out to Hackney. If he didn't find Inspector Ploddock he would return to the theatre.

Fluffy Yeoman's head snapped up when a knock came at their dressing room door.

'Yes?' said Granny Probyn.

The door rattled and another knocked.

'Yes?' said Granny Probyn a little louder. Fluffy Yeomans waited as the handle rattled some more. Suddenly the door swung open and Maltravers and Herr Delfger quickly entered the room closing the door quietly behind them.

Fluffy Yeomans hackles began to rise. He had placed himself between the two intruders and Granny Probyn.

'What do you want?' said Granny Probyn, her voice catching in her throat.

'We've come to make a bargain with you,' said Maltravers smoothly.

She quickly looked from Maltravers to Herr Delfger and back again.

He continued, 'I give you the whereabouts of Miss Plimple, you tell us where the papers are.'

'What makes you think, I know where the papers are?' asked Granny Probyn trying to instil in her voice an air of command.

'We know you're working for the British,' blurted out Herr Delfger, 'just gives us the papers and no one will get hurt.'

'What of Miss Plimple? I take it she is somewhere safe?' said Granny Probyn addressing Herr Delfger.

'The longer you prevaricate the worse it will be for Miss Plimple,' said Maltravers.

'You know that the theatre is surrounded by police. In fact I am expecting Inspector Ploddock at any moment.'

'My dear Mrs. Probyn,' said Maltravers, 'if you hand us over to the police, as you are threatening to do, I can guarantee that Miss Plimple will die. Surely you wouldn't want one of your confederates to perish in such a painful way.'

'No,' she said. After a short moment's pause she continued, 'what if I give you the documents, how can I be sure that Miss Plimple will be safe?'

'You have my word,' said Maltravers patronizingly.

Fluffy Yeomans hissed aloud. His tail standing straight in the air.

'Shush now,' said Granny Probyn admonishing him, 'Mr. Maltravers, Herr Delfger and I have just become business partners. One shouldn't talk to business partners like that.'

'I'm glad to see that we have come to some arrangement.' Said Maltravers.

'I don't trust her,' spat Herr Delfger, 'she's played us all off one another. Sweet little grandmother talking to her cat, she's had us running around in circles. She'll hand us over to the police as soon a look at you.'

'This is yer 'alf hour call Mrs. Probyn,' called Jimmy as he knocked on her door and made his way down the corridor calling out.

'It seems the show must go on,' quipped Maltravers to Herr Delfger, 'I think as a token of faith between our new business partnership, we take the cat. When Mrs. Probyn hands over the papers she gets the cat and Miss Plimple.'

Herr Delfger lunged at Fluffy Yeomans. Grabbing him before he or Granny Probyn realised what was happening.

Fluffy Yeomans spat and scratched as he was shoved hastily into his cage.

'I don't have the papers,' cried Granny Probyn, 'please don't hurt

Fluffy.'

'Shoes on the other foot now isn't it,' sneered Herr Delfger.

'Oh, dear,' Maltravers butted in, 'the audience will be disappointed not to see the star of the show; they'll have to rename the pantomime "Boots without Puss!"'

'Please, I don't have them, they are in the safe,' cried Granny Probyn again.

'Which safe? Whose?' Maltravers asked.

'The Miller's, they've been there all the time. Fluffy Yeomans found them. Please don't hurt him.'

'Who is this Miller, I've never heard of him?' asked Herr Delfger. 'Is this someone new we have to be aware of?' he asked Maltravers.

'Oh most assuredly,' laughed Maltravers. 'How very clever Mrs. Probyn. I have always said the best place to hide something is to put in plain view. To think I have looked in that safe hundreds of times and never noticed.'

'What!' Exclaimed Herr Delfger. 'You know where the papers are?'

'Oh yes,' replied Maltravers.

'Then what are we waiting for, let's get them and get out of here.' Herr Delfger was almost shouting.

'It won't be that easy my dear Delfger. I'm afraid the cat will have to do one more performance. If you please, kindly leave the cat.' He smiled at Granny Probyn. 'As a sign of our business partnership. Once I have the papers, you shall have Miss Plimple.' He said and quickly left the dressing room leaving a stunned Herr Delfger to follow.

It was very late in the afternoon when Karl and the professor approached the hotel receptionist. Curruthers had left instructions to give the professor whatever he wanted, unaware of course that the professor would want to go out, so the receptionist duly handed over some cash and arranged with the hotel porter for a taxi to take them to the Theatre Royal Drury Lane.

'Why does it always rain in England?' the professor asked the porter as they waited for the taxi. Dark clouds covered the sky and the rain poured down like water from a watering can.

The porter only shrugged in reply. He was used to the rain.

Mr. Marchmount was also used to the rain. Standing as he did outside the foyer he looked magnificent in his great coat and top hat welcoming the patrons of the theatre. As the audience arrived some holding umbrella's, some making a short dash from their taxi cabs, all wanting the cosy dryness of the theatre foyer which had been decorated to announce that this was to be the final performance.

There was an excited buzz in the theatre as the audience milled throughout the public areas and the bars. Business was brisk. Mr. Reed suitably attired in tails, circulated amongst the audience welcoming friends and well wishers.

The streets around the theatre were clogged with taxis and cabs all trying to deposit their passengers as close to the entrance as possible. Hessen's Rolls finally pulled up outside the portico of the theatre. Mr. Marchmount with his umbrella handy, opened the door then assisted Hessen's wife and daughter to the safety and dryness of the foyer as Hessen rushed in behind. Why for the life of him he had agreed that they should come to the pantomime he couldn't think. But his wife was used to getting what she wanted. He loathed the English sense of humour, with their boarding school jokes. He couldn't find anything in the least funny about men dressing up as women. He much preferred the hilarity of something like Wagner's masterpiece *Die Meistersinger*. But his wife had insisted. Thank God they had a box, he thought, he couldn't bear the idea of mixing with the hoipoloi, and he could put his seat at the back of the box and sleep.

Napoleon, Veronica, and Beauregard Henry along with their police escort took a cab from the station to the theatre.

Veronica complained bitterly that she would have preferred to go home, and at least freshen up a bit before being seen in public, but Napoleon had insisted there wasn't enough time if they were to make the beginning of the performance.

'Why does he want you at theatre?' she complained. 'Surely if you had to identify, the...' she didn't want to say the word 'body' in front of Beauregard, '...the you know what, surely you would do it at the... the you know where.' Again the word 'morgue' was missed out. Beauregard stared blankly out of the cab window.

'I'm sure the inspector has his reasons,' replied Napoleon, although he couldn't fathom out what they could be.

'And what if something...' Veronica replaced the word 'nasty' with the shake of her head in Beauregard's direction, '... were to happen while we watched the performance?'

Napoleon was having difficulty keeping up with his wife's sign language. 'I'm sure everything will be fine.' He said looking at the dozing policeman for encouragement. 'Inspector Ploddock said in his telegram that he would meet us at the theatre. What could possibly happen with the police there?'

Gerty put on her coat. She opened the door of the flat and looked at the weather. Taking an umbrella from the stand from behind the door she walked out into the rain without bothering to close the door behind her.

Tonight would be the end of it. This was something that she had planned since the death of her daughter Ashley. The police had called that night to break the news, but she had been expecting them.

Ashley's death had come as no surprise and now, tonight if all went according to plan, it would be all over. Walking quickly she tried to catch a cab, but the weather was against her. Nobody wanted to be caught in this downpour. She had no other choice but to wait for a bus.

Vincent and Lottie made a dash for the bus stop under the rain coat belonging to her husband. As Madam Delfger predicted, Vincent and Herr Delfger were of the same build and size and so, suitably refreshed and attired, they rushed down the street in the hope of catching a number 38 that would take them into the centre of town.

As luck would have it one was turning the corner into Dalston Lane just as they arrived and so they were able to jump onto the tail board before it set off down the road. Downstairs was crammed with wet steaming bodies so they made their way upstairs to find seats.

Hetty and Odel waited patiently in their cab to reach the portico of the theatre. Aware that Miss Plimple had gone missing that morning, they were both apprehensive about going to the theatre, but Inspector Ploddock had insisted. Hetty consoled herself that Mr. Pleach would be there if the need should arise and they needed protection, and of course Inspector Ploddock had assured them that he would be attending the theatre along with twenty police officers, so the theatre was probably the safest place in London.

Not two cabs behind sat Karl and the professor.

'Maybe we should get out and make a dash for it,' said Karl losing his patience with all the waiting about, 'it's not raining that hard.'

'We don't know where the stage door is,' said the professor trying to look ahead of the carriage. His view was obscured by the heavy rain hitting the cab window. 'I think it best that we wait for the driver to get us there. We would be soaked to the skin before we closed the cab doors and we are hardly dressed for the theatre or this English weather.'

Karl had to agree. They were still dressed in the clothes they had been wearing when they had left the German ship at Wilhelmshaven. 'Humph,' he said as he threw himself back onto the seat.

Vincent & Lottie got off the 38 bus at Museum Street. The rain was still pouring. They dashed across the road between traffic and almost ran the length of Drury Lane and turned into Russell Street under Herr Delfger's now sodden coat. Finally they reached the colonnade of the theatre and the relative dryness it offered.

'Our next problem,' said Vincent shaking the wet from the coat, 'is how do we get in? We don't have tickets.'

'Ve have to find the stage door and hask for Maltravers.' Answered Lottie.

'Well that's easy,' Vincent said as he turned to open the door in front of which they stood. The small vestibule was crammed full of wet people some with messages they wanted to pass on to members of the cast wishing them good luck etcetera. Some were autograph hunters who Walter was trying to extract before they managed to get into the theatre. Vincent forced his way through the small crowd. 'Excuse me,' he shouted to Walter above the general noise, 'could you inform Mr. Maltravers that Madam Delfger is here to see him please.'

'Yer'll 'ave to wait yer turn. Young Jimmy's rushed off his feet 'e is.'

Somebody else asked Walter a question and gave Vincent a withering look, as if to say how dare you push in? Madam Delfger stayed by the door, essentially blocking anybody's entrance and exit. Vincent made his way back to her.

'We'll have to wait,' he said. 'Show's about to start I think.'

'Ladies and gents,' shouted Walter above the noise, 'for those of you who have seats yer better takes yer place, the performance is about to start.'

'Told you,' said Vincent.

Scene 10

Most of the audience had already taken their seats when the third bell rang throughout the theatre. Gerty, loitered by the ladies toilets. She would wait until the usherettes had made their last inspection then make her way to the pass door.

Meanwhile the audience chatted away excitedly in the auditorium. The orchestra had finally made their way into the pit ready for the overture.

The stage door vestibule finally cleared of people, leaving only Vincent and Madam Delfger.

'Yer'll have to wait,' Walter warned. 'Mr. Maltravers is on in the opening scene. Once he's had his go, I'll get Jimmy to tell him yer here.'

Vincent thanked him. 'We'll wait inside if you don't mind. Dreadful weather out there,' he continued.

'Please yerself,' was Walter's reply as he settled into his chair and poured a cup of tea.

Vincent looked around for somewhere to sit, but the vestibule being so small, it wouldn't have allowed for any chairs. He looked at Walter who seemed to be deliberately ignoring the couple. 'We'll just wait over here then,' he finally said to no one in particular, and slouched against the wall.

At which point Jimmy rushed into the vestibule.

'Yer wanted to see me?' he asked Walter, short of breath.

'Aye,' said Walter, 'as soon as Mr. Maltravers has done his first scene, tell 'im he's a pair o' visitor's.' Walter cast a glance at Vincent slouched up against the wall and the huge frame of Madam Delfger who was still blocking the doorway, 'important like.' He added as an after thought.

'Right ho,' said Jimmy and rushed off to continue his work.

Inspector Ploddock had spent the day chasing the few leads he had in trying to find Miss Plimple. By 7pm he had to admit that his search had been pointless. She had simple disappeared off the face of the earth. He decided to make his way back to the theatre. If all had gone according to his plans, everybody involved with the secret papers would be in the theatre. He was taking a huge gamble, by asking the Oppenheimer's and the Dorfellwaffer's to attend the performance, in essence he was using them as bait hopefully to catch the murderer.

As the orchestra finished the overture it segued into the opening number of *I'm sitting on top of the world*, the great red velvet tabs swished open to reveal the village scene, and members of the chorus and dancers in their opening routine.

After that the dame made his entrance, always a great favourite with the audience. This was the moment that Gerty had waited for. She knew that all eyes would now be on stage and so she made her way to the pass door which led back stage. Opening it slightly to check whether anyone was on the other side she quickly entered and found the main staircase to take down to the lower floors. Above she could hear the performance going on.

'Well I wonder where my sons have gone to. Have you seen them, boys and girls? They're such a lazy lot, all except my Jack.'

Mr. Maltravers as the eldest brother Hovis then made his entrance on stage along with Mr. Percival Younger as the middle brother Be-ro. 'Hello mother,' said Mr. Maltravers.

'Oh you sauce pot, I'm not that old,' said the dame. 'What are you two layabouts doing here? You should be in the mill, working.'

'You should be proud of us, mother, we've ground enough flour and made some dough,' Mr. Younger said.

'Oh you silly parrot, I said dough, not dough, you know dosh, luca, money!'

This was the cue for Julian Pleach who played the youngest brother to make his entrance.

'Oh Jack, there you are,' said the dame, 'I've some bad news.'

'What is it, mother?' said Mr. Pleach.

'Oh, I've been a silly old goose.'

'Why? What's happened?'

'Well since your dear departed father left us all, he didn't leave any money so I went to the Black Baron, and borrowed bread.'

'Borrowed?' said Mr. Maltravers.

'Bread?' said Mr. Younger.

'Black Baron?' said Jack.

Gerty waited and listened. She needed the darkness of a scene change before she could pass unobserved under the stage to her hiding place as the stage crew went about their work.

'Yes Jack, Hovis, Be-ro, unless we pay back the money the Black Baron will take everything.'

'Don't worry mother, we'll sort something out,' said Jack.

'How?' asked the dame.

'I'll ask the cat,' said Mr. Pleach.

'Why didn't you use your loaf?' said the dame to her other sons, 'that's my Mother's Pride!'

The lights blacked out. Gerty could hear the crew struggling to lift the sets and props in preparation of the next scene. She quickly took her chance of not being noticed.

Inspector Ploddock arrived at the theatre after the performance had started. He was met by Sergeant Wiggins who had made sure that Mrs. Dorfellwaffer her son, Napoleon his wife and their son had been seated next to Odel and Hetty Oppenheimer.

'No sign of Miss Plimple?' Sergeant Wiggins asked.

'No,' Inspector Ploddock said.

'Look you, heres the thing,' said the sergeant eager to impart his news. 'We have a couple of foreign gentlemen, got them in the bar. One of them said they was related to Miss Plimple. Made an awful racket at the stage door. Thought you'd better see them.'

'Did they give you their names?'

'Said he was her uncle, professor,' Sergeant Wiggins took out his note book and looked at it. 'Meis.' He finally said.

'Why didn't you say so earlier.' Said Inspector Ploddock as he started to run to the steps to take him to the bar.

'Wait,' said the sergeant. 'That's not all.'

Inspector Ploddock stopped in his tracks and turned to face the sergeant. 'Our little German lady,' continued the sergeant, 'she's back stage with that Vincent fellow. Asked to see a Mr.,' he looked at his note book again and flipped a page or two. 'Maltravers.'

'Interesting, so it seems our spider is closing her web,' said the inspector. 'Anything else, before I see this professor?'

'Just one more thing, look you, it might be nothing,'

'Get on with it.' Urged the inspector.

'Constable Jones, said there was a furtive looking gentleman asking a lot of questions regarding Miss Plimple this afternoon.'

'Who was he?' asked the inspector.

Sergeant Wiggins, started to blush. He didn't take too kindly to making mistakes even if it wasn't his. But Constable Jones, was under his command at the time, and had let the stranger walk away.

'Well, look you, he didn't say.' Said Sergeant Wiggins rather feebly.

Inspector Ploddock nearly had a seizure. 'He didn't say, He didn't say! What was Jones thinking of, he didn't say?'

The front of house manager came running into the foyer at the sound of all the shouting. 'Shussh,' he said to a rather beetroot faced inspector.

'You mean to tell me,' continued the inspector trying to keep his voice down, 'that Constable Jones, probably talked to our murderer, and he didn't even ask who he was? He couldn't even get his brain to say "excuse me Mr. Stranger Sir, who are you and why are you asking questions about a young lady who has disappeared during the night and is believed to be dead?"'

Sergeant Wiggins, cringed where he stood. He had been expecting something like this. All he could manage was a shrug of his shoulders.

Inspector Ploddock turned in disgust and headed for the stairs. Sergeant Wiggins, followed quickly behind.

On reaching the bar, Sergeant Wiggins rushed to open the door for the inspector who glowered at the sergeant as he entered.

The inspector immediately introduced himself to the professor.

'Forgive me inspector let me introduce my assistant Karl, Karl Leibknecht. He has been travelling with me.'

The inspector shook the outstretched hand that was offered.

The professor continued, 'Is there any more information about my niece? The sergeant said that she has been missing since last evening.'

Now it was the turn of the inspector to cringe. He looked at Sergeant Wiggins and wondered how much he should tell the professor. 'I'm afraid we still have no news as to Miss Plimple's whereabouts,' he said, 'but I am confident that she will be found very shortly safe and well.'

After Mr. Maltravers' first entrance he had given orders that Madam Delfger and Vincent should be taken to his dressing room. Jimmy escorted them to the door and knocked. Maltravers opened the door quickly and ushered in his guests without any introductions and quickly closed the door in Jimmy's face.

Herr Delfger appeared from behind the costume rail. And Madam

Delfger sobbing fell into his arms.

'How very touching,' said Maltravers. 'Who is this?' nodding in Vincent's direction.

'*This* is Vincent,' said Vincent who took an instant dislike to being called *this*.

Madam Delfger only sobbed more. She was crushing Herr Delfger in her arms who was desperately trying to escape.

'Get a grip on yourself,' he said to her. 'We have work to do.'

'I thought you had gone, left me, I was convinced that mother was right.' She said through her tears.

'What is this Vincent doing here?' Maltravers asked again.

'He helped me,' sobbed Madam Delfger trying to gain control of herself. 'He got me released from the police otherwise I would have been in prison.'

'What do you mean, police?' Herr Delfger and Maltravers said together.

'Don't you think we have enough police hanging around here without you bringing more?' Maltravers was fuming.

'We haven't brought any police,' said Madam Delfger indignantly. 'They let us go. I got a little tipsy and then…'

Vincent didn't like what he was hearing. He interrupted Madam Delfger, 'I explained everything and we got off with a fine.'

There was silence from the two men. 'For being drunk and disorderly. Queenie's gonna kill me when she finds out I can tell you. Have a fit she will.'

Herr Delfger spoke first. 'What do we do with him?'

'Same as the others I suppose.' Answered Maltravers.

Vincent looked from one man to the next. 'What do you mean "same as the others?"'

Quick as a flash Herr Delfger had Vincent in an arm hold from behind. Maltravers brought out his bottle of Chloroform.

'Sorry old man, can't be any witnesses,' said Maltravers.

Vincent starred wide eyed at the approaching figure of Maltravers.

Too scared to scream out he just looked about taking the scene before him. He looked at Madam Delfger who had made a move to help but had stopped when her husband shook his head. He felt the cloth over his mouth as he breathed in the fumes. Queenies gonna kill me he thought.

Granny Probyn was in a state of high tension. Fluffy Yeomans first entrance had been okay, Mr. Maltravers acted as if nothing had happened between them. But Granny Probyn knew he was only biding his time until the last scene in act one when he opens the safe.

She was still awaiting a visit from Inspector Ploddock, but he hadn't turned up before the show had started and so she had no way of conveying to him that she knew where the papers where and who the killer was. She would just have to try and stop Maltravers herself from leaving the theatre before the interval.

Maltravers had just enough time to make his entrance for the last scene in act one. He had left Madam & Herr Delfger to secure the limp body of Vincent. This was the moment he had been waiting for. This was his chance of getting at the papers legitimately, without anyone suspecting. Hopefully he could slip out of the theatre during the interval without notice and be on his way to Liverpool. He had decided on Liverpool as he had some long standing friends who were working at the Empire Theatre there. He could stay with them until he booked a passage to America.

Of course he had no intention of mentioning any of this to the Delfger's, they could rot in hell for all he cared.

Maltravers rushed to the stage. The lights were just rising on the scene with the dame standing centre stage. Mr. Younger was fidgeting with nerves.

'Where've you been?' he asked. 'Nearly missed the cue, come on,' he ordered as he made his entrance followed by Maltravers.

This was the scene in which the three characters made dough from flour. Known as the slosh scene it became very messy. Each time the dame kneaded the dough one or the other of the brothers got covered in flour. The scene ended in the pair of brothers doing their tumbling routine which consisted of a chase ending with each brother jumping through a window up stage right as the sails of the windmill went past. This required perfect timing as they then made a return jump through another window this time stage left.

Mr. Younger went first as always. He landed perfectly on the trampoline placed behind the window out of view from the audience, which gave a gasp of delight. Next followed Maltravers.

As rehearsed the dame was ready with her rolling pin to try and catch the two young men as they tumbled their way back through the adjacent window stage left.

Timing had to be perfect, as the sail of the windmill passed the window Mr. Younger jumped through narrowly avoiding the dame's well placed choreographed strike.

Next came the turn of Maltravers, this time in reverse. He had to jump through the window, miss the dame's blow and then the windmills sail. Maltravers jumped, a little early just in time as the dame who had reappeared at the other side of the window cast her blow. It ricocheted off the back of his head. He could feel the thud as the wooden rolling pin crunched the back of his skull. Many of the cast waiting in the wings heard a loud crack as Maltravers had his skull broken. Standing dazed from the blow he was in direct line of the windmill's sail as it travelled on it course. Unaware of the danger, he turned slowly to face the dame. Her face swam before his eyes. He didn't recognise the features of the woman as he starred at her.

Suddenly the dame grabbed Maltravers by the shoulders, and turned his body 180 degrees as the sail of the windmill made it's decent. With horrifying slow motion he could see the edge of the sail bear down on him. He could hear the laughter from the audience as they thought this was all part of the routine. Only the stage manager and Mr. Younger, who was now standing downstage waiting for Maltravers to catch him, watched in horror as the sail caught Maltravers.

The dame jumped aside as the sail carried Maltravers up to the flies.

The stage manager cued the orchestra pit which began playing the play out music as he brought in the lush red velvet house curtains.

The audience applauded wildly.

As soon as the curtains had closed the stage manager and half the crew were waiting to try and catch the now limp body of Maltravers.

Granny Probyn watched, in horror as the body was carried to the stage managers office. Backstage was a chaotic mass of people wondering what had happened. Again people were presuming that it had been another terrible accident. That this pantomime must be cursed. Like a ship at sea with an albatross. The stage crew without any orders to the contrary started to strike the miller's set and prepare for act two beginners. It wasn't until the stage lift, which acted as a platform on which the bench and safe sat, was lowered that the real dame was found garrotted by a pair of ladies stockings.

The audience started to fill the bars and public areas. Many were queuing for the loos when Inspector Ploddock was summoned from front of house where he was still interviewing the professor and Karl. He left them with instructions to Sergeant Wiggins to collect Napoleon Packard and family and the Oppenheimers and take them all backstage to the green room and under no circumstances were any of them allowed to leave the theatre.

As Wiggins was instructing Constable Jones to fetch the Oppenheimers, Hessen and his wife entered the bar for their drinks which had been pre-ordered and awaited their arrival on a table set in the corner. A large bottle of champagne sat chilled in a silver ice bucket. Hessen needed a drink. He had sat through the first half of the pantomime without watching it, his mind on other business. His daughter was chatting merrily away to his wife about the story of the pantomime when Hessen stopped as he came face to face with Professor Meis.

Surprised by the fact that he had read in confidential reports from the NSDP that the professor was believed dead, Hessen smiled and introduced himself.

'Herr Professor, allow me to introduce myself,' he said extending a hand in greeting, 'we have not met before but I believe we have many close mutual acquaintances.'

Hessen's wife and daughter stopped and turned when she heard her husband speak.

'Oh forgive me, my dear, Professor Meis, permit me to introduce my wife and daughter.'

Professor Meis bowed slightly to the couple who politely smiled back. 'Take Unger to the table my dear, and have a glass of champagne while I have a word with the professor,' Hessen continued and then ignoring his family, gently took the professor by the elbow and led him in the opposite direction from their designated table. Karl, who was standing behind the professor, had not been acknowledged and the professor had not been given the chance to talk let alone introduce him. So, unsure of who this man was, he kept close to the professor without intruding into their space.

The bar was quite crowded now with people milling about chatting about the pantomime, the latest news about a possible war, the stock market and the thousand and one things that people chat about when they have absolutely nothing to say.

Hessen continued to talk in hushed tones, 'I understand from certain friends of mine that you have recently left Berlin?'

'Yes,' replied the professor turning to look Hessen squarely in the face. 'You seem to be remarkably informed. Just who might our mutual acquaintances be?'

'A man in my position needs to be informed, otherwise he cannot do business,' said Hessen.

'Just what sort of business do you do, Herr Hessen?' the professor rather testily enquired.

'Professor Meis, I… I mean *we* are not your enemy. Your work could be of great benefit to your country. You can share in its glory.'

'My work, Mr. Hessen if I continued working in Berlin would be used for evil,' said the professor growing irritated and raising his voice. 'I do not like the methods you and your people operate, with blackmail, threats, torture or worse.'

A few people standing around the professor turned to look at the two men who seemed to be having an argument.

'My dear professor,' said Hessen placatingly. He looked at the faces starring at them then returned to the professor. 'This is hardly the time nor the place to discuss such things. Might I suggest that we arrange a more suitable location and time when we can meet? I can assure you I do not need to resort to blackmail or torture. Think of it as a business deal.'

'Mr. Hessen, the only business I am interested in at the moment is locating the whereabouts of my niece. I suppose that her kidnapping has nothing to do with your appearance here this evening.'

Hessen looked genuinely shocked for a moment. A look that didn't go unnoticed by the professor.

'Professor, you have to believe me, that I know nothing of the whereabouts of your niece, or that my meeting you here this evening is little more than a coincidence. A happy one if I may say. Such is the way that fate lends a hand in the greater affairs of men. I'm sure we can come to an amicable solution while your niece is in safe hands.'

Sergeant Wiggins was desperately trying to get the attention of the professor, who happened to glance in his direction standing by the entrance doors to the bar.

'Herr Hessen,' said the professor holding onto his temper, 'if you will excuse me I have a previous appointment which I must keep. We may not be able to alter what fate has in store for us but we are given choices. I made that choice when my country decided that its glory was greater than the people who made it. Goodbye Herr Hessen, enjoy your champagne. Come, Karl.'

The professor turned to Karl who was waiting patiently behind him and then made his way through the throng of people towards the door and the waiting Sergeant Wiggins.

'Look you, what did he want?' asked Sergeant Wiggins nodding his head in the general direction of the bar.

'It would seem, sergeant,' the professor answered, 'that we have been followed. I have no doubt that I shall be contacted very soon about my niece.'

Inspector Ploddock rushed backstage making his way through the crowded doorway of the stage manager's office.

'How is he?' he asked as he looked at the lifeless body of Maltravers.

'Gone,' was the reply.

'Has an ambulance been called?' he asked.

'Walter has already done it.'

A great commotion was heard outside. The crowd which was nervously looking into the office turned as one to look behind them. Some of the backstage crew were shouting, others were trying to clear a way as the body of the dame was also carried into the stage managers office.

'Bloody hell!' Said the stage manager. 'There's no room in here. You'd better take him to the green room, he ordered, and everybody please go back to your dressing rooms.' He tried to sound authoritative but his voice was shaky.

Inspector Ploddock raised his voice above the crying and confusion of the chorus and young dancers. 'Can you all go back to your dressing rooms and stay there until a member of the police advises you to the contrary?'

Slowly the crowd began to disperse. Granny Probyn clutching Fluffy Yeomans to her chest at last had a chance of getting close to the inspector.

'I suggest that you do likewise, Mrs. Probyn,' the inspector said.

'Inspector, I need to talk to you, you see Mr. Maltravers is, was the murderer. Along with Herr Delfger, he's here. They threatened me you see the papers are...'

'You say that Herr Delfger is here?' asked the inspector cutting Granny Probyn off.

'Yes, before the start of the show, they came to my dressing room they were going to take Fluffy Yeomans...'

'Then he could still be in the building,' he said, cutting her off once again. 'Constable!' He shouted over the receding noise of the chorus, 'seal every exit to the theatre and get Wiggins here now. He should be in the green room. The green room!' He exclaimed and slapped his forehead. The inspector turned to the stage manager. 'Leave the body of Mr. Maltravers here, lock the door and allow no one to enter. Is there another room I can use that is close to the green room?' he asked.

'There's Mr. Reed's office,' answered the stage manager.

'Good,' replied the inspector and rushed off in the direction of the green room leaving Granny Probyn standing open mouthed.

The Delfgers waited quietly in Maltravers dressing room. Neither of them spoke. Vincent's body lay between them on the floor. He was breathing heavily in his enforced slumber. Madam Delfger felt guilty. She looked at the recumbent body with his hands tied behind his back and his feet strapped together with a belt.

'Couldn't we just let him go?' she finally said, not looking at her husband.

'Pah!' Was the only reply.

'Heinz, he helped me,' she pleaded. 'I don't know what I would have done without him. You had left me what was I to do?'

'Pah!' Came the reply.

'That brat was making such a fuss, and you didn't come back. I thought you had gone off with the money. How was I supposed to know that they…'

Her voice trailed away as she looked at her husband's face which had turned a sickly yellowy greeny colour which he had received from the battering of the frying pan.

'Always thinking of yourself. We've lost the boy and any chance of getting money to get away from this place, and you're worried about some pansy who held your hand while you get pissed at the cinema. Pah.'

'What about von Marenbach? He owes you money, we could leave with that. Tonight. We could get the train north, maybe even do a gig or two, then get the ferry to Denmark.'

'We can't even get the bus to Clapham Junction. Marenbach was pushed from his window. And we're going to be next. Our only chance is getting those papers from Maltravers and striking a bargain with Hessen to get our names of that list.'

'What list?'

'Maltravers, had been given an assignment. Unfortunately for him someone else is doing a better job of it than he is. He is as scared as we are, his name has probably gone straight to the top of that list. Our only hope is he finds the documents and we leave tonight, with or without him.'

Madam Delfger looked back down at the recumbent Vincent. 'I knew it would all come to no good,' she said quietly to herself. A vision of Levi Oppenheimer came back to haunt her. She closed her eyes but could still see the look of horror on Oppenheimer's face as he realised that he was falling.

'It was an accident,' she told herself. How had she allowed herself to get into this position? By agreeing with her husband to get rid of the body she had started on the road of no return. True they had got a hundred pounds but that seemed to go very quickly, bribing people, getting their things back from hock. Heinz was going to do one more job, make one more squeeze, and they would have enough money to get away. Where had it all gone wrong?

Vincent gave a snort in his sleep as he tried to change his position.

Herr Delfger looked at his watch. 'Something is wrong,' he said.

He quickly made for the door not bothering to step over Vincent who snorted again. Madam Delfger looked up at her husband.

'What?' she asked.

'Shush,' he said as he opened the door to listen at the corridor. He stuck his head out. He could hear muffled noise coming from the stage, but the corridor remained empty. He made his way to the open stairwell, and looked down. Madam Delfger followed and stuck her head out from behind the door.

'Heinz, what is it?' she whispered loudly.

'Shush,' he hissed back. He tried hard to listen to the commotion on stage. Something was wrong, he knew it. His instinct told him to run, and that was exactly what he did. Without a thought for his wife, Delfger started to scramble down the stone steps, his thoughts running wildly. He planned to make his escape through the scene dock where he had entered. Madam Delfger unsure what was happening followed her husband. She reached the top of the stairwell and loudly hissed, 'Heinz, Heinz what is it? Heinz!'

Madam Delfger looked down at the disappearing body of her husband who was already at stage level. 'Heinz,' she shouted forgetting all pretence of being quiet.

Herr Delfger ignored his wife's calls. His mind was racing. He could hear more clearly the commotion coming from the stage. He could hear shouting from the stage door entrance as Walter tried to get through to the emergency services. A couple of young girls who were part of the chorus hugged each other as they cried. Ignoring everything he made his way to the paint room. In the semi darkness all was quiet. He stopped inside the door. His heart was racing. More people were leaving the stage, he could hear the grief and worry in the voices of people as they were heading back to their dressing rooms. Nobody wanted to be by themselves, seeking comfort in the presence of others. What had happened? His was unable to think clearly. He knew something had happened to Maltravers. That meant somebody was in the theatre, somebody who had that list. He started to sweat. He could feel perspiration on his forehead. He wiped it away with the sleeve of his jacket. Then he heard it. A creaking. Ever so slightly by the large scene dock doors. He strained his ears to blot out the noise from the stage and concentrated on the far side of the room. There it was again. And again. Slowly he made his way passed the large paint frame which took up most of the left hand wall. Careful to keep to the handrail his foot slipped on something wet on the floor as he edged his way in semi darkness. He held out his hand in front of his body uncertain of what lay ahead. The noise grew louder. Stacked in the corner were costume skips presumably waiting to be filled. Herr Delfger knew that the production was to move on to Edinburgh next year so the costumes would be cleaned and packed ready for the journey and storage until they were needed again.

The squeaking happened again. In the shadows he could barely make out the shape of a basket as it moved slightly from side to side making the noise. His heart still pounding in his chest he slowly made to lift the lid. The basket stopped moving. He pulled away his hand and wiped the sweat away from his face again.

He could hear a noise behind him. He crouched behind the baskets, using them as cover as the door through which he entered opened sending a shaft of bright light into the room, before it was closed again with a bang as someone else entered the room.

Inspector Ploddock had reached the green room and had the body of the dame transferred to Mr. Reed's office just in time before Sergeant Wiggins arrived with the professor, Karl, the Oppenheimers and the Dorfellwaffers.

'Good,' he said quietly to Wiggins. 'Don't let anybody leave the theatre. Our killer is on the loose and somewhere here.' Wiggins' eyes widened. 'And, apart from Miss Plimple all the relevant people who are in danger are in this room.'

'Look you,' said Sergeant Wiggins. 'Where's Mrs. Probyn?'

'Why she's just here...' Inspector Ploddock looked around expecting to see Granny Probyn. 'Damn, where is she?' he cursed to himself. 'Go and fetch her Wiggins,' he ordered, 'I left her on the stage.' The sergeant nodded and quickly left.

Professor Meis approached the inspector. 'Forgive me for interrupting, inspector, but I thought you ought to know. I have just been approached by a gentleman in the bar before we left. He introduced himself as Mr. Hessen and alluded that my niece was in safe hands. I expect that someone will try to contact me to secure Jane's release.'

'Hessen, is here?' asked a surprised inspector. 'Well, well well, things do seem to be taking quite a turn.'

'You know the man?'

'Yes, yes, but for a totally different matter, or so I thought.'

Everybody had tried to make themselves comfortable in the green room. Veronica and Ethel Dorfellwaffer fussed over Beauregard Henry who, still recovering from his kidnapping shock, sat quietly staring into space. Napoleon, Odel, and the professor were having a conversation about the properties of the stage hydraulics and their uses in commerce, while Hetty fidgeted with her reticule. Karl sat separately on the other side of the room but his attention was constantly being drawn back to Miss Oppenheimer.

Hetty blushed as she rummaged through her reticule once again.

Karl blushed himself and looked away trying to listen to the professor and the conversation. Slowly his eyes would drift back towards Hetty's direction.

Sergeant Wiggins returned without Granny Probyn. In all the confusion that had been happening on stage and in the wings nobody seemed to know where she was.

Mr. Reed had been summoned backstage. Act two would have to be cancelled. The audience although still unaware that anything was amiss on stage would have to be told. The front of house manager and Mr. Reed were discussing the possible backlash if they didn't offer to return the audiences money. Never one to let a crisis get in the way of running a business Mr. Reed with the backing of the management were discussing the possibility of continuing the second half when they were interrupted by Inspector Ploddock.

'Gentlemen, if you please,' he said, 'someone will have to make an announcement. Calm must be kept while an orderly evacuation can take place.'

'But, inspector,' boomed Mr. Reed, 'why must we cancel?'

'With respect, Mr. Reed, I appreciate that in theatrical circles the show must go on at all costs, but I have to insist it is too dangerous to continue. There is a murderer on the loose in your theatre and if he is not stopped there could be many more casualties. If necessary I will invoke the law and close this production forcibly.' Inspector Ploddock was incandescent with rage.

Mr. Reed, for the first time in his life, was struck dumb as to what to say under the visible force of the inspector's speech. He opened and closed his mouth like a fish out of water before he finally managed a nod of his head.

'I shall leave you gentlemen to make that speech while I organise the evacuation.' He nodded to the men as he left, still seething with the stupidity of the men who gave no thought to others apart from their own greed and glory.

The inspector summoned Sergeant Wiggins to oversee the removal of the audience and to make sure that their murderer didn't leave with them. An impossible situation as neither of them had any idea of who that murderer was.

'Damn,' said Inspector Ploddock again. 'Where is Granny Probyn and her little old lady?'

'Inspector?' queried Wiggins.

'Wiggins, I've made a terrible mistake, and I think that Mrs. Probyn and Miss Plimple may pay the price of it.'

'Sir?' Wiggins said, he didn't want to interrupt his superior.

'We must find them as quickly as possible.'

'Yes, Sir. But Sir, all the men are supervising the clearing of the auditorium. There's over two thousand people in there. It's going to take some time. We don't have enough men to do that and search backstage.' Wiggins was stating the obvious and he knew it. He just wanted to clarify his own position. Should he take some men and search the backstage area again?

'We'll just have to commandeer help from our friends in here,' indicating the green room, 'and some of the backstage crew we can trust. You look after the audience I'll handle back here.'

Sergeant Wiggins nodded and turned to go to muster his men.

'And bring Herr Hessen backstage,' he shouted as an afterthought.

'Rightho,' said Wiggins as he disappeared down the corridor.

Scene 11

An unearthly quiet had overtaken the backstage of the theatre. After the recent chaos and noise only a slight hum of whispered voices as the chorus, cast and dancers who, had stayed together rather than going separately to their dressing rooms, discussed the situation. It seemed a general consensus of opinion that there was safety in numbers.

Having their dressing room closest to the central stairwell, von Stutlz, Mr. Pleach along with other members of the company were waiting with the door open to catch any news.

Madam Delfger had returned to Maltravers' dressing room and barricaded the door. Now that her husband had shown his true colours she had no other option, she wasn't going to be taken alive. She looked down at the sleeping figure of Vincent and for the first time in her life a wave of motherly affection steeled her nerves. She would fight like a mother lioness protecting her cub.

Leaving the ladies under the protection of Professor Meis, Inspector Ploddock assisted by Napoleon, Karl, Odel, Walter, Jimmy and a few of the crew went in search of Granny Probyn.

'I suggest we split into two groups,' he suggested. 'One start at the top of the building checking all rooms while the other work their way up.'

There was a general nodding of heads.

'Right then,' said the inspector as if he were weighing up teams for a five aside football match, 'Napoleon, Odel, Karl, take young Jimmy and start on the upstairs dressing rooms. Meanwhile, myself Walter and the others will start under the stage. Hopefully we should meet in the middle with our man.'

Again a nodding of approval all round as they set off to their respective tasks.

Granny Probyn fumbled around in the dark. She could feel the comforting presence of Fluffy Yeomans as he pushed against her left leg. Inspector Ploddock obviously had too much to think on and after seeing Herr Delfger fleetingly pass a group of chorus girls she determined that he shouldn't escape justice. Granny Probyn swallowed her fears and followed him into the dark scene dock area and paint room.

As the door to the paint room closed behind her she stood for a moment to let her eyes adjust to the dark.

Herr Delfger could only glimpse the outline of a shadow before the door closed shutting out any further visibility. He crouched further behind the costume basket.

Then to his consternation the basket began to creek again as something inside jostled. Convinced that the murderer was following him Herr Delfger was sweating, preying that the gentle squeak from the basket wouldn't betray his position and that it couldn't be heard across the room.

Fortunately for Herr Delfger Granny Probyn wasn't that good when it came to her aural senses, and so remained quite literally in the dark as to his whereabouts. Fluffy Yeomans on the other hand was more adept in these situations and focusing his attention made a beeline in the direction of the sound. His eyes wide, allowing him to see what others couldn't, he made his way quietly towards the stack of baskets.

Miss Plimple was aware that someone was in the room, she had heard a door open and close. Wriggling her body as much as she could made the basket creak against it's corners. Closing her eyes to the pain in her shoulders and legs she wriggled as much as possible.

She thought she could hear breathing, stifled gasping coming from somewhere close to her head. She tried again to wriggle causing the basket to creak more. Surely someone must be able to hear.

She tried to shout but her voice caught in the rag that had been stuffed into her mouth.

Granny Probyn gasped as she felt Fluffy Yeomans leave her. Frightened to call out she fumbled her way to the wall, feeling her way back towards the door. "Surely there must be a light switch?" she thought as she ran her hands in a wide arc across the wall. After several attempts she finally managed to locate the large Bakelite knob with it's familiar switch in the centre.

The switch gave a satisfying 'clunk' as the paint room was instantly bathed in light.

Granny Probyn felt a little more secure now that she could see. 'It's no use hiding Herr Delfger,' she called, 'I know you are here. There is no escape. The building is surrounded by police. I suggest that you give yourself up before it is too late.'

Herr Delfger blinked as the light blinded him for a second, at the same time Fluffy Yeomans struck.

Like a banshee with his claws armed Fluffy Yeomans attacked. Herr Delfger screamed as his face already damaged with bruising received a vicious swipe of lethal talons.

Spitting and hissing Fluffy Yeomans kept up a barrage of blows as Herr Delfger desperately fought off the wild beast.

Miss Plimple could hear a mass of commotion inches away from her head. She joggled and wiggled as much as she could to attract the attention of whoever was on the outside.

Granny Probyn rushed to the corner of the room where the costume trunks where stacked. Shouting at Fluffy Yeomans to stop, Herr Delfger finally managed to free himself from the claws of his assailant and buried himself into the corner of the room. Fluffy

Yeomans blocked his escape as Granny Probyn joined them. Catching her breath she sat upon the basket which held the now overwrought body of Miss Plimple.

'Well done, Fluffy,' Granny Probyn gasped, 'you've just caught yourself a big fish.'

Fluffy Yeomans his fur on edge meowed a "thank you" but remained blocking the escape of Herr Delfger.

'Please, please,' said Herr Delfger, 'please I never meant to hurt you, honestly. It was Maltravers. He did it, he said if I didn't help him he would kill me, please! You have to believe me.'

'Why should I believe you, Mr. Delfger?' replied Granny Probyn. 'Every time there has been a murder you have had a hand in it.'

'Murder!' Exclaimed Herr Delfger.

'Yes, murder Herr Delfger. And you are the murderer.'

'No, no, you've got it all wrong.' Herr Delfger's mind was racing. 'I didn't kill anyone. My wife, she killed him, Oppenheimer I mean, Maltravers, he killed the boy. Please I didn't kill anyone.'

'We shall leave that for the police.' Granny Probyn said.

Miss Plimple was desperate to make her presence known. Making one last immense effort she kicked hard on the wicker work basket.

'Who's that?' said Granny Probyn turning in surprise as the noise of someone kicking the basket had happened near her. Fluffy Yeomans was also on the alert.

Granny Probyn got off the basket and walked to the other edge.

'Fluffy, you keep an eye on Mr. Delfger, while I find out...'

The basket was kicked again.

Granny Probyn's heart was fluttering.

'Something's in here,' she mimed to Fluffy who was looking at the basket.

Granny Probyn slowly opened the lid which gave a squeak of protest in it's hinges.

The basket jumped again causing Granny Probyn to jump as well.

'I know you're in there,' she said as the costumes wiggled in the trunk. 'Come out before someone gets hurt.'

The costumes wriggled some more.

Finally, when she had got no response, Granny Probyn started to slowly take off the top layer of costumes. The basket was now rocking furiously as Miss Plimple in a last ditch effort was trying to communicate her whereabouts.

Finally the last layer was removed revealed a very dishevelled Miss Plimple crying with relief.

Granny Probyn quickly undid the tape that was fastened around Miss Plimple's mouth.

'Oh, thank God you're all right!' said Granny Probyn as she released the tape. 'We have been so worried.'

Miss Plimple, overcome with emotion, burst into tears once again.

Herr Delfger was still cornered. His eyes were out on storks as Miss Plimple emerged from the trunk.

'Well, it seems that we have Herr Delfger to thank for your release, although I fancy, if Fluffy Yeomans hadn't interfered the outcome would have been far different,' said Granny Probyn.

'It wasn't Mr. Delfger,' said Miss Plimple through her sobs, 'it was Maltravers. I was so stupid, after all the warning's I didn't think!'

'That's right, Mrs. Probyn,' said Herr Delfger, stepping forward only to step back again as Fluffy Yeomans hissed loudly. Herr Delfger cowered again in the corner. 'It wasn't me, Maltravers, he did it, ask him. He's the one you're looking for.'

'Unluckily for you Mr. Delfger, we are unable to do that, unless you know of a good medium?' replied Granny Probyn.

'You mean he's dead!' exclaimed Miss Plimple and Herr Delfger as one.

'Please! Please, Mrs. Probyn, you have to help me. They'll kill me too.' Herr Delfger crying slumped back into the corner of the room. His life as far as he could see it was over, his only possible escape from death was Granny Probyn and the police, 'Please, I'll do anything, anything, don't let them kill me please!' He begged while sobbing to himself.

Fluffy Yeomans relaxed his guard, his fur no longer standing on edge he was his normal small self, as he sat.

'Well Fluffy,' said Granny Probyn, 'you keep an eye on Mr. Delfger while I go and get us some help.'

Fluffy Yeomans meowed.

'There's a good boy. Now, Jane,' she said addressing Miss Plimple who was still slumped in the basket, 'I think we should try and move you to more comfortable surroundings. Do you think you can walk?'

'I'll try,' said Miss Plimple as she attempted to stand but her legs gave way again. 'Please could I have a glass of water?' she asked as pins and needles attacked her arms and legs.

'Of course, dear,' said Granny Probyn, 'you sit there and try to gather your strength while I go and get some help.'

'Thank you,' said Miss Plimple trying to hold back more tears.

Napoleon and his group left the inspector and almost ran up the central staircase to the top floor.

Napoleon and Karl stood at either end of the corridor while Jimmy and Odel opened every door and searched each room before moving on to the next.

After two rooms containing props and furniture Odel made his way to the third door.

'Don't open that door,' called Jimmy as Odel had turned the key in it's lock.

Odel taken by surprise looked back up the corridor to the sight of a worried looking Jimmy.

Before either had a chance to say anything more, the door flew open and two whirling dervishes whistled past Odel in their bid for freedom knocking him against the opposite wall.

Mac and Morag raced in opposite directions from each other. Karl and Napoleon hearing the commotion both turned to see Jimmy spreading his hands as wide as possible like a shepherd trying to herd his flock into a pen. Odel, dazed by the quickness of the twins, stood looking up then down the corridor after the two tykes.

Karl taking his cue from Jimmy spread his arms wide in the vain hope that Morag, who was quickly closing the gap between them, would stop. Morag on the other hand merely side swiped Karl and was free and running down the stairs at the end of the corridor. Mac on the other hand had tried to out-manoeuvre Jimmy who managed to grab hold of the woollen tank top Mac was wearing which sufficiently slowed him down enough for Napoleon to catch and hold the squirming child.

Karl started to give chase to Morag whose skinny legs were jumping the stone steps three at a time. Odel seeing that Napoleon and Jimmy had managed to curtail Mac went in pursuit of the other two. Odel had just reached the main stairwell to see far below him Morag reach the first floor and Karl trailing far behind her on the second story landing. Shouting down the stairwell to Karl that the girl had already reached the ground floor Karl stopped to look up at Odel who was looking down.

The noise and commotion had brought Julian Pleach, Herr Stutlz and the rest of the cast who had huddled in their dressing room out into the corridor.

'Don't let her get away,' Odel shouted down the stairwell.

Karl nodded, and was immediately set upon by Julian Pleach and other members of the cast.

'We have him!' Cried a joyous Mr. Pleach back up the stairs to Odel.

251

Odel who had started down the staircase in pursuit stopped at the third floor on hearing the cries from Mr. Pleach.

'No!' He shouted, 'let him go, get the girl!' He cried in return.

'What?' answered Julian.

'The girl, the girl!'

Karl was fighting off the cast who held him fast. 'You have the wrong person.' He was shouting as confusion broke out among the rest of the cast. Odel reach the first floor as Julian and Karl finally managed break free of each other.

'You let her get away,' said Odel.

'Sorry,' said Julian, 'we thought, well... we heard all this shouting, and well you see I didn't recognise this chap and well...'

Julian trailed off and looked around for support from the rest of the cast who nodded their assent.

'Well she's gone, whoever she was,' said Odel.

'She must be one of the twins,' said a young dancer.

'One of the twins?' Odel queried looking at Julian.

'Hmm,' Said Julian. 'Mr. Reed returned from Edinburgh with a couple of feral Scots twins. He intends to star them in next years panto of "Babes in the Wood." I believe they were locked in a room somewhere, out of harms way, as they caused havoc in the paint shop.

'Well Napoleon and Jimmy have managed to hold onto one of them so the other won't go too far I suppose,' said Odel.

Meanwhile below, Inspector Ploddock, Walter and some of the crew searched yet again beneath the stage when the sounds of shouting reached the depths of the theatre.

'Sounds like they've caught somebody,' said the inspector to the group. He decided to divide his group leaving Walter to finish off the search while he and the rest made their way back up to the stage level and the commotion happening above.

Walter continued methodically looking behind and into all

the storage areas beneath the stage finally coming to a small room where the electricians kept their lanterns and cables. The room was normally locked with a padlock and when he saw that the lock had been smashed he decided to investigate further. Walter slowly opened the wooden door. Inside the small room all was dark. He could make out from the light bleeding through the doorway shelves specially made so that the lanterns could hang rather than rest on them.

Walter flashed his torchlight across the shelves. All seemed quiet. Cables hung in great coils from hooks along one wall as he made his way to the back of the storeroom. Keeping his torch ahead of him the beam cut through the darkness like a knife. The soft glow of the working lights lit the door way behind him but didn't pierce the darkness this far back. Satisfied that there was no one in the room Walter tuned and made his way back to the open door.

Suddenly a figure moved past the light of the door, Walter shone his torch trying to keep up with the moving figure. But the light only bounced off the hanging lanterns.

'Who's there?' he called. 'I know's yer in 'ere. Yer may as well give up now,' he said, keeping the torch moving through the shelves.

Walter turned. He had heard a noise from behind him. The light from his torch slashed through the dark and came to rest on a face.

'You!' he exclaimed, 'but you're supposed to be Mrs. Probyn's friend. Why?'

The question died on Walter's lips as a heavy iron bar cracked his skull.

Walter dropped to the floor like a sack of potatoes. The torch spinning from his hand smashed against the shelves breaking the glass and sending the storeroom back into darkness.

Scene 12

Granny Probyn was sent flying as the door to the paint room burst inwards catching her on the arm. Morag raced past like a bat out of hell, into the paint room, climbed one of the frames and finally came to rest hanging like a chimpanzee with a huge grin on her face. Granny Probyn tried to lift her arm to open the door but a pain shot through her making her feel decidedly weak.

Miss Plimple and Herr Delfger watched with surprise as Morag happily swung from the paint frame without a care in the world.

'Are you all right?' Miss Plimple finally managed to ask as Granny Probyn eased herself onto a bench while she held her now throbbing right arm.

No sooner had Granny Probyn managed to sit than the door to the paint room was once more thrown open. This time Inspector Ploddock stood blocking the door followed by Julian Pleach, Karl, Odel and most of the cast.

The inspector could hardly believe his eyes as he looked around the room. Not only had he found Granny Probyn, but Miss Plimple, and the murderer safely guarded by Fluffy Yeomans.

'How did you do it?' he asked Granny Probyn as she sat on a bench.

'Do what?' replied Granny Probyn.

'Save Miss Plimple for one and catch the killer?' he said.

At this Herr Delfger, Miss Plimple and Granny Probyn all began to tell their side of the story.

Inspector Ploddock looked from one to the next trying to concentrate on each of their stories. 'One at a time please.' He said. 'But first I think we had better get you fixed up,' nodding towards Granny Probyn's arm.

Inspector Ploddock turned to the crowd behind him. 'Everybody could you please go back to your dressing rooms,' he shouted, then addressed Julian. 'If you would be so kind as to help Mrs. Probyn to the green room, Odel, if you could help Miss Plimple, I shall take care of our other guest.'

'I didn't do it, I swear I didn't do it,' pleaded Herr Delfger falling to his knees.

'He's right, inspector,' said Granny Probyn. 'It was Mr. Maltravers. He kidnapped Miss Plimple.'

The inspector looked at Miss Plimple. She in turn nodded and burst into tears.

'I was so stupid after all the warnings that you and Mrs. Probyn gave us,' she sobbed.

Odel pushed past the inspector and made his way to assist Miss Plimple, still weak from her ordeal.

'Come along, Miss Plimple,' Odel said helping her from the basket.

'You too,' said Julian taking Granny Probyn by her left arm and steadying her as she stood.

Inspector Ploddock nodded to Mr. Perry the assistant stage manager and a couple of the crew who picked Herr Delfger off his knees.

'But this leaves me with a rather sneaky feeling in my stomach, Mrs. Probyn. You see, if as you say Mr. Maltravers was our murderer, then who murdered Mr. Maltravers?'

'And Mr. Beleno,' piped up Mr. Perry.

'Indeed,' said the inspector. 'Maltravers couldn't have done that murder as he was on stage at the time. It seems our murderer is still at large.'

'Then who could it be?' asked Granny Probyn. 'I mean there are no other little old ladies.'

Twenty minutes later everybody was seated in the green room. Miss Plimple had been reunited with her uncle Professor Meis, Julian had been reunited with Hetty who shyly avoided glancing in Karl's direction. Granny Probyn had been seen by the company doctor who pronounced that her arm wasn't broken only badly bruised and that Miss Plimple was only dehydrated and in need of lots of rest but otherwise was okay.

Sergeant Wiggins and his team had finally managed to take the names and contact details of the audience and cleared the theatre before returning to the inspector with Mr. Hessen and his family backstage.

'Boyo, that was a job!' He said to the inspector as he joined them outside the green room. 'I've brought Mr. Hessen as you asked.'

Inspector Ploddock nodded then addressed Hessen and his family. The little girl was bored and disappointed as they never saw the second act and was in no mood to be kept hanging around.

'I'm sorry that you have been kept waiting, Herr Hessen,' said the inspector, but it seems that you haven't been entirely honest with me.

'In what way inspector?' asked Hessen with no sign of politeness. 'I answered all of your questions truthfully. If you cannot ask the right question how am I supposed to answer?'

The inspector bridled at this remark but decided to let it pass as Hessen was obviously livid that he and his family had being kept waiting.

'Perhaps I should get a constable to escort your wife and daughter home while we have a little chat,' suggested the inspector. 'That way no one is inconvenienced any further.' As the girl was trying to squirm free from her mother's hand.

'I think that would be an excellent suggestion,' said Mrs. Hessen then to her husband, 'I shall take the car.' With which she turned on her heels and dragged her daughter behind her.

Inspector Ploddock nodded to Sergeant Wiggins to follow Mrs. Hessen then continued talking, 'You see Mr. Hessen I have a problem, and I think that you may have the answer.'

'What makes you say that? I have already told you of my business relationship with von Marenbach, what else is there to know?'

'Well for instance, how is it you come to know of a certain Professor von Meis?'

'As I said before, inspector, I am a business man and it is my business to know people. The right sort of people.' He added. 'I had not met the professor until tonight.'

'So you admit that you talked with the professor?' asked the inspector.

'Since when is it a crime to talk to a mutual acquaintance in the bar of a theatre, or is it that Great Britain is not the land of free speech.'

'Quite,' said the inspector, 'would you mind telling me what your conversation was about?'

'Let me see, I introduced myself and my wife and daughter then I suggested that we have a meeting at a more appropriate time and place to discuss a business proposition.'

'I see, and what was his reply.'

'Rather rude, if I may say so, accused me of kidnapping his niece I believe.'

'And why would he do that?' asked the inspector.

'I haven't the slightest idea. I have never met his niece,' said Hessen smugly.

'Then maybe I can introduce you?' said the inspector.

Hessen looked rather taken aback.

'You seem surprised,' said the inspector.

'Not at all, inspector, only... well obviously the professor is suffering from a paranoia complex. Of course I'm no expert on these matters but if I were you, inspector, I would take anything that the professor says with a pinch of salt. Isn't that what you English say?'

'Indeed, Mr. Hessen, indeed. But, if as you say that Professor Meis has a paranoia complex, how can you account for the number of dead bodies which seem to be accumulating in the city morgue and certain missing documents of his?'

Hessen smiled and opened his arms wide in a gesture of search me. 'I have no idea, inspector,' he said.

'Well, it seems to me that your business associate Mr. von Marenbach was somehow involved with these papers, and I have it on good authority that a certain Mr. Maltravers was also in your employ. He is another of those bodies. Doesn't it seem a coincidence that two of your associates have ended up, how shall I put it? Dead!'

Hessen was getting hot under the collar, but kept his cool for the inspector. 'I do not know where you have got your information about this Mr. Maltravers. He has never worked for me.'

'Are you saying that you have never met him?' asked the inspector.

Hessen, aware that the inspector was trying to trap him thought quickly through his options and decided to tell half the truth.

'He came to several meetings my wife held at our house, I believe I met him there, in fact that is the reason why we are here tonight. My wife is a great patron of the arts, inspector. Did Mr. Maltravers not give the performance of his life this evening?'

The inspector couldn't take this line of questioning any further. He had a statement from Herr Delfger that Maltravers was working for Hessen but no proof, and with his chief breathing down his neck he needed to do everything by the book so, until such time that proof could be found, he had to let Mr. Hessen go.

'I take it that our little conversation is over,' Hessen said.

'One last thing, before you go, I believe that you gave Mr. Maltravers a list. Could you tell me what was on it?'

Hessen couldn't help himself and blushed red, 'I er... well it was ...'

'Good night Mr. Hessen,' said the inspector and returned to the green room smiling to himself.

Jimmy came bursting into the green room, 'Inspector, inspector, quick, it's Walter, 'es been hurt!'

'What!' came the cry from nearly everybody in the room.

'Down under the stage by the lighting store room,' gasped Jimmy, 'done 'im in good and proper. Mr. Perry is brinin' 'im up now wiv a couple of crew.'

The inspector lunged for the door. 'Wiggins,' he shouted, 'WIGGINS!'

'Yes, Sir,' Wiggins said rushing up the corridor from the stage where he was trying to console a distraught Mr. Reed.

'Where are the men?' he asked.

'Still in their positions a couple have gone across the road to the Butchered Calf for a quick half. But...'

'Then get them back here and quick. He's still here. By god, the nerve of the man. Well don't just stand there man. Quick!'

Sergeant Wiggins ran to the stage door shouting at Constable Jones.

'What happened to your search?' the inspector asked Napoleon who was among the crowd behind him.

'Well... we sort of got interrupted by the twins and then Mrs. Probyn and Miss Plimple were found and well we didn't get any further than...'

'Fine, Wiggins, where are those men?' he shouted down the corridor.

'Coming, Sir,' shouted Wiggins from the stage door vestibule.

'You had all better stay in here, until we find this killer. He's still on the loose and I don't want any more bodies tonight.'

Mr. Perry and a couple of men were carrying Walter on a make shift stretcher.

'Did you call an ambulance?' Mr. Perry asked Jimmy.

'Lor, I forgot,' said a shamed Jimmy.

Inspector Ploddock and the rest looked over the frail body of Walter.

'He's lost a lot of blood,' said Mr. Perry.

'Can you hear me, Walter? Do you know who did it? Who did this to you?'

Walter opened his eyes and tried to focus. He looked at the crowd of people starring down at him. Karl and Professor Meis, then he recognised the faces of Miss Plimple, Mr. Pleach, Odel and Hetty, Napoleon Packard and his wife holding their son and behind them Ethel Dorfellwaffer, and Granny Probyn.

'It was her! She did it!' cried Walter and fainted back onto the stretcher.

'Quick get him to the hospital,' said Inspector Ploddock to Mr. Perry, as all eyes turned to Granny Probyn.

Ostracised by Walter's accusation Granny Probyn sat in the green room by herself with Fluffy Yeomans on her lap. Ethel Dorfellwaffer, Napoleon, Veronica and Beauregard Henry sat as a group as far away as possible. Odel and Hetty with Mr. Pleach sat quietly together, the only conversation was from Professor Meis and Miss Plimple who had so much to catch up on.

They could all hear shouting coming from the rest of the building as the police checked and searched once again for the killer.

Granny Probyn wracked her brain as to why Walter should accuse her of hitting him. Why would he do that? Maybe he was in concussion and not thinking properly she reasoned, but the others had suddenly turned cold towards her, even her oldest friend Ethel. Granny Probyn looked across the room to where she sat huddled in a group with her family.

Granny Probyn looked at the family. She almost hated the way that Veronica smothered that brat Beauregard Henry and how utterly soppy Napoleon was. Her mind drifted to her own family, her mother and father, her two lost boys, Beryl with whom she had never been close. The same as she had never been close to her mother. Was that the reason Beryl and her husband now chose to live so far away? Since her own husband Abercrombie had died, and having no brothers or sisters, she had to admit it, she was all alone in the world, apart from Fluffy Yeomans. She really had no reason to get up in the morning.

Sitting, holding back the tears, she tickled the chin of her only comfort in life while he gently kneaded her lap.

Then slowly, as if a fog lifted from her mind a thought occurred to her. Of course, who else could it have been? Maybe Miss Christie had been right all along, maybe there was another old lady who had been jilted at the church. How could she have been so dimwitted, Miss de la Mouche had said it so many times. 'Mother!'

The twins had been reunited, or to be frank Mac had been released into the paint room where the two youngsters hung from the frames as if they had been born in the trees. As they showed no sign of wanting to come down or escape, Inspector Ploddock gave instructions that they could stay where they were, he had more important things to worry about. Somewhere loose in the theatre was a madman, a ruthless killer. Now with the building empty he had at his command all of his officers. He sent Sergeant Wiggins with half the contingent to the top floors to check and work their way down while the other half was to work upwards. He would stay at stage level and co-ordinate the search. On command as each room and floor was checked it was secured by an officer. All the exits had been sealed and officers placed strategically so that the killer could not leave the building. It was only a matter of time before the net closed in.

'All clear on the top floor,' Sergeant Wiggins shouted down the stairwell.

'All clear under the stage,' came another voice.

'All clear on the third floor,' another voice called.

Sergeant Wiggins left an officer guarding the top floor and made his way with his men to the second floor where the chorus girls, boys, dancers and others members of the cast had their dressing rooms.

Madam Delfger sat with Vincent's head in her lap as she stroked his head. Vincent now released from his restraints slept like a babe. She could hear the police closing in. She knew that she would be caught. There was nowhere for her to hide. As long as Vincent was safe she said to herself. She thought of her husband and spat on the floor. How could she have ever been in love with him. Perhaps they had just drifted apart, to late for that now. She could hear the shouts of the police as they checked each room. Suddenly the knob turned. Rattled, turned again. There was a loud knock. Voices called outside.

Sergeant Wiggins on the other side of the door asked who's dressing room was this.

'Mr. Maltravers,' piped Jimmy.

'Right, lads, break it down,' said the sergeant to his men, 'we don't have time to waste.'

Two officers each struck the door with their shoulders, each time the door lurched in its frame but held.

'Look you, boys, put your backs into it,' said Sergeant Wiggins.

The door slowly opened. Madam Delfger filled the doorway.

'My, my, look what we have here.' Said the sergeant. 'We've got him sir, or should I say we've got her,' shouted the sergeant. Madam Delfger and the sergeant walked quietly through the throng of police officers to the stairwell.

'Sergeant, we've got another body,' said Constable Jones as he looked into the dressing room and seeing Vincent lying on the chaise lounge.

'We have another body Sir,' Wiggins called down the stairwell.

'Damn,' swore the inspector. He could just hear his chief "three dead bodies and one critical in hospital!" as he started up the steps to the second floor.

'Well, well well,' he said as he reached the top step and saw the dejected frame of a woman, 'if it isn't Madam Delfger. You'll be pleased to know that your husband is safe in the hands of my officers and is as we speak on his way to Scotland Yard where, I'm glad to say, you will join him and be charged for the murder of well let me

262

see...' the inspector held up his hand and pointed to his first finger, '... Mr. Maltravers,' to the next finger, 'Mr. Beleno,' the next, 'Mr. von Marenbach....'

'I never did any of those things,' she said. 'Neither did my husband, he's too much of a coward.'

'And what of Levi Oppenheimer and our friend in the dressing room?' Inspector Ploddock nodded down the corridor.

'Herr Oppenheimer was an accident, he made to grab me and fell down the stairs, I never meant to kill him and Vincent,' she said, 'he's not dead, only sleeping.'

'Take her away,' he order Sergeant Wiggins and walked down the corridor to Maltravers' dressing room.

Gerty sat in Granny Probyn's dressing room idly playing with a tassel on one of the cushions of her armchair while she waited. Unconcerned, she also could hear the shouts of the police officers as they worked their way throughout the theatre. She would bide her time and, be either caught by the police or, if she was lucky, kill that interfering old woman. Gerty waited.

As Inspector Ploddock entered the green room all eyes turned to look at him. He in turn looked at each of them then said, 'We have caught the second murderer, none other Madam Delfger.'

Cries of relief came from all around.

'It is only a matter of time before we work out who killed who.'

Hetty sniffled into her handkerchief.

'As for your uncle, Miss Oppenheimer, I believe that his death was an accident. As to the rest, we shall have to wait until I have interrogated our suspects.'

'Does this mean we are free to go?' asked Karl.

'You have always been free to go, Mr. Leibknecht. I only wanted you here for your own safety.'

'What about Beauregard Henry?' asked Veronica.

'I'm sure under your loving care he will be fine,' said the inspector.

'Yes, yes, but what if they should try and kidnap him again?'

'I hardly think that is likely, you see...'

'What about the professors papers?' asked Odel cutting in. 'We still don't know who took them or where they are. There could be others still waiting in the wings as it were.'

'Indeed,' said the professor, 'what about that Hessen chap he could quite easily be one of them.'

'As to Mr. Hessen, I believe I will have sufficient evidence to arrest him. For the papers well,' the inspector shrugged. 'I think the secret may have died with Mr. Maltravers.'

'Not quite,' said Granny Probyn.

All eyes turned to Granny Probyn, although exonerated by what the inspector had just said there was still some frostiness in the air.

'I believe I may know of their whereabouts and I agree with Veronica. There is still a killer at large.'

Scene 13

How very clever of you,' said Gerty standing in the doorway holding a Luger pistol pointing at Granny Probyn. 'It's a shame I didn't finish you off before. It would seem you have brains in that thick skull of yours.'

'Gerty!' Said an astonished Ethel. 'Why?'

'Hello, Ethel, it's been a long time.'

Everybody was confused, here was a strange woman the spiting image of Ethel and they both knew each other.

'Would somebody like to explain,' said a bemused Inspector Ploddock.

'Shall you tell them or shall I, Ethel, or maybe your old friend here? Maybe she could show us how clever she really is,' said Gerty pointing the gun once more in Granny Probyn's direction.

'Well,' Granny Probyn ventured, 'I'm not sure what I should call you, I mean, I only know you as Mother! or should I say the mother of Miss de la Mouche. But what I don't understand is why did you kill your own daughter?'

'She was weak, she was going to plead with that Plimple woman for the papers, instead of doing her duty,' Gerty said.

'And Mucus, I mean Mr. Drillby what about him?'

'He was easy. He wouldn't tell me where the professor was intending to go, even though the two of them had been in communication. You see the party knew all about the professor's plans to escape. We couldn't let that happen. Not with such important work for the fatherland.'

'Pah,' shouted the professor. 'It wasn't the Fatherland that wanted my work, it was the Nazi thugs in charge...'

'I'm still confused as to who gave the orders,' said Granny Probyn cutting off the professor, 'Herr Delfger and his wife, if you don't mind my saying inspector were hardly, well...'

'He's a petty crook, I would have dealt with them sooner or later...' said Gerty.

'What about Mr. von Marenbach?' asked Granny Probyn.

'He was an upstart, he wanted to take over the party, I couldn't have that you see I needed Hessen's protection. He is going to get me back to the Fatherland.'

'How could you Gerty, you're my little sister,' asked Ethel again, 'why?'

'I couldn't do what you did Ethel, bowing and scraping to those Jews. Look how they treated you. Like dirt. Their dirty little slave girl, clean out the fire, polish the silver, wait at tables.'

'It was a job, Gerty, I took that job so that you wouldn't have to. I took that job because they were good kind people Gerty. They helped you. They helped me.'

'They used you, Ethel. They sat with their millions in their big houses telling the rest of us what to do. Letting the rest of us do the dirty work. So I thought if I had to do dirty work I may as well do the dirty work of the party. The bourgeois government weren't all that happy so the party helped me escape.'

'And you think that the party will help you again?' said a voice from behind.

Gerty turned to see Curruthers holding a gun standing in front of her blocking the door.

Without a moment's pause Gerty fired two shots, and dashed from the room as Curruthers held his stomach and collapsed to the floor.

Fluffy Yeomans jumped from Granny Probyn's lap as Hetty and Miss Plimple screamed, Inspector Ploddock after a moments hesitation, gave chase while Napoleon and Mr. Pleach were the first to reach Curruthers.

'Not a very good spy am I?' he said.

Gerty ran down the corridor, she knew that the police were still covering the exits. Her only chance of escape would be through the scene dock. Inspector Ploddock, followed by Odel and Karl, was soon on her tail. She stopped at the door to the paint room turning to fire her gun again. With nothing to stop the bullets Inspector Ploddock threw himself onto the ground, as Fluffy Yeomans ran past and the bullets went whizzing over his head. One hit Karl in the shoulder who was spun around by the force of the bullet as it shattered his collarbone leaving him slumped in a heap against the wall.

'Are you alright?' shouted Inspector Ploddock back down the corridor to Odel.

'Yes,' Odel shouted, 'don't let her get away,' as Gerty disappeared into the paint room followed closely by Fluffy Yeomans.

Inspector Ploddock was scrambling back onto his feet and as he reached the door he heard another two shots fired.

Gingerly he opened the door of the paint room and looked inside. The twins were both climbing down from the frame nearest the door.

'It weren't our fault mister,' said Mac.

The inspector followed their path and noticed that Fluffy Yeomans was sitting unperturbed on the floor next to the open trough where the paint frame travels into the floor licking his paw and cleaning behind his ears.

'It was the cat,' Morag said, 'he tripped her up.'

Next to Fluffy Yeomans was the bloated purple face of Gerty de la Mouche as she hung by the neck, her body in the trench caught in the ropes of the paint frame.

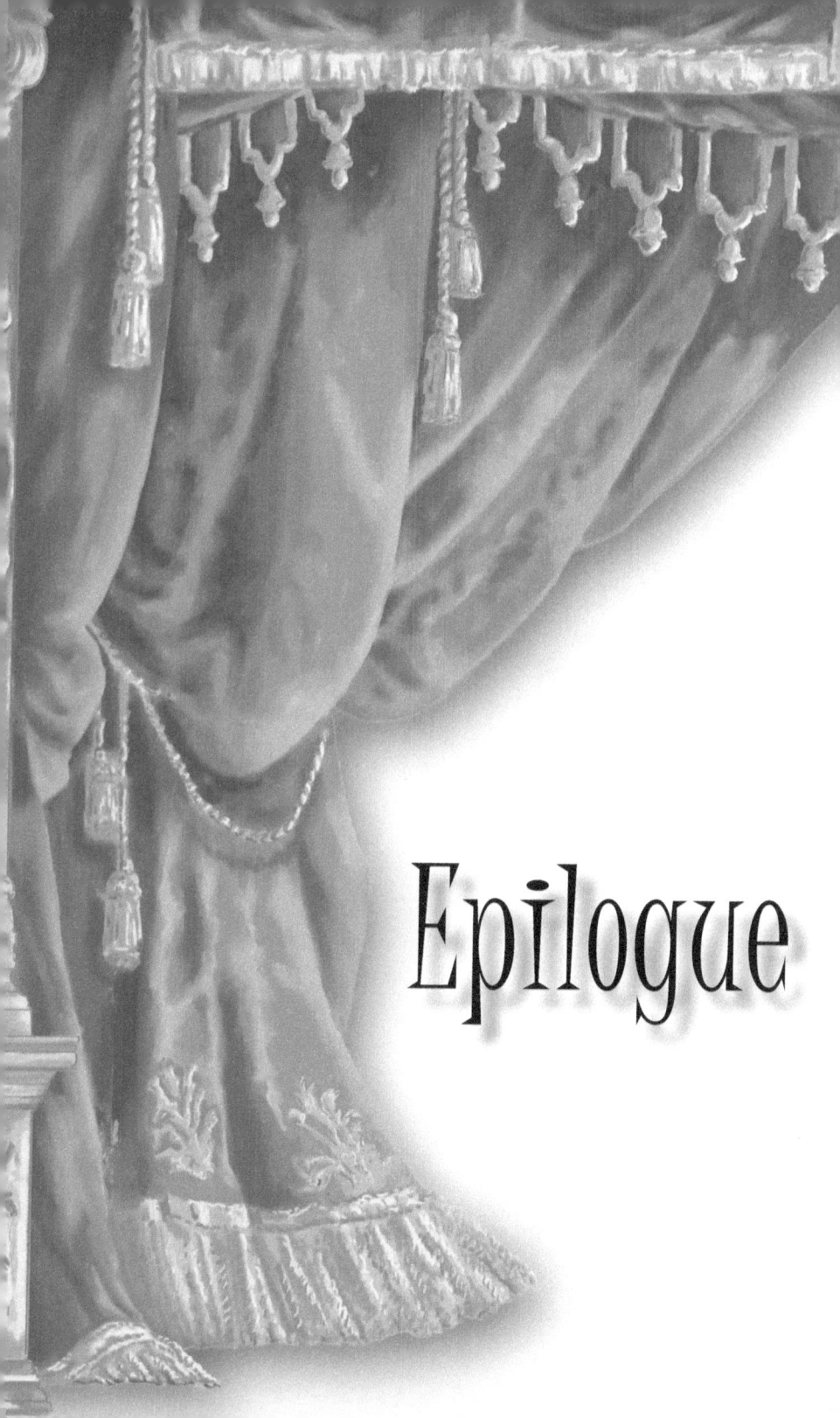

Epilogue

After being questioned by Sergeant Wiggins, Vincent was eventually allowed to go home the next day. Nursing a humdinger of a headache from the morphine and chloroform which Maltravers had administered, Queenie almost dragged him up the stairs to their little flat above the café as he tried to explain the reason why he had stayed out for a second night. This time Queenie wasn't so forgiving.

Odel cancelled their plans to travel to America and Hetty began arranging for her forthcoming wedding to Mr. Pleach.

Miss Plimple and the professor on the other hand decided that America would suit them better, and Karl was happy to follow.

As the saviour of her baby, Beauregard Henry, Veronica looked upon her heroic husband Napoleon in a new light. While Beauregard Henry himself recovered enough from his ordeal and returned to his old classmates a hero. His stories got bigger on each retelling.

Ethel Dorfellwaffer cried a lot for her long lost sister but could not forgive what she had done.

Inspector Ploddock finally got rid of that sneaky feeling in his stomach, until of course it would return with his next case. And Granny Probyn?

Well Granny Probyn had had enough of show business. She closed

Fluffy Yeomans' scrap book which had lain open on her lap.

'I think, from now on, we leave acting to the professionals,' she said to Fluffy as he curled up on a tartan rug in front of the wood stove.

Fluffy Yeomans yawned in agreement. His mother was right he thought, the theatre is full of pesky vermin, and closed his eyes.